Butterfly Kisses

The Orange Blossom Series — Book 1

LEIGH DUNCAN

BUTTERFLY KISSES
The Orange Blossom Series #1

Copyright © 2016 Leigh D. Duncan

This book is a work of fiction. The characters, events, and places portrayed in this book are products of the author's imagination and are either fictitious or are used fictitiously. Any similarity to real persons, living or dead, is purely coincidental and not intended by the author.

Print ISBN: 978-1-944258-09-2
Gardenia Street Publishing

Published in the United States of America

Books by Leigh Duncan

HEARTS LANDING SERIES
A Simple Wedding
A Cottage Wedding
A Waterfront Wedding

THE ORANGE BLOSSOM SERIES
Butterfly Kisses
Sweet Dreams
Broken Road

HOMETOWN HEROES SERIES
Luke
Brett
Dan
Travis
Colt
The Hometown Heroes Collection, A Boxed Set

THE GLADES COUNTY COWBOYS SERIES
His Favorite Cowgirl
Rancher's Lullaby

SINGLE TITLE BOOKS
A Country Wedding
Journey Back to Christmas
The Growing Season
Pattern of Deceit
Rodeo Daughter

Dear Reader,

Welcome to Orange Blossom, a town that owes its existence to the early settlers who were stubborn enough—or foolish enough—to brave the mosquitoes and hurricanes until their wives and children finally started calling this part of Central Florida "home." That was four generations back, and since then the town has grown a mite. Orange Blossom currently boasts a population of nine hundred and forty-three quirky characters, ornery cusses and staid leading citizens. Make that nine hundred and forty-four once Mary Beth and Deputy Sheriff Jake Sparling's baby boy puts in his appearance.

For more than a hundred years, people around here have—in one way or another—earned their livelihoods from the citrus groves that once stretched for miles in every direction. But in the late '90's and on into the new century, a canker infestation put most of the citrus growers out of business. Residents worried that nearby Orlando, where theme parks sprout on every corner and tourists crowd the streets, would gobble up their small town like it did Kissimmee and Saint Cloud. Others feared a big juicing conglomerate would snatch up the last family-owned-and-operated orange grove around these parts.

Either scenario was sure to drive every store in Orange Blossom out of business. And what would the town be without Miss June's Pie Shop on Main Street, or the Book Nook down on the square?

But threats to the town don't only come from the outside. Young folk go off to college and never return. Some of the town's finest citizens have been tempted by the kind of big business that would destroy their laid-back way of life. An influx of new blood will fix things right up, as long as those who move to Orange Blossom understand that, around here, folks like things just the way they are, thank you very much.

Pull up a chair and sit a while,
Leigh

To outsiders, Justine Gale's five-year-old daughter looks healthy enough, but the single mom knows the awful truth—a serious medical condition threatens her child's life. Justine struggles to give her little girl all she deserves, but a dead-end job and a growing mountain of debt darken both their futures...until a courier delivers an unexpected inheritance. Justine returns to the small town of Orange Blossom, Florida, where she spent idyllic summers determined to do whatever it takes for her daughter's sake—even sell the citrus grove her family sweated blood to preserve through four generations. But the rekindling of childhood friendships offers fresh hope, while the boy she left behind threatens Justine's future.

Nate Rhodes traded ten years of sweat equity to own the citrus grove he's worked in all his life, only to learn the owner never recorded their gentleman's agreement. Now, his old flame wants to sell the land—his land—to a competitor. But there's far more at stake than his own dreams. From the owner of Miss June's Pie Shop to Bill down at Smalley's Hardware, everyone in Orange Blossom earns their living from the area's last, family-owned citrus grove. Without Castle Grove, the town will wither and die, just like the love between the caretaker's son and the owner's niece did years ago.

For my niece
Genna Rose Taylor Lute
The bravest young woman I've ever known.

PROLOGUE

Ten Years Ago
Orange Blossom, Florida

"It's not fair." In a move perfected during her first summer at Castle Grove, Justine slid over the twin bed, landing with a flourish in her usual spot on the floor between Sarah and Penny. "We're eighteen, almost adults. We should be able to stay here if we want to."

"Well, maybe not *right* here." Scooting over a bit, Penny tugged strands of her red hair loose from where Justine's shoulder had pinned it to the bed.

"There's nothing fair about this at all." Sarah's dark curls shook.

"What is this?" Justine plucked at the heavy sweater Penny wore despite the heat and humidity of a Central Florida summer. "Aren't you hot in all those clothes? And what's with the glasses? They make you look dowdy."

"Leave me alone, Jus," Penny grumbled. "I'm cold and my contacts were bothering me, okay?"

"Okay, okay." Justine backed off. The last few days had taken a toll on all of them. Though, come to think of it, Penny had been out of sorts before Aunt Margaret...before she...

Justine cleared her throat. "It was bad enough that this was going to be our last summer together," she huffed. College would put an end to the practically carefree days spent at her aunt and uncle's Florida home. Every year since first grade, she and her mom had driven south from Virginia the day after the school year ended. Her heart always thumped when, ten miles past the Orange Blossom town limits sign, they'd turn beneath a crowned archway onto the gravel track that led through the heart of Castle Grove. At the main house, she'd basked in the expected half hour of *oh my, how you've grown*. The minute her mom and Aunt Margaret retreated to the kitchen for tea and pound cake, though, that was her cue to race down the hall to the room she and Sarah had shared from the beginning. They were just going into seventh grade when Penny's dad moved to town, and the room was rearranged to accommodate Orange Blossom's newest teen. Sarah had dubbed them the Three Musketeers, and the name had stuck.

But this year, only ten short days after Justine had traded welcome-back hugs with her besties, it was all over. The doors were closing on the informal camp her aunt and uncle ran for kids who had nothing better to do than get into trouble over the long, hot summers.

What about all their plans?

Emails had been flying between her and her friends for months. Knowing it'd be their last chance before life took them in different directions, they'd put together an insanely long bucket list of all their favorite things to do—from feasting on hand-churned ice cream, to riding bikes into Orange Blossom, to skinny-dipping in the clear spring at the edge of the orange grove. They'd only begun to check items off their list when everything came to a grief-stricken halt.

"We should talk to our folks, convince them they're wrong." Penny stuck a bookmark in a well-thumbed novel.

"That might work for you, Pen. Your dad will do anything for you." As a widower, Mr. Kirk doted on his only child. "My parents won't budge. They're sending me to Dad's office in Rome till the week before I move into the dorm at Georgetown." Her dad had said she might as well take advantage of the opportunity to learn the family business.

"Ooooh, Italy. So tragic." Adjusting the dark-rimmed glasses that hid her hazel eyes, Penny pretended to swoon.

"Think of all the new dishes you'll try while you're there." Sarah absently licked her lips.

"She better be thinking of all the weight she'll gain if she spends three months eating pasta and cannoli." Despite the summer heat, Penny burrowed into the heavy cardigan that hid her own washboard-straight figure. "If you aren't real careful, you'll get a head start on the Freshman Fifteen."

"Not gonna happen." Justine elbowed her friend in the ribs. "Besides, you're missing the point. Which is, this was supposed to be our last summer of freedom, and now it's ruined. My folks said it wouldn't be *proper* for us to stay here without Aunt Margaret to chaperone. As if." She choked up, unable to banish the image of her only aunt keeling over in the middle of the roomy, farmhouse kitchen. One minute, Aunt

Margaret had been slicing lemons for a fresh batch of lemonade. The next, she'd been...gone. Dead before she hit the floor, according to the paramedics who'd taken forever to arrive.

Sarah plucked a thread from the rough edge of her cutoffs. "I get where they're coming from. There's not much to do in Orange Blossom besides gossip. Rumors, they tend to stick like glue."

Justine's face warmed. If anyone would know how life worked in small-town USA, it'd be Sarah. How many times had the three of them had to listen as some bleached-blond matron eagerly repeated the story of how Sarah's mom got caught behind the bleachers with the captain of the football team? She supposed they meant well, a lesson in what not to do and all that, but jeez. If Sarah wanted to be reminded of her mom's mistakes, all she had to do was look in the mirror.

"I'm worried about the garden," Sarah, the consummate foodie, continued. "We haven't even picked the first crop of tomatoes. The vegetables need to be hoed. There'll be food to can and freeze all summer. Uncle Jimmy won't be able to do all that himself."

"That's another reason we should stay." As if she could see through the closed door, Justine stared in the general direction of her uncle's bedroom. The man who'd buried his wife of thirty years that morning had disappeared into the orange groves as soon as they'd come back from the cemetery. Returning hours later with red-rimmed eyes and a tear-streaked face, he'd retreated to his room and refused to join them for dinner at the dining table crowded with funeral food.

"I guess my dad agrees with your folks. He says your uncle can't be expected to ride herd on a bunch of teenagers. Not while he's grieving." Penny rubbed her finger along the spine of her book.

Justine heaved a sigh. It was time to face facts. Her time at Castle Grove had come to an end. There'd be no more laughing over jokes or sharing secrets with her girlfriends while they plucked juicy, sun-ripened blackberries from the vines that grew along miles and miles of the fences. No more sitting on the front porch on rainy afternoons snapping beans or shelling peas and singing old gospel hymns while Aunt Margaret played the piano. Or watching Uncle Jimmy and the guys trudge across the lawn after they finished tending to the two hundred acres of prime citrus that surrounded the house. She wished she'd known when they held that last bonfire that she'd never again roast marshmallows on a downed branch. That she'd never have another chance to flirt or share a secret kiss with her first—and only—boyfriend.

Speaking of which... Crap.

Justine shot a glance at her watch. She was supposed to have met Nate at their special place by eight. It was already ten minutes past. She sprang to her feet. "I'm late. I have to go."

Penny's lips pursed. "Your mom will have an absolute cow if she finds out."

"They're wrong about Nate." Much as she didn't want to admit it, her love for the grove manager's son was the other reason her parents had insisted on an early end to her summer. Maybe, though, just maybe, this wouldn't be good-bye so much as *ciao.* Because, whether or not Camp Castle Grove closed its doors, her love for Nate would endure. "Cover for me?"

"Of course," Sarah gushed, placing a hand to her heart.

"Take a walkie in case your folks come looking for you." Penny unclipped a radio from her waistband and handed it across.

Without giving her friends a chance to try and talk her out of it, Justine removed the loose screen from the window and slipped onto the porch that wrapped around her aunt and uncle's wood-framed crackerbox. She stared across the dirt track that ran between rows and rows of orange trees.

Is Nate still waiting for me?

Shoes in hand, she padded silently down the unpainted steps. A rough board gouged her big toe. She grimaced but kept moving, willing herself not to stop until she reached the waxy green leaves and gnarled brown trunks that marked the first row of the grove. Leaning against a tree, she propped one foot on her thigh, licked her fingers and dug at a sliver of wood. Okay, maybe her parents had been right about insisting she wear shoes instead of running around barefoot like a Florida native, she admitted while she flexed her feet against the thick green grass until she was sure she'd gotten out the splinter. But just that. Nothing else.

Certainly not about Nate. Who cared if he was *just* the son of the grove manager? If he worked for Uncle Jimmy instead of getting a part-time job dishing out ice cream or collecting movie tickets like all her friends? Nate had drive, intelligence, purpose. He'd overcome his humble beginnings. One day, he'd go places. And if not, well, that was fine. She loved him just the way he was.

Fifteen minutes later, she burst into a clearing ringed by the oldest trees in the grove. Just as she'd hoped, Nate hadn't given up on her. She hurried to him, buried her face in his shoulder, certain the boy who'd shared her first kiss would come to her rescue.

"My parents are sending me to Italy. They won't let me stay without Aunt Margaret here. Dad got me a job in his office in Rome until classes start in the fall," she nearly wailed. Her parents owned and operated Gale Enterprises, an international firm that specialized in government contracts.

"You're kidding, right?" Nate's admiring whistle sounded in her ear. "You are one lucky, lucky girl."

Justine waited. When her folks had sprung the news on her, she'd been excited, too. For precisely thirty seconds. Until she'd realized their new plan put an end to the long, kiss-filled days and nights she'd dreamed of spending with Nate.

"Think of all the sightseeing you can do. The Roman Forum. The Colosseum. Me, if I ever get to Europe, I want to see the Alps. I've heard the snow never melts on some of the mountains. Not ever."

Of course he'd be impressed with snow. Growing up in Florida, Nate probably imagined big, white flakes, snowball fights and skiing. He'd never worn a puffy coat that turned him into a big, blue marshmallow. He didn't know how quick those beautiful flakes turned to ice that latched on to jeans and made them weigh a ton. His frame of reference wouldn't include salt trucks, treacherous sidewalks or how gray and dirty the world turned days after a winter storm. Or how much the bitter cold made her long for heat. For him.

Unable to wait any longer, she pointed out the obvious. "Nate, it means we can't be together."

Silence.

She wondered if he was thinking the same thing

she was thinking. It had taken Nate months—the whole fall, winter and spring between her junior and senior years—to create the oasis in the center of her uncle's grove. Ten days ago, he'd led her to this very spot. Where bright red lantana blossoms and purple petunias attracted clouds of butterflies. For her. When the first one landed in the palm of her outstretched hand, she'd known. Known that Nate loved her. Known she truly and completely felt the same way. He was the only one for her, and he always would be. They were Anthony and Cleopatra. Rhett and Scarlett. Mr. Darcy and Elizabeth. Someday, poets and authors would write about *them*.

In an instant, they'd gone from being lifelong friends and sometime adversaries to something else, something more. From the girl with a crush on a college boy to a couple in love. When she'd let him kiss her for the first time, she swore the ground beneath her feet had moved. No, it hadn't been perfect. She'd bumped his nose. He'd missed her lips and planted one right on her cheek. With practice, they'd gotten better.

That first week, they'd had lots and lots of practice. Until three days ago, when, without warning, Aunt Margaret died. Since then, there hadn't been time for kisses, only tears.

"Not at all?" Disappointment freighted the voice that normally sent delicious shivers through her. "Not even when you get back?"

"That's just it. I won't be back. I start at Georgetown in the fall." Fifteen hundred on her SAT's, a stellar GPA, plus all kinds of extracurricular stuff mandated by her parents, had practically guaranteed her early acceptance to the top-notch school of her choice. Nate had spent his first two years at the local college, but that was only because he played football. As quarterback for his intramural team, he'd set a school record for touchdowns. Now that he had his AA, the big schools were probably begging him to play for them. Wouldn't it be great if they ended up at the same school? She closed her eyes and imagined crisp fall afternoons when she'd sit in the stands, cheering for Nate, followed by long winter nights when they'd hold each other close.

"You'll look amazing in Hoya blue. Have you spoken to the coach yet?"

Nate rested his chin on the top of her head. "Much as I'd like to, there's no sense even talking to him. Georgetown is three-deep in quarterbacks."

"What about someplace close by? UMD is a good school. So's UVA, but it's a couple of hours away." When Nate didn't answer, she stopped herself. While Sarah and Penny had been bragging about their acceptance letters since she got here, Nate hadn't even mentioned his plans for the fall. An appalling thought occurred to her. She tipped her head until she saw his face. "What, exactly, are you going to do?"

"I thought I'd probably finish up at Florida."

Probably? "I thought..."

Much as she didn't want them to, the doubts her mother had raised wiggled to the surface. She rubbed the spot dead center between her temples where a headache threatened. What was she worried about? UF had a good prelaw program. Maybe it wasn't as good as Georgetown's, but it was decent. She took a steadying breath and let the words spill from her mouth. "I could transfer to Gainesville next year."

Nate snorted. "Sorry, but I don't see you as part of

the Gator Nation. At least, not as an undergrad. Maybe for your master's."

She sniffled so softly she was certain Nate would never suspect she was crying.

"Hey." Nate's voice whispered into her hair. His hands caressed her shoulders. "It'll be all right. We'll have a lifetime together. So what if we don't go to the same college? I'll graduate in two years. Then I can work and save till you get your degree."

"It's...it's more than that," she breathed. "There's law school and summer internships."

Nate's hand stilled, but only for a moment. She snuggled deeper into his embrace, certain that loving Nate didn't mean an end to her dreams, her future. Once she passed the bar, she'd land a great job with a top firm and he'd...he'd...

"I know. But one day you'll have your own office on Main Street," he said, naming the street that ran through the heart of Orange Blossom. "All our friends will come to you for advice. Uncle Jimmy will send you all of Castle Grove's legal work."

For one brief second, she pictured her name painted on a plate-glass window overlooking the town square, saw herself standing at the doorway to her office while the band warmed up for a summer concert in the small park. She blinked the image away. Though she loved spending summers at Castle Grove, a tiny practice in Central Florida was pretty far from the corporate world. In fact, it was about as far away as she could get from the kind of career she wanted and still call herself an attorney. She shook her head.

"Nobody needs a high-powered litigator in the middle of citrus country." The tears she'd blinked away earlier rushed back and brought friends. "Don't you want something more out of life?"

"More than what, baby? Everything I want is right here in Orange Blossom." Nate's gesture took in the grove and beyond. He hugged her close. "Especially when you're here. As long as we have each other, nothing else matters."

Justine brushed the tears from her cheeks.

He was right. This was all her parents' fault. They were the ones who insisted that only the best was good enough for their daughter. In return, they expected perfection and, for the most part, she lived up to their expectations. But she hadn't needed to be valedictorian of her class, she didn't have to attend an Ivy League college or go to a prestigious law school— not to earn Nate's love. In his arms, she felt something she'd never felt before. That she was perfect, exactly as she was. From her board-straight blond hair, to the tiny birthmark on the inside of her right calf. From a chest that seemed to grow every day, to legs that didn't. Nate loved her the same way she loved him. It'd be years before she had to decide where to hang her shingle.

For now, her last summer before college loomed. Thanks to her parents, she wouldn't spend it in Florida. But that didn't mean she and Nate couldn't make plans of their own.

"About that trip to Europe. I was thinking…" She stepped out of his arms, tilted her head to study the eyes of the man she intended to spend the rest of her life with.

"Yeah?"

"Why don't you come, too? I'll have to work, but on the weekends, we can explore Italy. There's a self-guided tour that promises 'a hundred churches and art museums in sixty days,'" she quoted from one of the brochures her parents had shown her that afternoon. "It'll be a lot more fun if we're together."

"Wow, Justine. That's insane. Crazy good, but it's not—"

"Wouldn't it be awesome?" she interrupted. She couldn't stand to hear one more person tell her she couldn't have what she wanted. Not even Nate. "We could see Michelangelo's David. Touch the frescoes in the Piccolomini. We can even play tourist and throw coins in the Trevi Fountain."

And at night, we can...

"Justine, baby. That sounds..."

Like heaven.

"Totally boring. I mean, statues and museums? Yawn." When she stiffened, he shrugged. "Anyway, I can't. Dad's arthritis is acting up. He's counting on me to help him out in the grove this summer. I'll be lucky if I can swing a week at the beach before classes start in the fall."

She gave him another chance. "Italy has beaches. Topless beaches," she said, ignoring the heat that crawled up her neck and into her face. "Miles and miles of them."

"You don't know how much I'd like to go to one with you," Nate said, his voice one part earnest, two parts strained. "But when I think of the beach, it's more like Daytona than the Riviera."

Time to pull out my best argument.

She cleared her throat and stared up at him through lowered lashes. "I was thinking, you know, about you and me and someplace totally romantic for our first time and..."

"I was kind of thinking right here"—his arm stirred the floral scent that drifted in the air—"is pretty romantic."

"It is. But can't you just picture it?" She hurried, trying to ward off the confusion that crept across Nate's features. "You and me in a quaint little inn overlooking a vineyard. Surrounded by the rolling hills of wine country. Instead of orange juice, we'd toast with real champagne. We could have real flowers on the nightstand instead of weeds."

She blinked. She hadn't really said that last part out loud, had she? Judging from the shocked expression on Nate's face, she had. Her arms dangled, cold and empty, at her sides when he eased out of reach.

"Is that what you really think?" A muscle along his jaw twitched. "Are you saying *this* isn't good enough? That *I'm* not good enough?"

His challenging tone put her on the defensive. "Oh, no. I didn't mean it that way. I meant..." Her voice trailed off. What had she meant? Three days ago, she'd wanted nothing more than to lie down on a blanket with him right here. But what were wildflowers and butterflies compared to soft sheets and room service? There had to be a hundred more romantic places for their first time. She took a breath. Her thoughts, like their conversation, had veered seriously off course.

She gazed into hard, flinty eyes that stared back at her without a touch of their usual tenderness.

"I guess the rest of the guys were right all along. You really are a spoiled, little rich girl, aren't you? I should have known better than to think you were different."

The accusation stung. The sneering tone cut. She kicked at one of the plants. Red blossoms showered the ground. "Bunch of overgrown caterpillars, that's all this is." Nate could stuff his butterfly garden.

Without a word, he wrenched a clump of flowers out by the roots. Pitching the offending plants to one side, he yanked hard on a second handful. A third followed. Then a fourth.

A burst of static at her hip competed with the whir of cicadas. "Justine, your mom was just here. I told her you were in the bathroom, but you'd better get back. Pronto. Over."

Penny's voice on the walkie-talkie broke through the fog that had wrapped around her while Nate fumed. Horror lanced through her chest at the damage he'd done. The garden—and their love—lay in ruins, and their time had run out. Tears stung her eyes. She wondered if Nate felt the same regret as his shoulders slumped. The armload of plants he'd jerked from the dirt fell to the ground at his feet.

"I guess this is it, then," he said and turned away.

Before she could say how sorry she was, or even whisper good-bye, the boy she'd intended to love forever disappeared into the trees beyond the clearing.

Justine brushed a hand through her hair. She didn't know which was worse—learning that Nate didn't want the same things out of life as she did, or that her parents, once again, had been right. She clutched her aching chest and wondered if it hurt so much because her heart was breaking.

With nowhere else to go, she stumbled toward the house. Now, more than ever, she needed to be with her friends.

Present

Justine Gale pulled into one of two parking spaces assigned to the cramped third-floor apartment she called home. She turned off the engine. The car shimmied and grumbled.

"Timmy Burroughs said our car is ugly," Margaret Grace chirped from the backseat.

"He did, did he?" Justine shifted so she could see the five-year-old still safely buckled into her booster seat. A tiny scowl marred the little girl's mouth.

"Yeah. I don't like him anymore."

"Why do you think he said that?" The urge to grin at her daughter's crossly folded arms tugged at Justine's lips, but she kept her tone neutral. Timmy was Gracie's best friend at day care. In all likelihood, their spat would blow over in a matter of minutes, if not days. As for the car, well, the kid had a point.

"His mom has a new van. It has doors that slide open all by themselves. It's silver, and it has a TV

15

screen. Timmy gets to watch *The Muppets* on the way to school." The awe in Gracie's tone proclaimed Timmy the luckiest boy in the world.

"*The Muppets*, huh? I bet he likes that." Justine held her breath while her own bucket of bolts gave a last wheezing shudder. Lately, she'd begun to fear the vehicle was on its last set of tires. Her salary as a paralegal at Jacoby & Sons barely covered the bills and her portion of the rent. What would she do if her only source of transportation needed major repairs? No way could she fit *that* into her already-tight budget.

"I wish our car had a DVD." Gracie heaved a sigh dramatic enough to jiggle her dark curls.

We all have our dreams, kiddo.

She'd had a few of those herself. She gave the steering wheel a tap. There were all kinds of things she'd planned to do by the time she got within hailing distance of thirty. Make partner in a big law firm. Buy a house. Spend vacations traveling the globe—anywhere but Italy, that was. She'd never go there again.

Life hadn't exactly turned out the way she'd planned. Not that it mattered. She stole another look at Gracie and smiled. She had new hopes, new dreams now. But it would take more than dreams to pay for a DVD player. As for a new car with all the bells and whistles, that was so far down her priority list, it didn't even make the first page. Unfortunately, her dog-eared copy of *Raising Your Child as a Single Parent* didn't include a chapter on explaining red ink to a preschooler.

So she didn't.

Instead, she stretched every dime of her salary by haunting consignment shops for secondhand clothes for Gracie and gently used suits she could wear to work. At the supermarket, she pushed her shopping cart past the expensive cuts of meat without a second glance. She fixed macaroni and cheese three times a week and had almost convinced herself it was her favorite meal. As for her car, there were advantages to driving a ten-year-old sedan. For one, she didn't have to worry about getting carjacked. No self-respecting thief would bother with a vehicle whose air conditioner had given up the ghost two summers ago. Plus, having to roll down the windows let her put her suspicious neighbors at ease so much faster.

Catching sight of a white-haired woman who had halted by her front bumper and was pinning the new arrivals with a dark look, Justine leaned out the open window. "Afternoon, Mrs. Morrison." She threw in an extra welcome for the well-behaved Sheltie sitting at his owner's feet. "Hey, Brutus."

"Oh, Justine, is that you?" A hand appeared from Mrs. Morrison's pocket where, no doubt, the busybody's thumb had hovered over the speed-dial key for the neighborhood watch commander. Apparently satisfied that muggers weren't going to spring from Justine's rattletrap, the older woman tugged on her dog's leash. "Come along, Brutus." She waited while the ever-friendly pup scrambled to his feet, before moving off with a brisk, "Have a nice evening, dear."

Not likely.

Justine swept a glance from the unevenly mowed grass to the wind-blown newspapers that rattled against the iron rails of an open staircase, one of a hundred in the sprawling apartment complex in Fairfax County, Virginia. She swallowed, hard. She was a long way from the two-story Colonial she'd grown up in and farther still from where she'd thought she'd be by this stage of her life, but there wasn't anything she could do about that now. For now, she had to make the best of what she had for herself, for her child. Starting with seeing Margaret Grace's pediatrician in—she checked her watch—one hour. Dr. Lassiter's nurse had been quite insistent that he expected her in his office—without her daughter—at four p.m. sharp.

What's that all about? She sighed. Bills, probably. But what if...?

"Mommy," Gracie called insistently. "Can we get a new car?"

"Not today." Or tomorrow. Or next year.

"Oh-kay. There's Aunt Penny. Hi, Aunt Penny!" Gracie frantically waved from the backseat.

"Use your inside voice, sweetie." Justine rubbed her forehead where a headache threatened. "We're too far away for her to hear you." She stared up at the severe silhouette of the woman at the window of their apartment on the third floor. Where would she and Gracie be now if they hadn't had Penny's help five years ago when they'd had nowhere else to go? On the streets? Or worse, separated? She owed her childhood friend more than she could ever hope to repay.

"Let's see who can race upstairs the fastest," she suggested, knowing she'd lose on purpose. "If you beat me, you can stay with Aunt Penny while Mommy goes to an appointment."

"But I want to come with you," Gracie grumbled, all the while unbuckling her seat belt. "When we play games, Aunt Penny always wins. She won't let me watch TV till I practice my letters. Can't you stay home and play with me?"

Justine swallowed a sigh. Working double shifts and counting on other people to help raise her child wasn't what she wanted either. Not that it mattered. Despite her efforts, the chasm between *want* and *need* widened a tiny bit more every day. She tugged on one earlobe. She could live on stale bread and water for the next ten years, and she still wouldn't pay off the medical bills that had mounted—high and fast—during Gracie's first three months of life. Not unless she gave up her job and started robbing banks.

She shrugged. She had to try, didn't she?

"Tonight, Mommy has to go out, and tomorrow, I have to work late. But I'm off on Sunday. We can go to Evans Farm in the afternoon on our way to the grocery store." Though the gristmill and petting zoo had been replaced by brick homes and pavered walkways, the pond remained a popular spot for ducks and geese.

"Promise?"

Quickly, Justine ran through the list of chores she'd planned to tackle on the one day Jacoby & Sons closed and locked its doors. Penny would be in Chicago next week for a big book fair. She wouldn't care whether the floors got swept and mopped. The laundry could wait till another day. "We'll take some bread and feed the ducks," she announced.

Pronouncing the trade acceptable, Gracie scrambled out of the car.

"Careful," Justine warned before the girl could charge up the walkway. "Go slow so you don't fall."

Watching her daughter turn the sloping sidewalk into a game of hopscotch, Justine grinned. They might not live in a fancy house or drive a gas-guzzling SUV, but she and Gracie had made significant strides since the day, five years ago, when she'd stuck her gloved hand through an incubator's port in the neonatal intensive care unit. From the moment Gracie's tiny fingers had wrapped around hers for the first time, she'd devoted every thought, every prayer, every fiber of her being into making sure the small figure in the crib overcame the doctors' grim predictions. And it had worked. Not only had Margaret Grace thrived, she'd escaped every one of the dire complications—ranging from cerebral palsy to blindness—that were often associated with premature births.

From her glossy brown curls to her sturdy little legs, her daughter was the picture of good health. Which made the doctor's call earlier today all the more puzzling.

Justine drummed her fingers on the wheel. Maybe the latest round of labs had cost more than her insurance would cover. If so, Dr. Lassiter could just add it to her tab. She'd find a way to pay the bill. Not right away, of course, but somehow, someday.

"I'm beating you, Mommy!"

The reminder derailed her thoughts and put her in motion. She caught up just as her exuberant little girl bounded up the stairs toward the apartment they'd shared with Penny ever since Justine—empty-handed, hormonal and scared to death—had been discharged from the hospital. A door opened as they reached the third-floor landing. Gracie barely slowed before she plowed straight into Penny's knees.

"Ooof!" her roommate exclaimed, retrieving Gracie's backpack and bending to give the girl a welcome-home hug. "There's that little munchkin I've been waiting for. I've missed you! There's a pile of books on my chair. Want to read before dinner?"

"That's my favoritest thing to do in the world,"

Gracie declared, scrunching her face into a big smile.

"Give your mom a good-bye kiss, and we'll get started."

"Bye, Mommy."

The two thin arms that curled around her neck tempted Justine to skip the appointment with the pediatrician and play hooky with her daughter. How long had it been since she'd taken Gracie to the zoo or driven into the District to watch the pedal boats in the Tidal Basin? Too long, she admitted, and wished for the umpteenth time that a fairy godmother would suddenly appear and wave a magic wand over her...life. Knowing that wasn't going to happen and that she did, really, have to go, she settled for giving her daughter an extra cuddle.

"See you later, sweetheart," she called as Gracie darted inside. Standing, she glanced at her friend. "I'd better get moving if I'm going to make that appointment on time."

"The doctor didn't give you any hint why he wanted to see you?" When Justine shook her head, concern flashed in the hazel eyes Penny nearly always hid behind heavy-rimmed glasses. "I'm sure it's nothing."

"From your lips to God's ears," Justine whispered as she retraced her steps down the stairs.

For once, fate smiled on her and her car's engine sprang to life without the usual complaints. Afternoon traffic in the DC suburbs flowed smoothly for a change. She even caught a few green lights, and less than an hour later, she pulled into the parking structure near Fairfax Hospital.

Going through what she owed, she trudged along the short walk from the parking lot to Lassiter's office. She'd need a stick of dynamite to make a real dent in the mountain of outstanding bills left over from Gracie's extended stay in the NICU. Just this minute, she didn't have one, and she'd looked for one everywhere she could. Her salary, meager as it was, kept her from qualifying for state assistance. Well-meaning friends said she ought to file for bankruptcy and get the load off her back once and for all. They didn't understand that the ultra-conservative law firm she worked for would fire her the minute her case appeared on the court docket. Or how badly she needed to keep her job.

Because change was coming.

In the fall, her little girl would start all-day kindergarten in one of the country's finest public school systems. Weeks later, thanks to Jacoby & Sons' educational assistance program, Justine would return to school, too. Starting over and attending law school as a part-time student meant it'd be years before she passed the bar, but once she did, the bump in salary would wipe out her debt. One day, there'd even be enough for a house with a yard where her daughter could play.

Her fingers crossed, Justine squared her shoulders and opened the door to Dr. Lassiter's office. Stepping into the waiting area, she took in the bare tables where busy two- and three-year-olds usually colored in books or built block houses. Her stomach tightened as the glass window over the receptionist's desk slid open.

"Ms. Gale."

Spiky black hair framed a pair of dark eyes that refused to meet Justine's gaze. With none of her usual exuberance, the pediatrician's longtime assistant said, "Dr. Lassiter is wrapping up a phone call. He'll be right with you."

"That's okay, Lisa, I'll just—"

But the woman she'd been on a first-name basis with for more than five years had already retreated. The frosted glass slid into place with a snap.

"—wait here," Justine finished and sank onto a hard chair.

She tugged her lower lip between her teeth, her concern mounting that today's meeting was about more than payment schedules. A shiver raced down her spine. She rubbed her hands together and grabbed a magazine off a nearby coffee table. A sense of doom thickened the air while she flipped pages without reading a word.

She'd traded one uninteresting magazine for another by the time the door to the exam rooms opened. Standing, she scanned the pediatrician's deeply lined face. Even in Gracie's first critical days, she'd found reassurance and hope there. Today, his wrinkles looked more pronounced, the brackets around his mouth deeper. Her heart stuttered.

Surprised that her knees didn't buckle, she crossed the room, her hand outstretched. "Dr. Lassiter?" She raised one eyebrow.

"Justine," he said, easing some of her trepidation with the same firm grip she'd grown to expect. "You came alone? Wasn't there someone you wanted with you?"

"No. Just me," she said, trying to maintain a brave front. But she'd spent enough time in hospitals following Gracie's birth to recognize the code for bad news. She dipped into her purse for her cell phone while she tried to think of someone she could call. Someone who might wrap their arms around her and tell her everything was going to be all right...despite her growing fear that it wasn't. There was no one, and she squared her shoulders.

Just tell me what's wrong, and I'll deal with it.

For her daughter's sake, she'd do anything, even slay a dragon if that's what it took.

"Margaret's blood tested positive for protein during her last physical. Remember the extra blood work and tests I ordered?" Lassiter asked as he led the way to his office.

"I thought you were just being careful," she protested. The pediatrician had been ordering one test or another for so long that she hadn't even questioned the need for an ultrasound. Why bother when the results were always normal?

Not this time, it seemed. In the well-appointed office, she sank onto a leather chair. The air around her grew too thick, too hot.

"Now that we have the results, I took the liberty of consulting with a colleague, Dr. Paul Shorter, the head of the Pediatric Nephrology Center." Lassiter took his place on the opposite side of a wide desk. He struck a few keys on an open laptop. "He's quite concerned about Gracie's eventual renal failure."

"I'm sorry. Her what?" She eyed the computer screen where a vague bean shape emerged from the background static.

"Think of the kidneys as a filtration system." Lassiter interlaced his fingers and leaned forward, his arms tented. "Every day, poisons build up in our bodies. The kidneys filter out all the bad stuff and turn it into the harmless urine we eliminate."

"Bottom line." She gave the man the best no-nonsense look she could manage under the circumstances.

"Nature gave us two kidneys, a built-in redundancy. If one goes bad, the other can handle the load. In Gracie's case, her left kidney is badly damaged. It probably has been from birth. Maybe earlier. The other isn't doing as well as it should."

Her head swimming, she sucked in a breath of much-needed air while the doctor waited, giving her a chance to absorb the blow. Not that it mattered. There wasn't that much time in the world.

"We see this condition sometimes with children who were born premature." Lassiter opened a thick patient chart and rifled the first few pages. "Sometimes these babies start out fine, but as they get older, their kidneys can't keep up. With proper care, we should be able to get your daughter to puberty before hers give out. Perhaps a few years more." Eventually, he explained, hormonal swings and growth would put so much strain on Gracie's weakened kidneys that they'd fail completely. "Once that happens, we'll put her on dialysis until an organ becomes available for transplant."

Before she could blurt, *Take one of mine!* Lassiter shook his head. "We already know you're not a match. Gracie's blood is O positive. And yours is"—once more Lassiter referred to the chart—"yours is A."

She'd been the first in line when doctors suspected her daughter might need a transfusion shortly after her birth. Finding out she couldn't give blood to her own infant had been devastating. But this, this was so much worse. In a split second, she was back in the NICU, where tubes and wires ran from every opening in her baby's body. She'd gotten through the experience then by constantly reminding herself that her little girl was too young, too new, to know what was happening to her. A giant fist squashed her heart as she considered putting Gracie through all that now that she was old enough to feel, to understand, what was happening.

"I'm afraid there's more bad news." Lassiter removed his glasses, took a handkerchief from his pocket and began polishing the lenses. "Transplants are expensive. And knowing your financial situation as I do..."

Money?

Unwilling to believe they were discussing costs when her daughter's life was at stake, she peered at the doctor. Didn't he know she'd do anything to ensure Gracie's health? Her car was on life support, but she'd make it last. As for law school, she'd put that off for another year. Or three. Once Gracie started kindergarten in the fall, her day care costs would drop. As a last resort, her employers were always looking for people to work overtime. She usually refused in order to spend more time with Gracie, but if it would help—

"We're talking roughly a quarter of a million dollars in out-of-pocket costs, Justine. There are programs you can apply for when the time's right. Medicaid. Public assistance. But for now, you need to prepare yourself."

Her mouth dropped open, and there wasn't a damned thing she could do to stop it. The number might as well have been a million, for all the hope she had of ever reaching it. Suddenly, slaying dragons seemed like a walk in the park compared to the ordeal that lay ahead. Uncertain when her tears had started to fall, she mopped her cheeks. Dreams of someday watching her daughter cross a high school stage to receive her diploma or—God help her—walk down the aisle wavered.

Please, please tell me this is all some kind of cosmic joke, she silently begged.

The painful truth was etched on Lassiter's somber face. "For now, all we can do is monitor her condition. Make sure she eats a balanced diet. Gets plenty of rest." He came around the desk, helped her to her feet. "Keep everything as normal as possible. And try not to worry."

Fear rippled through her, scattering her thoughts like a flock of buzzards at the edge of the road. What else could she do but worry?

Nate Rhodes tossed a quick look over his shoulder at the swath he'd cut through the tall weeds. Between the whitewashed fence and the main highway, the mowed edge ran straight, nearly straight as a plumb line, until it disappeared in a distant heat mirage. He drew in a satisfied breath that tasted of orange blossoms mixed with the sharper tang of fresh-cut grass. In his book, a job worth doing—even a simple one—was worth handling right. He faced forward, only to shift the John Deere's gears into neutral when a shiny new pickup sent up a spray of gravel as it pulled to the side of the road. The driver's window glided down.

"Morning, Nate." Everett Grimes's voice rose over the tractor's engine. "Hot enough for you?"

"Reckon so, Mr. Grimes." Amused that Everett considered the weather worth a comment, Nate blotted sweat on the sleeve of his shirt while he hid the smile that tugged at his lips. Heat and humidity were nothing new for May in Central Florida.

"Have you seen your uncle Jimmy this morning?" White hair topped Everett's lined face when the retiree crooked an age-spotted arm over the window frame.

"No, sir." Nate resettled his baseball cap. Only someone born and raised in Orange Blossom would know he and James Castle weren't actually related. Everett, having moved to town a scant six years earlier, was a relative newcomer and thus not privy to all the town's history. "I spoke with him last night, though. He was his usual self. Why? Something wrong?"

"It's probably nothing, but he missed our Wednesday breakfast at the Ham Hut. We were all looking forward to hearing the latest about the Orange Fest." The winter event drew visitors from all over the country.

"Come to think of it, I didn't see his car go by this morning." Nate frowned. In the ten years since Aunt Margaret's passing, the owner of Castle Grove had rarely skipped the weekly gabfest at the town's only restaurant. Shielding his eyes against the bright spring sun, Nate studied the dirt road that cut between neat rows of citrus trees. Once stirred, the thick, moisture-laden air trapped dust in a tight grip, refusing to let it settle for several hours. But only clear blue shimmered above the lush, green leaves. If he'd gone to town, Jimmy hadn't taken his usual route.

Nate pulled his cell phone from his shirt pocket. With one swipe, he checked for missed calls, anxious voice mails. A prickle of concern faded when no messages appeared on the screen.

"You're welcome to go on up to the house, if you want," he told Everett.

"Nah, nah. I'll head on. I'm taking a sausage biscuit home to the wife. Can't let it get cold. Besides, you know how Jimmy gets when people check up on him." Like a turtle, Everett pulled his head back into the safety of his truck cab.

"I hear ya." Nate nodded. James Castle personified every cliché ever coined about crotchety old men. Long and lean, the octogenarian fiercely guarded his independence. Even after his hip replacement three years back, he'd insisted on doing his own laundry and fixing his own meals, refusing to hire any one of the dozen or so women in town who would have been glad for the work. Or the chance to catch the widower's eye.

"He probably fell asleep watching the news last night." Jimmy's television often blared late into the night. Sometimes, the sound had disturbed the peace and quiet when Nate carried his morning coffee onto the front porch of the small cottage near the main house. "I'll knock on his door when I'm finished."

As Everett pulled back onto the road and aimed for home, Nate let his hand linger over the gearshift. He eyed the remaining grassy strip where fat bees buzzed lazily over knee-high growth. He ought to spend the best part of the day mowing beyond the fence line that surrounded the two hundred acres of prime citrus groves, but the uneasy feeling in his gut called for a change of plans. His stomach turned over as he thought back to the last time Uncle Jimmy skipped breakfast with his cronies without giving his pals a heads-up. Late that same afternoon, Nate had discovered the old man moaning on the living room floor in the big house, one leg sprawled at an awkward angle.

It was one thing to give the man his space. Quite another to risk needless suffering.

His decision made, Nate feathered the gas. The

tractor roared to life. He'd finish this side of the driveway. After that, something cold and wet might be just the ticket. And if he happened to run out of sweet tea and had to ask Uncle Jimmy for a glass, well, the old man could hardly accuse him of hovering, could he?

An hour later, Nate eyed Jimmy's ancient Ford pickup parked in its usual spot in the shade. His shoulders tightened as he climbed the steps onto the wide porch surrounding the clapboard house that had been home to four generations of Castles. Leaving the door for the moment, he crossed to an open window.

"Uncle Jimmy, you in there?" Hoping to spot movement, he leaned down to peer through the tattered screen. A gap between panels of heavy drapes offered only a tiny glimpse of the darkened living room. Nothing moved in the shadowy recesses.

He called again. When there was still no answer, he tried the handle. The slick brass knob turned half an inch before stopping, and Nate tugged his ball cap from his head. He slapped it against his thigh, exasperated. Even in the heart of Orange Blossom, any kind of break-in was more likely the result of a high school prank than the work of a real burglar. But five miles stretched between Castle Grove's property line and the town limits. Reason enough to leave the house open in case someone—someone like him—needed to check up on things. Besides, why bother locking up and then leave a key in the first place a robber would look? Reaching beneath the mat, Nate pulled out the spare.

The door swung open, and he froze. Awareness skittered down his spine on icy feet. His nose crinkled at the fetid odor of trash that had lingered inside far too long. He waved a hand through the stale air before yanking the curtain cord. Light poured through the grimy window, and Nate blinked uncertainly at wood that had once gleamed from weekly polishing. A thick layer of dust coated every surface. He sniffed again, this time picking up the unmistakably sour smell of mildew.

How long had it been since James Castle last invited him in for a game of checkers or to watch TV? Far too long, judging from the piles of mail that sat unopened on the coffee table.

"Uncle Jimmy?" Calling, he picked his slow way through the dining room to the kitchen, where his boots made sucking noises as he walked across the sticky tiles. He swore softly. How had things gotten this bad?

He hated to think how long it had been since anyone broke out a vacuum or mop. He shook his head, but guilt had settled on his shoulders where it refused to budge. They might not be related by blood, but Jimmy was more than an employer. The old man had walked the waiting-room floors with his dad the day Nate was born. He was the closest thing to a grandfather Nate had ever known. More than that, he was a friend.

And I'll be a better one. Starting right now.

With grim determination, he forced his feet down a long, narrow hall. Outside the master bedroom, he slowed to a halt. The old man hadn't gone anywhere, not with his truck parked right where he'd left it last night. So why hadn't he answered?

A host of possibilities rose. Not liking any of them, Nate drew in a ragged breath. Hinges that could use a good dose of WD-40 protested when the bedroom door swung wide. Nothing but dust stirred when he called Jimmy's name. Sheets draped a mound on the bed. The uneasy feeling that had formed in his stomach dropped lower, but Nate moved closer. Sweat trickled down his back as he prodded the mattress and got no response.

Minutes later, he strode onto the porch where he retrieved his phone and reported what he'd found.

"I'm sorry to hear that, Nate," said Connie, the sheriff's dispatcher. "You sure he's, you know, gone?"

"I'm sure." He swallowed, mopped his cheeks and dried the back of his hand on his jeans. In the back bedroom, the man who'd helped raise him lay cold and hard beneath a sheet gone soft from countless washings.

"The sheriff's out on Route 46. I'll pass the message along to him. He'll be along soon's he can. He'll want to make notifications. How 'bout rustlin' up a list of next of kin while you wait?"

"Yeah. Sure." Nate shrugged. Going back into the house held no appeal whatsoever, but it had to be done. Only, there wasn't anyone to tell, was there? An only child, Jimmy had inherited the grove that had been in his family for generations. He and Margaret hadn't had any children. The Castle line ended with them. Was there anyone else?

Margaret's sister and niece, Nate guessed, though no one from that side of the family had visited in...

He removed his cap long enough to rake his fingers through his hair. All hell had broken loose between him and Justine following Margaret's funeral. Had it really been ten years ago? It had, and the date had marked the last time any of Jimmy's extended family had paid even the briefest of visits to Castle Grove. He closed his eyes, imagining the thin, willowy girl he'd once loved.

Where is she now?

Justine had always been ambitious. In all likelihood, she was sitting behind a big desk in some corner office where diplomas and awards dotted the walls. She'd married, hadn't she? Nodding, he resettled his ball cap. Word was she'd had a kid a few years back. By now, photos of two or three smiling children probably decorated her bookshelves.

Nate straightened. The idea that Justine might show up for Jimmy's funeral twisted the knife in his gut, but she wasn't the only one who might drop by. Word of James Castle's passing would spread quickly—Connie would see to that. Before too long, people would converge on the grove to pay their respects.

What would they say when they saw the place?

He shook his head. The old man's memory deserved better than the gossip that would drip, like cane syrup from a biscuit, if anyone saw how low the owner of Castle Grove had sunk. As for Jimmy's relatives, well, the homestead never had been up to their standards. No more than Nate had lived up to Justine's.

Squaring his shoulders, Nate walked through the house, raising the windows and drawing open the drapes. In the streaming light, he took a hard look at a house that had gone far too long without a good cleaning. Clearly, the situation called for a mop and a bucket and plenty of elbow grease. Without that much time, he rooted through the cupboards on the back porch until he came up with dust rags and a box of thirty-gallon trash bags. Then he set to work tidying up the place.

By the time plumes of dust rose from behind the first of several cars that turned off the main road, he'd made some headway. True, the house would never be featured in *Better Homes & Gardens*, not without a total makeover. But at least the stale air no longer reeked of spoiled food, while bills and magazines stood in some semblance of order on the desk in Jimmy's office. In a bathroom that could benefit from a blowtorch, Nate overlooked blackened grout while he washed his hands. The grubby towel on the rack was another matter. He opted to air-dry on his way to greet the paramedics.

A short while later, Nate propped one shoulder against the peeling paint on the front porch. His arms crossed, he stared into the distance as EMTs wheeled the stretcher bearing James Castle's lifeless body through the house.

"He lived a good life." Deputy Sheriff Jack Sparling removed his hat, revealing hair that had thinned a bit in the years since he'd played wide receiver to Nate's quarterback.

"That he did." Nate's throat tightened, and he cleared it. "He managed to hang on to the place when canker drove most every other grove out of business. He was a smart man, savvy 'bout citrus and business. Well-respected." Jimmy had served on the town council for the past fifteen years and had been mayor of Orange Blossom for the last five.

"We're sure gonna miss him."

Metal rattled as men in dark uniforms carried the stretcher down the front steps. Efficiently, if not reverently, they loaded their burden into a waiting ambulance. Doors thudded closed. One of the men trudged up the stairs with a clipboard while the other went around to the front of the vehicle. The engine started. The deputy scrawled his signature where the young man pointed and returned the paperwork.

"Sorry for your loss." The kid, so wet behind the ears that acne pimpled his chin, aimed his comment at no one in particular.

Nate gulped. It didn't seem fitting, somehow, that Jimmy's life should come to such an inauspicious end. "What happens next?" he asked.

Jack hitched his gun belt higher on wide hips. "In a case like this, the coroner doesn't usually bother with an autopsy. Not considering Jimmy's age and the circumstances." He glanced over his shoulder at the interior of the house. "Looks like he was kinda failin' there at the end, you know."

Nate rubbed the spot where guilt dug a hole in his heart. "Wish I'd known how bad things had gotten for him. I'd have sure helped out more."

"It happens with a lot of old folks. Remember my aunt Tilly? She was the same way," the deputy commiserated. "Shocked the entire family when we saw it. Much worse than this. You gonna handle the funeral?"

Nate blinked. There wasn't much to handle. Ten years ago, Jimmy had purchased adjoining plots and prepaid all the expenses after Margaret collapsed while working in the kitchen. An aneurism, the doctors had said. "I'll call the funeral home. They'll see to all the details."

"Place could use some sprucing up, but the roof looks to be in good shape. Think you'll move in?"

It didn't feel right, dividing up the estate before James Castle was laid to rest. Until there was a reading of the will and everything was official, he'd go to work overseeing the planting and harvesting of Castle Grove the same way he'd always done. The way his father had done before him. One day, he'd own the land he'd worked all his life. One day soon, but not today.

"Royce Enid's been Jimmy's lawyer for as far back as I can remember. I'll check with him, but I'm not in any hurry to change things." There wasn't any rush. Everyone in town knew about the deal Jimmy had offered him.

"You do that." Jack scanned the land on which Orange Blossom depended for its livelihood. "Meantime, town's gonna need a new mayor. We can't afford to wait, not with the Orange Fest to plan for." Months of preparation went into the annual fundraiser. In his dual role as mayor and owner of the grove that underwrote most of the start-up costs for the event, Jimmy had headed up the planning committee.

"I hear ya." Nate flipped through a short list of available candidates. The people of Orange Blossom would never accept a relative newcomer like Everett Grimes. Born and raised in the area, Jack would make a good fit, but his duties already kept the deputy so busy he didn't have time to fish, much less run the town. Nate shook his head. Finding someone to follow in Jimmy's footsteps wasn't going to be easy.

"Seems pretty clear you ought to take the job," Jack said. "You're already on the council. A local boy. Someone everybody likes. With all this land"—he made a sweeping motion—"you're the obvious choice."

"Me?"

"I can't see anyone else rushing forward to take the job."

Nate turned the idea over. In a place the size of Orange Blossom, serving as mayor mostly meant staying on the good side of more than half the thousand or so who called the hundred square miles smack-dab in the middle of Florida their home. Planning for the Orange Fest, though, that involved real work. And failure, well, that simply wasn't an option. Not with the local high school students dependent on the money the event raised to help cover their college costs.

On the other hand, how could he turn down the position? He wasn't one to shirk a little hard work, was he? Besides, shouldering Uncle Jimmy's responsibilities was one way to repay the debt he owed the old man, considering he'd soon inherit the land under his feet.

"If that's what everyone wants, I guess I could." Nate hauled himself erect. "Least ways till the next election."

"Why don't you sit? Take a load off. The laundry can wait till tomorrow. Or never." Penny flopped down on the oversized recliner closest to the TV, aimed the remote and began flipping channels.

Justine finished folding a towel, placed it on the stack, then bent to retrieve the next item from the clothes basket. Relaxing wasn't on her agenda tonight any more than it had been on any given day since Gracie's birth.

She eyed the pile of clean clothes. Once she put the laundry away, there were lunches to pack for tomorrow. She needed to get a spot out of her second-best black skirt. The cute pair of jeans she'd bought

Gracie at a thrift store had to be hemmed. And that was just the start. She'd log at least four hours of overtime by researching the latest pleadings in the Peterson case before she climbed into bed tonight. If she was lucky, Gracie would sleep through the night, and she would, too. Either way, the alarm would still go off at five, plunging them into the chaotic routine of getting an active preschooler and herself fed, dressed and out the door to school and the office.

How would she manage if she got sick? Or if Gracie did?

Worry, a constant companion of late, ate at her, and Justine rubbed her stomach. When the flu had made the rounds at day care, she'd kept Gracie home for a week rather than risk exposure. She'd begun carrying packs of antiseptic wipes wherever she went...and she wasn't afraid to use them, on doors, shopping carts, anything, in fact, that Gracie might touch. She watched their diet with a fervor that would make a religious zealot proud. But, no matter how much overtime she put in, no matter how hard she worked, she was bailing water with a can full of holes.

Her eyes squeezed shut against tears that always hovered just below the surface while she mechanically folded another towel and added it to the growing stack. Fear rippled through her, scattering her thoughts like buzzards at the edge of a busy highway. Her chest tightened.

Her mother would say the situation was her own damn fault. *People have to face the consequences of their mistakes,* Nola had harped over countless family dinners.

Justine shook her head. She'd made mistakes—who hadn't? Falling for Marco was probably the worst choice she'd ever made, but even that had an upside, because it had given her Gracie. Still, she hadn't killed anyone. Hadn't scammed little old ladies out of their life's savings. Hadn't set fire to a house. So why did life have to be so damned hard?

"Breathe," she told herself. "Just breathe."

She was struggling to do just that when the doorbell rang. Justine flinched and dropped the T-shirt she'd been folding. She shot a quick glance across the room. "Are you expecting someone?"

Penny plucked at the blousy sweatshirt she wore over her sleep pants. "I'm not exactly dressed for company."

While her roommate muted the television, Justine hurried to the door. Peering through the peephole, she studied a uniformed figure on the landing. Still cautious, she left the security chain in place while she eased the door open a crack.

"Ms. Gale?" the delivery man said without looking up from an electronic keypad. "I have a package for you."

Her gaze dropped from the man's bright yellow shirt to a matching envelope, and deciding he was legit, she opened the door wide enough to accept a thick envelope. Her brow wrinkled as she studied the unfamiliar return address. She wasn't expecting anything. She certainly didn't know anyone in Florida who'd pay for expensive courier service. But when the delivery man held out a stylus, she tucked the parcel under one arm and scribbled her name in the blank.

"What is it?" Penny asked, lowering the footrest on the recliner before she crossed the room.

"I don't know, but it can't be good." Not if the last month was any indication.

Caution drove her to the couch where she sank onto a worn cushion. Had one of her creditors filed suit despite the small, but steady, payments she'd been making against the mountain of debts that had accumulated during Gracie's stay in the NICU? Not sure she had the strength to deal with more bad news, she forced one finger under the flap. A dozen sheets held together by a heavy black clip fanned onto the coffee table when she tipped the envelope.

She flipped past a handwritten note requesting a phone call at her earliest convenience and stared at letterhead belonging to one Royce Enid, Attorney at Law, Orange Blossom, Florida. Her heart thumped against her ribs. A quick scan of an official-looking cover letter informed her that Royce was the executor and representative of James Clayton Castle, deceased.

"It's from Uncle Jimmy's lawyer," she announced. Relieved that none of her many creditors was taking her to court, she relaxed the tiniest bit.

"Why would he—oh, that's right." Penny straightened. "You were related to him, weren't you? Sarah and I and Nate and Jake and the rest—we all sort of ended up at Castle Grove each summer, but you were his niece."

"By marriage. Aunt Margaret was my mother's sister. I should've gone to the funeral." But she hadn't. The news about Uncle Jimmy had reached her while she and Gracie had been waiting for yet another lab technician to draw blood. She was pretty sure that was the same day her car had sputtered to a stop just off I-66. By the time she'd covered her portion of the lab work and the repairs, her checking account had been bone-dry. With no hope of heading south to pay her respects, she let the memories of those long-ago days at Castle Grove wash over her. Inhaling deeply, she almost smelled the faint scent of orange blossoms.

"I miss those summers we spent with your aunt and uncle." Penny pushed her glasses higher on her nose. "We all grumbled about doing chores, but we had the best times! My favorite was when we picked blueberries."

"Of course it was. You always ate as much as you picked. Sarah and I, we'd tote full baskets back to the house, and you'd only have a few berries in yours." She laughed, recalling how mercilessly they'd teased Penny about her blue tongue.

"Remember when Jimmy got all dressed up in his beekeeper outfit to harvest the hives?" Penny's eyes crinkled.

Justine's throat ached for the taste of the clear, golden honey that dripped from frames her uncle had called supers. "I'd give my eyeteeth for another piece of that honeycomb," she said, her voice wistful. They had chewed the thick wax like gum, making it last for hours.

Her roommate cupped one hand over her mouth. "I can still see Nate that time he bit into a bee. He danced around like his mouth was on fire."

"Nate Rhodes, I haven't thought of him in ages," Justine whispered, removing the pins from her hair, one by one. She'd once loved a boy who had run his fingers through the long, straight strands. But that had been years and years ago, back when she'd spent her summers among the orange trees on her uncle's farm. A wisp of smoke from her last painful encounter with Nate stung her eyes. "I wonder what he's doing these days."

"Dad says he comes into the store from time to

time," Penny said slowly. Not long after he moved to Orange Blossom, a bad wreck had ended Mr. Kirk's truck-driving career. With the money he'd gotten from the insurance settlement, he'd opened the Book Nook on Main Street. "I think Nate took over as the grove manager after his father retired. We could ask Sarah...if you're interested." Unlike her and Penny, their friend had remained in Orange Blossom where she worked in the bakery named after her great-grandmother.

"Nah, that's okay." Long strands of hair brushed her shoulders as she shook her head. She'd closed out that chapter of her life the summer she graduated from high school.

Penny pointed at the thick raft of papers on the coffee table. "Do you think your uncle might have left you something?"

A bright spark of hope flared in her chest. It died, guttering as quickly as it had burst into flame. "Uncle Jimmy and Aunt Margaret were land rich and cash poor. At one point, they asked about stock in Gale Enterprises, but they didn't have enough money for a buy-in."

"Good thing," Penny murmured without a trace of malice.

"Yeah," Justine agreed with a half laugh. "Good thing." Her dad's company had gone belly-up shortly after his death.

Leaning over the papers, she scanned through page after page, her experience at Jacoby & Sons helping her cut through the legalese like a hot knife through cold butter until she reached a copy of her uncle Jimmy's will. She ran one finger along the italicized script.

I, James Clayton Castle, being of sound mind...leave all my worldly goods to my wife, Margaret Elizabeth Castle.

She looked up from the papers. When she'd headed home at the end of each summer, Aunt Margaret had always loaded her down with boxes of canned fruits and vegetables. Months later, when icicles dripped from the eaves and snow blanketed Northern Virginia rooftops, opening one of those glass jars had filled the room with the sunshine and the scent of homegrown tomatoes. Wishing the woman had lived to see her namesake, Margaret Grace, Justine returned to the page.

In the event her death precedes mine, I name my niece, Justine Gale, as my sole beneficiary.

The will slid from her boneless fingers. She stared blankly at Penny.

"What?" her roommate asked, alarm filling her face. "What is it?"

Justine inhaled a huge shuddery gulp. Her arm jerked. In one halting movement, she toppled the neatly folded clothes from the coffee table to the floor. Spreading the papers on the scarred wooden surface, she backtracked to the beginning to make sure she hadn't overlooked some important detail that would negate what she'd just read. She hadn't.

"I need to go to Florida," she said at last. "As soon as possible." Air seeped across her lips as she reread the section naming her the sole beneficiary of two hundred acres of land in Central Florida.

A citrus grove. *Castle* Grove.

She tugged her bottom lip between her teeth while her heart struggled to accept what she'd read. Aware that Penny stared at her like she'd lost her marbles, she explained, "Royce Enid needs to see me right away. If I'm reading this right—I'll have one of the attorneys in the office look it over, just to be sure—but if I am, Uncle Jimmy left everything to me. The land, the grove, tractors and more farm equipment, the house...everything." Her thoughts churning, she found it hard to concentrate. What should she do next? "If I can scrape up the money to pay for the trip, can you watch Gracie for me for a weekend while I go down there to check things out?"

"You know I will, but oh my God!" Penny jumped to her feet. "You own Castle Grove? That's fantastic! We should call Sarah, get her in on this."

"Wait. Hold up on that for now." In spite of the hope that flared anew in her chest, Justine held up one hand. "Let's be sure it's not all just a mistake before we tell anyone else."

"Yeah. Okay. You're right." Penny's eyes widened. "But if it is true, you don't know anything about raising oranges. What are you gonna do with a citrus grove?"

"I'll sell it," she said, making a snap decision. She bet eager buyers would line up at the chance to own the large tract of land. By now, the acreage had to be worth a small fortune. Enough to erase her debts and provide for Margaret Grace's future.

A laugh floated out of her before she had a chance to stop it. She bit back a second one, willing herself away from the slippery slope that would lead to hysteria.

"Thank you, Uncle Jimmy," she whispered.

Clutching the copy of her uncle's will to her chest, she let her tears flow.

"Nate, why didn't you tell me?" A high-pitched squeal punctuated Erlene's distinctly Southern drawl.

Nate held the phone at arm's length. His on-again/off-again relationship with the freckle-faced redhead had grown cold enough that the midday call had caught him off guard. Wary of damaging his eardrums, he angled the mouthpiece to his lips.

"Tell you what?"

"You don't know?"

Another shriek proved he'd been right to keep the receiver as far from his head as possible. "Why, Royce Enid walked into the courthouse as pretty as you please this morning. He filed the probate papers on Jimmy's estate. That's what!"

The news was startling enough to risk another of Erlene's frequent screams. According to Florida law, nearly every estate had to pass through probate court before its assets were distributed to the beneficiaries. But who had given Royce leave to start the process?

"You're positive?" Doubt colored his tone. He pressed the phone to his other ear. If there'd been a reading of the will, he sure as heck hadn't been invited.

"Sure as I'm sitting here." Here being the county tax collector's office in the courthouse where Erlene's primary focus was keeping up with all the gossip while she sold hunting and fishing licenses. "He turned in the paperwork first thing. It won't be long now. A court date's already been set for October. By the first of the year, Castle Grove will be all yours."

"Some of it already is," he corrected. Leaning against the kitchen sink, he gave the healthy grove beyond the window a satisfied look.

"Either way, it's a dream come true. People are already saying what a good job you're doing as mayor. As the owner of Castle Grove, you're a cinch to win the election next fall. I hope you'll remember me when."

He didn't say anything in the pause that followed. After a minute, Erlene's voice dropped into a slightly more subdued register. "What's the matter?" she asked. "Aren't you excited?"

Not exactly.

Her news gave focus to the feeling he'd had lately that something was wrong. As heir apparent to the grove that was the main industry in Orange Blossom, he'd moved one seat over on the city council, shouldering the job of mayor and plunging into the planning of the Orange Fest. The rest of the time, he'd gone about the business of trimming and mowing and fertilizing, the same way he had for most of his life. Secure in Jimmy's promise—and out of respect for the dead—he'd put off having a conversation with Royce about the estate. Now, he wondered if he'd made a huge mistake. Shouldn't he have heard from Royce before this?

A letter? A phone call? Something?

"Nate, you there?"

He reined in his drifting thoughts. "Yeah, I'm here. I'm just, ah, a little surprised that things are moving so quickly, I guess." He used his free hand to take a glass from the cupboard by the fridge. "I have to go now, but thanks for the heads-up, Erlene." The sooner he got off the phone, the sooner he could call Royce. Or better yet, stop by the lawyer's office over the hardware store.

"Sure thing, but..."

If he'd thought the latest gossip was the only reason Erlene had reached out to him, he'd been wrong. He held his breath, prepared this time, for the question he hoped she wouldn't ask.

"You want to get together this Saturday? That new Jake Jackson movie's playing at the Bijou over in Oviedo." A muffled rustle meant Erlene had cupped her hand over the speaker. "You know how a good romantic comedy puts me in the mood."

Oh, he knew all right.

Trouble was, he hadn't been in the same mood where Erlene was concerned for quite some time. They'd had a few laughs, tumbled into bed together more than once. But his attraction had waned once he realized her idea of deep conversation stretched no further than the latest blockbuster movie. Wanting more, he'd let the time between calls and Saturday nights stretch a bit.

"Sorry." He shook his head, knowing the tepid relationship had run its course. For now, he was content to roll out of a bed that seemed far too large for one person each morning. Sure, in the minutes before he poured his first cup, he wondered what it'd be like to have someone to share his coffee, his life. Mostly, though, he pushed those thoughts aside, tugged on a pair of jeans one leg at a time and went to work overseeing the citrus grove and the town that depended on it.

"Some other time?"

"Probably not," he said, softening his words to cushion the blow. He gave her a minute to let the news sink in. Then, because they'd been friends long before they'd started stepping out together, he asked, "You okay with that?"

"Right as rain," Erlene quipped. "We both knew what this was from the start and that it would end one day. It's not like we were ever going to march down the aisle together."

Nate caught the wistful note and felt a guilty pang. "You will, Erlene. You just have to, you know, find the right guy."

"There's plenty of fish in the sea," she agreed, her voice overly bright.

Through the receiver, Nate heard a short buzz announcing a new arrival at the tax collector's office. Two seconds later, Erlene mumbled, "Sorry to cut this short, doll, but my next Mr. Potential just walked in, and he's a doozy. Be seeing you."

With a heart even bigger than her well-endowed chest, Erlene had no shortage of eager men waiting to dance her around the local pool hall. Which, Nate had to admit, was also part of the problem. Sooner or later, someone richer, smarter, *better* than he was was bound to catch Erlene's fancy. He'd taken the initiative, but she could have just as easily been the one to call it quits. Still, he'd stop by the courthouse in a day or two for a quick chat, just to make sure there weren't any ill feelings between them. Keeping the peace with a former girlfriend—no matter how shallow the relationship—was important in a town the size of Orange Blossom, where far less than six degrees separated any two people on Main Street.

Nate poured sweet iced tea and carried the glass out onto the porch. It felt odd, being in the house in the middle of the day with nothing to do. Ordinarily, he had plenty to keep him busy, but a sudden downpour had curtailed his plan to track down a problem with the irrigation system. The rain dripping from the eaves and the gurgle of water in the downspouts meant he could shut off the pumps. Thinking of Erlene's news, he leaned on the railing and stared out at orange trees he hoped to call his own before too long.

"Jimmy, you old codger," he whispered. "Did you pull one over on me?"

Margaret's death, coming on the heels of a canker epidemic that had wiped out half of Castle Grove's citrus trees, had made Jimmy more aware of his own mortality. The arthritis that forced Nate's dad into early retirement only reinforced Jimmy's feelings. Soon after Nate graduated from college and took over as manager of the grove, the old man had knocked on his door. "I'm not a young man anymore," the owner had said. "It's time I start thinking about the future."

"Yes, sir," Nate had acknowledged. Was Jimmy going to sell the land and put him out of a job? Castle Grove had been in the old man's family for four generations. A Rhodes had managed the estate for nearly as long. Nate had swept a quick look over the cottage he'd made his own after his dad retired. He'd taken his first steps across these hardwood floors, learned to play the guitar in the small bedroom down the hall. The scar over his right eye came from a run-in with the kitchen counter. He hated the thought of leaving, especially when there was little hope of landing a job on another grove. Faced with rising costs and diseases that threatened Florida's citrus industry, most independent owners had given up, planted pines or, worse, sold out to a conglomerate or developer.

"I'm gonna have to pour every dime back into the groves for the next several years. Gotta plant new trees to replace the ones we lost to disease. It'll be years before they mature and bear fruit." The man Nate had called Uncle Jimmy since he'd learned to talk had leaned heavily on his cane.

Knowing the old man didn't usually bring up a topic without knowing exactly where he wanted to go with it, Nate had bided his time and heard the man out.

"I'm getting on in years. Margaret and me, we didn't have any children. My niece, Justine, she's got other plans for her life. I want to leave this land to someone who'll love it, same as me, and there ain't no one else wants Castle Grove the way you do. So, how 'bout we do this... For every year you manage the place without taking a bonus, I'll deed ten acres to you. The rest, well, the rest'll be yours when I'm gone."

Nate had stared at the spry octogenarian. "Uncle Jimmy, you're probably going to live to be a hundred."

The remark had tugged a smile from the rail-thin figure. "Nah, but even if I did, by then you'd own all this." He'd hitched an arthritic thumb over his shoulder, pointing to fields that still lay empty, stripped naked of diseased trees. "What do you say?"

Studying the landowner's lined face and watery blue eyes, Nate had managed to take a breath. It wasn't money he'd wanted, it was land. Land that had grown more dear than diamonds once theme parks had sprung up on every corner of Orlando, thirty miles to the south. Though both his father and grandfather had talked of establishing a grove of their own, they'd never had the means to pursue their dream, one they'd passed along to him. Since graduation—before that, even—he'd been saving to buy his own place. But, despite the tidy nest egg in his bank account, he'd never save enough to make his dream a reality. Jimmy had offered just that chance.

"I'd say you have yourself a deal," Nate had agreed. A chance to put sweat equity to work—that had been an offer he couldn't refuse. The two-bedroom cottage that had come with the manager's title offered ample space for a bachelor.

"Good." They'd shaken hands, and the deal had been struck. "I'll throw in the first ten as a measure of good faith," Jimmy had added.

And Nate had lived up to his end of the bargain. Dug a thousand holes on each acre. Planted seedlings. Tenderly grafted sweet buds to the sour, but hardier, root stock. He'd poured his life into rebuilding the groves. In spite of that, had Jimmy decided he didn't measure up? Looking out over trees laden with fruit that would see their first harvest this winter, Nate swallowed another gulp of tea and tried to ignore the way it sloshed loosely in his stomach.

The memory of his first love drifted in the air like smoke from a dying fire, a reminder that the owner wouldn't be the first Castle to turn their back on him. But to see Castle Grove through the lean times, he'd worked twice as hard as any man.

Why, then, would Jimmy cut him out of his will?

He wouldn't, Nate told himself. They'd had a gentleman's agreement, and if there was anything he knew about James Clayton Castle, he knew the patriarch of his clan had been a man of his word.

Erlene had to be mistaken. It was as plain and simple as that.

He removed his hat and ran a hand through hair that was a few weeks overdue for a cut. With the rain expected to continue for the rest of the day, this was as good a time as any for a trip into town. He'd see the barber, swing by the town hall, then pick up a few groceries. While he was at it, he'd stop in for a chat with Royce. Content with his plan, he dashed the dregs of his iced tea onto a hibiscus bush at the edge of the porch and headed inside.

A shower, a shave and a haircut later, Nate ambled into a storefront on Main Street. He'd barely made it through the door before Karen Smalley peered around her computer screen to call out a cheery, "Afternoon, Mr. Mayor. Sure is nice to see this rain, isn't it?"

"Afternoon, *Madam Secretary*." Nate aimed an amicable smile toward the petite, dark-haired woman. When Karen's lips pursed and her brows knitted, he smothered an urge to laugh.

"Thought we'd decided to leave all the formalities for the council meetings," he prodded. If all went well with the Orange Fest, a fall election would make his position as interim mayor permanent. Until then— and, truth be told, afterward—he'd rather be called Nate, same as always.

"I hear ya, Mr.—Nate."

"That's better, Karen." He let his grin widen. "How's Bill?"

"Bill's good." She nodded, her features settling into the pleased expression she wore whenever someone mentioned her husband of twenty years. "He said to tell you those saw blades you ordered came in."

"Great. I'll stop by before I head back out to the grove and pick them up." Bill ran the town's only hardware store. "And the boys? I passed by the high school. Coach Martin has them doing two-a-days already."

"Had to start early if we're going to win another state championship." Maternal and school pride danced in Karen's eyes. The Smalley twins, seniors this year at Orange Blossom High, played first-string offense.

"They decide where they're headed next?" Nate asked.

"Too early to tell. What I do know is, it's pricey as all get-out. Putting both of them through school would bankrupt us if it wasn't for scholarships and loans. Thank goodness for Orange Blossom's grant money. It'll really come in handy." The creases in the secretary's face smoothed. "They'll be the first in our family to get their degrees, you know."

Even more reason to make sure the Orange Fest was a huge success. The money the town raised during the event provided a five-thousand-dollar grant to each college-bound graduate of Orange Blossom High. Nate moved on to the purpose of his visit. "Think I could get a copy of the agenda for next week's council meeting?"

Karen lifted one shoulder before her computer

screen once more snagged her interest. "It's already sitting on your desk," she said absently.

"Anything I should pay particular attention to?" He moved toward a desk far more suited to Jimmy's stature than his own six-foot, three-inch frame. Sure enough, the agenda sat, centered, on the blotter.

Karen's chair squeaked. "Mostly, we'll be talking about plans for the Orange Fest. We have a slew of vendor applications to look over. One from Fresh Picked Citrus." She pointed, making a face. "Another from a time-share we'll turn down."

Nodding, Nate thumbed through one of several stacks of paper on the desk. Visitors from all over the country poured into Orange Blossom the second week in January. For two days, booths filled with homegrown fruits and vegetables or handmade arts and crafts lined both sides of every street. Every year, one or two mass marketers tried to crash the party, and every year, the city council rejected their applications.

"Clara Johnson will be there with the usual request for start-up money."

He lowered the agenda to the desk blotter. In the past, a generous donation from Castle Grove had funded the 5K race that kicked off the weekend's festivities. He ran a hand through his hair and wondered if he needed Royce's permission to approve the expenditure.

All the more reason to talk to the man, he decided.

He glanced at Karen. No one within Orange Blossom's ten square miles could so much as walk down Main Street without her knowing about it.

"I hear Royce was over in Oviedo this morning." The tension in his shoulders eased a bit when Karen gave a nonchalant shrug and returned to her typing.

"I had coffee with Mary Beth a little while ago," she said, referring to Royce's receptionist. "Royce told her he'd been retained by Mr. Castle's heir." Karen's fingers slowed until they rested on the keyboard. Concern etched a frown across the face she turned away from the monitor. "I just assumed that meant you. It didn't?"

Nate's shoulders went as rigid as a two-by-four. He swallowed an acidic bitterness. "I think I'm about to find out," he answered quietly.

Ignoring the questions that clouded the secretary's eyes, he turned on one heel. Across the street, he ducked into a narrow alley between the hardware store and the diner. At the end stood a flight of wooden stairs. He took them two at a time, his boots striking each tread with a thud that echoed in the small space. On the landing, he fought for composure before he grasped the knob. Only when he was certain he'd hidden a chest-tightening mix of anger and fear, only then did he open the door.

A light floral scent floated in the chilled, dry air that blasted him as he crossed the threshold into Royce Enid's waiting room. Nate ran a quick glance over the empty side chairs flanking a red leather couch in the outer office. Thankful that none of the 943 other residents of Orange Blossom required the services of the town's lone attorney at the moment, he turned away from a local artist's rendering of the quaint downtown area before he aimed a hopeful smile toward the woman seated at the reception desk.

"Afternoon, Mary Beth." Observing the usual protocol chafed a bit, but he detoured from his original purpose long enough for a polite, "How're you and the little one doing?" He let his eyes bounce off her rounded middle.

"We're just—oof." Mary Beth grimaced and rubbed a hand over her bulging midsection. "To tell the truth, I'll be a whole lot better after this little guy pops out."

"A boy, huh? Jack must be over the moon." Nate flicked aside the tiniest sting of envy. Not everyone could be as lucky as the wide receiver who'd married the prom queen. He certainly hadn't been. He stuck his hands in the pockets of his Wranglers.

"Uh-huh, and I think he's going to be a linebacker." Mary Beth slipped one hand around to the small of her back and straightened in her chair. "Nate, what can I do for you?"

"Royce in?"

"Oh." Mary Beth's head tilted to one side. She gazed up at him over the top of dark-framed glasses. "I didn't realize you had an appointment."

"I don't. I was over at the town hall and thought I'd drop by. If he's not too busy."

Nate concentrated on maintaining a confident, casual air as the receptionist flipped open a leather-bound book. Paging to the first week in August, she tapped a pencil on the edge of a calendar that, from what he could see, contained nothing but white space.

"He's pretty busy. But if this is town business..." Mary Beth's voice trailed off to leave the suggestion hanging.

Nate hesitated. The juice of Castle Grove oranges went into the orange meringue pies Miss June's Pie Shop shipped all over the state. Peels of grapefruit harvested from Castle Grove trees went into the candy made right here in Orange Blossom. Take away the income the hardware store earned from the two hundred acres just west of town, and Bill would have to close his shop. When Nate added up all the people whose livelihoods depended, in one way or another, on the grove, any threat to its existence sure sounded like official business to him.

"Tell him it is," he hedged. Lying to an expectant mother would probably earn him a special place in hell, but he needed to see Royce and he wasn't willing to wait. Minutes later, as he shook the age-spotted hand of one of Jimmy's cronies, Nate came straight to the point.

"I heard you opened probate on the Castle estate this morning."

Loose flesh beneath Royce's chin jiggled as the man's head swung up and down. His hand tightened slightly before his fingers slipped from Nate's grasp. Stepping behind a massive mahogany desk, the attorney eased himself onto a well-padded leather chair. He gestured toward one of two others. "Have a seat."

Nate folded his arms across his chest and locked his knees. "I think I'd rather stand, if you don't mind. So it's true? You filed the papers?" His last hope that this had all been a terrible mistake faded when Royce's head bobbed again. He took a breath.

Royce flashed a mouthful of sharp white teeth. "It's a royal pain, I know, but probate shouldn't take too long. Three, maybe four months. Then, according to the terms of Jimmy's will, all his assets will be transferred to his heir."

His heir, but not me?

Nate had played poker with the lawyer often enough to recognize the nervous twitch Royce developed whenever the man bluffed with a pair of twos. It was time to lay his own cards on the table. He let his eyes narrow.

"I was more than a little surprised that you didn't check with me before you went to court."

Royce cocked one white eyebrow. His thumbs slipped beneath the straps of black suspenders. "I know you were expecting to inherit some, maybe all, of Castle Grove, son. But Jimmy didn't leave so much as a blade of grass to you."

A thin, high whine swirled inside Nate's head. "If not me, then who?"

Royce's face flushed bright red. "You remember Justine, don't you? Blond hair. Big blue eyes. Little bit of a thing, she was. She used to spend summers here when she was a child."

The dismissive hand Nate waved through the air said only that he didn't care. Not that he'd forgotten the girl he'd given his heart to. Or how, a long time ago, she'd walked out of his life, out of Orange Blossom, out of the state without so much as a single backward glance.

"Jimmy left everything to her."

Despite the soothing way in which he said them, Royce's words delivered a blow straight to Nate's gut. His breath abandoned him, and his knees buckled.

"Guess I'll sit, after all," he grunted, sinking onto the chair. His head bowed, he took a minute to get his wits about him before peering up to ask, "You're sure about this?"

"As a judge." Royce nodded. "He named Justine Gale as his only heir."

Nate gave himself points for not raising the rafters. "He wouldn't do that," he argued softly. "She didn't care about him, much less about the land. If she had, she'd have come back here from time to time. Hell. She didn't even bother to show up for the funeral."

Royce tsked. "Mr. Castle was well within his rights to leave his land to a relative. I'm afraid that's what he did."

Anger, hot and red, boiled up from Nate's midsection. He gripped his thighs, felt his color rise with the effort it took to control his temper. His thoughts turned sluggish, but he managed to hang on to a single hope of convincing the lawyer to see his side.

"Royce, you and everyone else in town know about the deal Jimmy and I struck," he said, his words coming in a rush. "Just last year, after the grapefruit harvest, you were there when he raised that toast at The Crush."

The only bar in town, The Crush threw its doors wide open for an annual end-of-the-season party after the last truckload of citrus headed to the packing plant. While most folks came for the free hors d'oeuvres, hot wings and live music, those who earned their living directly from Castle Grove showed up for all that plus to get their bonus checks. For the past eight years, the elderly gentleman who sat at a small table in a back corner had hoisted his beer in Nate's direction as the evening wore down.

"He told everybody there I'd earned another ten acres. That made eighty. Nearly half the estate. He promised to leave the rest to me in his will, but I'd consider settling for what's owed me." A grove that size would provide a comfortable living.

"And I wish I could give it to you. But the fact is, since Jimmy never transferred any land to you while he was alive—"

"He was trying to keep Castle Grove afloat," Nate protested. "It seemed a whole lot more important to pay for fertilizer and pickers than to lay out thousands of dollars for taxes and legal fees. Especially since I was eventually going to inherit the land anyway."

"In hindsight, that was probably a mistake." Royce blew a huge breath out over his even larger stomach. "It doesn't matter how old we are, sometimes we think we're going to live forever. Jimmy probably intended to change his will one day. For whatever reason, he never got around to it. What we're left with is the one he wrote out before Margaret died. That one leaves everything to Justine."

Nate clenched his fists and ground out his words. "But you know that wasn't what he said, what he meant. There has to be some way to make this right."

"What can I tell you, Nate?" Royce's cupped hands held no answers, only air. "Maybe if he'd written it down..."

Nate's heart sank. When it came to growing citrus, Jimmy had been all green thumbs, but the man hated record keeping with a passion. He swallowed. "Guess I'll have to hire my own lawyer."

The squeak of hinges badly in need of oil sounded through the room as Royce folded his hands across his belly and tipped back in his chair. "You can do that, hire your own attorney, file a suit to assert your claim. The case will drag through the courts for years. In the end, you'll lose. While it's true that a man is only as good as his word, the law doesn't consider a handshake and a gentleman's agreement legally binding."

"What else can I do?" Walls decorated with framed

photos of an ever-thickening lawyer posed with influential clients were closing in. He needed to get up and get out before he did something he'd regret. "There's no way I'll let the land I've worked for go to an outsider without putting up a fight."

Royce tipped his chair forward, sending another rusty squeak through the shrinking space. He rested his elbows on the desk and settled his chin atop his closed fists. "I spoke with Justine earlier this week. She's coming down to check things out. You could approach her, tell her your story. If she believes you, she might be willing to sell you the land you want at a reduced price."

"Pay good money to buy what I've already paid for with sweat and hard work?" Nate's voice shook. He rose to his feet, his determination to get what belonged to him growing with every step he took toward the exit.

At the door, a quick glance out the window overlooking the town halted his flight as, across the street, Karen Smalley turned her key in the lock before she left the town hall for the night. All along Main Street, lights flickered in the line of mature oak trees that, on a hot summer day, provided shade for shoppers. On his next inhale, he caught the faint scent of baked goods coming from Miss June's Pie Shop. The odor mingled with the smell of fried chicken, tonight's special at the Ham Hut. The sights and smells of the small town he'd lived in all his life served as a sobering reminder that more than his stake in Castle Grove hung in the balance.

Wondering how Jimmy's death and a battle over his estate would affect Orange Blossom, he stabbed Royce with an appraising look. "What about the

Orange Fest? The 5K race? Castle Grove always covered the start-up costs and the prize money."

Royce sighed. "I'll put it on my list of things to discuss with Justine when she gets here. In the meantime, as Jimmy's executor, I'll need to approve all large expenditures. There's a goodly amount of cash in checking, and your name's on the account. Should be enough for day-to-day operations. You'll handle that, same as always. But save all your receipts so we can true things up at the end."

"What about the pickers for the orange harvest?" The migrant workers were paid, in cash, at the end of every day.

"Let me know when you plan to start. I'll make sure to come out every night at quitting time to pay them. That's the best I can do."

Seconds later, Nate felt a momentary pang as he barged out the door and into the reception area. A quick glance told him he had nothing to worry about. Mary Beth had left for the day.

Nothing to worry about? He barked a short laugh.

Sure, he had nothing to worry about. Nothing more than getting stabbed in the back by a man he'd called his uncle since he was old enough to talk. Or having the land he'd sacrificed to own slip from his fingers. Disaster would befall Orange Blossom if ownership of Castle Grove remained in doubt for too long. And then there was the Orange Fest, and the kids who might not go to college in the fall unless he came up with a way to underwrite the fundraiser that helped cover their expenses. He thundered down the stairs.

Nope. Not one damn thing to worry about. Instead, he had a whole slew of them. And at the top of his list was Justine Gale. The woman had broken his heart. Now, she had stolen his land.

As she neared a once-familiar turn off the highway, Justine's throat constricted. Though Royce Enid had urged her to come, though he'd tempted her with photos of lush citrus and substantial outbuildings, each of the last thirty miles had eaten away at her hope that Castle Grove was the answer to some, if not all, of her prayers. Abandoned groves where weeds grew nearly as tall as the gnarled skeletons of dead trees had mocked her decision to come to Florida ever since her plane touched down in Orlando. Add that to her mother's insistence that the trip was another in a long line of foolish mistakes, and it was no wonder her chest clenched so tight she could barely breathe.

And what about Gracie? Was she okay?

Anxious, Justine ran a finger over the cell phone in the cup holder. The last bar on the display had disappeared soon after she'd crossed the Seminole County line. Her heart ached at the thought of being out of touch. Of leaving Gracie with Penny, even if it was only for a long weekend. Was Penny feeding her all the right foods? Would she do as she'd promised and follow her instructions to the letter? Was Gracie using a hand wipe after she touched a doorknob, a toy at day care? If she didn't, and she got sick...

Justine shook her head, refusing to travel down that path. She was here to secure her daughter's future, and that's exactly what she'd do.

In the distance, sunlight glinted off a freshly

painted white fence. She blinked, certain her eyes were deceiving her. But the fence was no mirage. Behind it stretched row after row of orange trees, each so green and healthy the picture belonged on a postcard.

Her lips gaped open. Relief softened her shoulders.

The thriving state of Castle Grove would let her demand top dollar for the land.

She needed every penny she could get.

Reassured she'd made the right decision, after all, she squinted at the sign that had greeted visitors to Castle Grove for as long as she could remember. The cast-iron crowns adorning each side triggered memories of long summer afternoons spent playing in the shade of the main house. Dressed in her aunt's castoffs, she'd been a princess, while Sarah and Penny had taken on the roles of ladies-in-waiting. Nate, a threadbare towel knotted around his neck, had been her Prince Charming. The strands of plastic beads he'd spray-painted had become their crown jewels. For years after they'd all outgrown their make-believe kingdoms, she'd pulled those beads from their special box to wear at the traditional end-of-the-summer cookout.

She pictured the gingham curtains at the windows of her room in Castle Grove, the old-fashioned dressing table where she'd dreamed about the future, the nightstand where she'd kept her diary. Would everything be the same as it had been back then? Would the jewelry, even after all these years, still be tucked in a bottom dresser drawer?

When the rental car nosed past an unmanned fruit and vegetable stand as she turned onto a dirt road, her lips firmed. Wherever the beads were, the gold flecks had long since rubbed off, just as surely as her dreams of a fairy-tale existence had faded. Now, her only hope for the future lay in getting a good price for the land her uncle had left her. And, with that in mind, she determined not to let memories of idyllic summers or the first boy who'd broken her heart cloud her judgment.

Her hands on the steering wheel tightened, though the long drive between orange and grapefruit trees didn't seem as bumpy as she remembered. She rolled down her window, anticipating the tangy scent of maturing citrus. Money in the bank, Uncle Jimmy used to call the green, unripened fruit.

The smell poured into the car along with a heavy dose of August's heat and heavy humidity. Immediately, her nose wrinkled. Nothing felt quite the same as it had back when she'd been a teenager. The thick carpet of freshly mowed grass between the trees looked greener. The trees, shorter.

She shrugged and rolled the window up again. Who cared if the air swaddled her like a wet blanket? She'd barely be in Orange Blossom long enough to notice. One day off was all she could manage. That, plus the weekend, gave her just enough time to attend a meeting or two, handle the details of the estate and make sure Nate agreed to stay on through the harvest. With any luck, she'd be on the last flight back to Virginia Sunday night and home in time to drop Gracie off at day care on her way to work Monday.

Ten minutes later, the glimpse of a sharply pitched roof above the trees announced she'd nearly reached the end of the road. Despite a reminder that her purpose in making the trip was business, all business, her heart rate kicked up the same way it had at the beginning of every childhood summer. She glanced toward the barn, half expecting Uncle Jimmy to hurry out of it, a spring in his step and a smile on his face. She saw the screen door slapping shut behind Aunt Margaret. As often as not, her aunt would still be wiping her hands on a dish towel when her mom braked to a stop at the end of the driveway. Over orange pound cake and tall glasses of lemonade, thick with slices of Castle Grove lemons, they'd spend the afternoon filling everyone in on the news from home and catching up on the latest happenings around Orange Blossom.

Justine dampened her lips. She could use a glass of ice-cold lemonade, but from the looks of the old homestead, it had been a long time since anyone had come rushing through the front door. Mounted on brick footers, the house hadn't aged as well as the barn or the fence. The windows along the front were intact—thank goodness—but the white clapboard siding, where it wasn't cracked or chipped, had faded. Wooden stairs leading from the drive to the wide, wraparound porch tilted precariously. At some point, the railing had disintegrated. The few remaining posts leaned drunkenly.

Warped floorboards creaked beneath her heels as she crossed the porch. Standing well to the side, she gripped the empty frame of the screen door between two fingers and eased it open. A breath she hadn't realized she'd been holding seeped between her lips when nothing darted or slithered out. She raised her hand, but stopped. Why knock when Royce had assured her the house had been sitting vacant and unused since Jimmy's funeral? Instead, she gave the handle a twist. It refused to budge.

Locked?

Gingerly, she lifted one corner of a frayed welcome mat. "Well, crap," she sighed when she didn't find a key. She eyed the double swing, but one look at the wasp nest on the ceiling hook made the decision not to wait there an easy one. Besides, she told herself, at four thirty on a Friday afternoon, the few people who worked the grove this time of year were most likely home with their families.

That left only Nate, and she ran a hand over her wrinkled skirt, wishing she'd had a chance to freshen up before she faced him. Above the chirp of cicadas, sharp clangs broke the breathless air. The sound seemed to originate from somewhere in the grove, and wanting to get settled before nightfall, she squared her shoulders and headed for the trees.

A few steps past the first row, her heels punched through the sod and mired deep in the sand. She kicked off her useless shoes and wiggled her toes in the cool grass. Carefully, she picked her way through the grove, avoiding spider webs that stretched between the trees, until she spied a faded blue shirt draped limply over the ends of a post-hole digger. Beyond it, she caught movement. Her gaze narrowed in on a sweat-dampened T-shirt that clung to a much broader pair of shoulders than she remembered.

Nate?

She lingered in the shade, watching tanned, glistening muscles alternately cord and flex as he shoveled gray sand into a hole. It was hot, heavy work for an afternoon when temperatures soared past ninety, yet he kept a rhythmic pace until the last of a knee-high pile disappeared. Justine felt a bead of sweat roll between her breasts when he bent, giving the level patch of dirt a final pat with the flat side of the shovel. She jumped when he spoke.

"You going to stand there all day? Or was there something you wanted?" He plunged the shovel into the ground and turned to face her.

The instant she caught sight of a wide jaw that tapered into a familiar rounded chin, Justine stifled a groan. Of all the conversations she'd planned on having with her old boyfriend, she hadn't imagined a single one that began with her getting caught gawking at him like a schoolgirl. Any more than she'd ever dreamed Nate would grow into the shoulders that had once topped his wiry chest like a coat rack. Straightening, she did her best to ignore the heat that climbed into her cheeks while she flipped through a dozen openings. At last, she found one that sounded innocuous enough.

"Hey, Nate," she said, forcing a casualness she didn't feel. "Hot enough for you?"

His movements slow and methodical, he leaned on the handle of his shovel. The brim of his baseball cap cast shadows across his eyes, making them unreadable, but she didn't need to peer into their dark depths to recognize the angry scowl on lips she'd once considered perfect.

Why? she wondered. She refused to believe that, after all these years, he still bore a grudge over their breakup. Her own pain about that fateful summer had long since faded. Surely his had, too. But something had gotten under his skin, and deciding it was up to her to make the first move, she stepped forward, her hand extended.

"It's good to see you again."

Nate's brusque, "Missed you at the funeral," took

her by surprise. Stung, she dropped her hand. Her fingers curled into a fist.

She shoved a wayward strand of hair over her shoulder and gave Nate her best who-do-you-think-you-are glare. Not that it was any of his business, but she could barely scrape up the money to keep her daughter fed. At the time, a trip to Florida had seemed impossible.

"I wish I could have been here," she said, grinding out the truth between clenched teeth. The night of Uncle Jimmy's funeral, she'd paged through the photo albums she'd kept every summer and, with tears on her cheeks, lifted a glass to his memory. "I bet there was a nice turnout."

"Pretty much the entire town showed up." The first hint of humor played around Nate's mouth. "It's Orange Blossom, after all."

Now that was more like it, she thought, flexing her fingers.

"So what's new around here?" she asked, sticking with the seemingly safe topic. She hadn't come all this way to fight with the man. "Does the band still play the same old songs on the square every Sunday afternoon? Did the Ham Hut finally change their menu, or are they still serving navy bean soup on Wednesdays?"

A look she could describe only as strangled passed over Nate's face. He jerked the shovel out of the ground and stood holding it. "Orange Blossom is fine, just the way it is. If you don't like it, you're free to leave."

And how, exactly, am I supposed to respond to that?

She peered up at him, trying to figure out his attitude. Neither of them was a star-struck teen anymore—she got that—and she sure as hell didn't want to pick up where they'd left off. She'd been hoping the intervening years had brought perspective, but the signals he was sending made it clear that any sort of friendship with the man she'd once considered her soul mate was out of the question.

Fine, then.

If he was determined to shoot down her every overture, she'd adapt, keep things strictly business. She gestured to the leafy green surrounding them and dug deep, reaching for the conciliatory tone her bosses used around the office. No matter how much potential he'd shown as a teen, Nate had chosen a life of menial labor on land that didn't even belong to him. He was an employee, nothing more. At least until her uncle's estate passed through probate and she sold the place.

"I hear you took over as manager when your dad retired. Everyone says you've done a great job with the grove. Looks like there'll be plenty of oranges this harvest."

Nate studied trees fairly dripping with dark green balls. He scuffed a booted foot through the grass, his frown melting. "So long as Mother Nature does her thing, we should do all right."

Her gaze skimmed over the topmost branches of trees that had been mere twigs when she'd last seen them. "What happened to all the other groves in the area? Coming in, all I passed were miles and miles of dead and overgrown trees."

The question earned her an appraising glance accompanied by a tight-lipped smile. "Most of the other owners around here had big mortgages. When the canker hit, it put 'em out of business. Uncle Jimmy, he owned Castle Grove outright." He gestured toward the trees. "We tightened our belts, replanted and moved on. Those new trees'll have their first harvest this year."

She'd heard her aunt and uncle talk about canker, of course. The disfiguring disease had swept across Florida, and in an effort to stop it, the government had torched groves left and right. Her uncle had lost half his trees by the year she'd graduated from high school. She nodded toward the circle of wide gray sand where Nate had been working.

"Guess it keeps you busy. Even on a Friday night."

"Irrigation pipe was plugged up. It took me a while to figure out where the problem was." He hefted the shovel. Just in case she hadn't gotten the hint, he asked, "So, did you want something, or are you just here to reminisce?"

Not about to let him know how closely he'd come to hitting the mark, she aimed for breezy nonchalance and was pleased when her voice remained smooth and steady.

"Actually, I'm hoping you have the keys to the main house." Before he could ask why, she gave him the answer she'd decided to give anyone who asked about her purpose in Orange Blossom.

"I have some business in town and thought I'd stay there for a few days."

She crossed her fingers, hoping Nate would never have to know she couldn't afford to stay anywhere else. Airfare and the cheapest rental car she could find had already bent her credit card nearly to the breaking point. And with a cold making the rounds at the Bowen house, she'd had to scrap her plans to crash on Sarah's couch.

Nate removed his hat and ran a hand through

dampened hair that curled at the nape of his neck. "Door's not locked, probably warped shut. Have your husband put some muscle into it. It'll pop open."

"My hus—" Years of practice helped keep the sharp sting of failure from twisting her smile into a grimace. Her non-marriage and Gracie's birth were the kind of fodder the local grapevine thrived on. She was surprised their story hadn't already spread all over town. Opting for a much-abbreviated version of a story Nate probably didn't want to hear any more than she wanted to tell, she spread her ringless fingers wide and held them up. "No husband. It's just me this trip."

For a second, Nate's features softened. She waited, wishing he'd say he was sorry to hear about her troubles. From there, he'd ask about her job, her home, her family. She'd ask the same things, too, the way old friends did after a long time apart.

But Nate remained silent, and Justine studied the face she'd once known as well as her own. The stubborn set of his jaw, the rigid way he held his mouth told her he'd decided against getting reacquainted. She smothered a sigh.

"Royce said it'd be okay for me to stay at the house," she said, hoping to diffuse a situation that had grown uncomfortably tense.

Nate only shook his head. "Jimmy wasn't much for keeping things neat and tidy. You'll be better off staying someplace else. A hotel in Orlando or Oviedo."

"I'll be out of your hair soon, Nate," she said softly. "I'll be so busy meeting with buyers and Royce, you'll hardly know I'm here. After that, I'll leave. You can forget I was ever here."

She realized her mistake when Nate reeled as if she'd slapped him. Quickly recovering, he thrust the shovel into the ground so hard the blade slid into the dirt clean up to the handle.

"You can't sell Castle Grove."

His words carried such absolute certainty that she took a second to regroup. The man needed reassurance, that was all. He probably thought she meant to put him out of a job, but she had no intention of stripping away his livelihood. She'd considered his history with the land and rushed to let him know.

"Don't worry." She dredged up her most disarming smile. "You'll stay on as manager. No matter which offer I accept, I'll make sure your job is a condition of the sale."

"No." Nate's jaw worked. "You don't understand. The land's not yours to sell."

"Not yet," she agreed. She wasn't foolish enough to think everyone in Orange Blossom would be thrilled with her plans. Nate, for one, obviously didn't like change. But he, like the others, would have to adjust. "Once we get through probate, though..."

"Not then. Not ever." Nate shook his head. "Eighty acres of this land is mine. The rest was promised to me."

Justine thought quickly. She'd read the will and knew she was the only beneficiary. "I don't—"

"Jimmy and I had a deal. I expect you to honor our agreement."

Justine bit her lower lip. She searched every inch of Nate's broad features and gray-blue eyes. Deception hadn't been part of his makeup when she'd known him, but she had to look only as far as her ex to know how quickly men could change if there was something else they wanted. Marco had wanted so badly to immigrate to the US, he hadn't cared what he had to do to get there. Nate apparently wanted land, her land. Well, he wasn't going to get it. She stared at the man who was making quick work of tearing apart the thin wisps of friendship they had left.

"I haven't heard word one about any *deal*." She framed the word in air quotes and hiked an eyebrow to let him know she doubted his claim. "Whatever you thought you worked out with him, Uncle Jimmy left Castle Grove to me. And the minute I can, I intend to sell it to the highest bidder. Right now, that's Fresh Picked Citrus. If you want the land, you'll have to beat their price."

Protests rose from Nate's gut, roared through his head and clogged his throat. He worked his jaw. No matter how hard he tried to free the words, they jammed, refused to break loose. More than ten years ago, he'd fallen head over heels for the boss's niece only to watch her walk away when he didn't live up to her expectations. True, he hadn't attended an Ivy League college like Justine, hadn't spent summers bumming around Europe, hadn't gone to law school. But his ag degree from the University of Florida should count for something, shouldn't it? He'd kept up with changes in the agriculture business through extension and online courses.

He stared out at the trees he'd coaxed from seedlings into maturity. He'd spent more days than he could count sweltering in the heat to mow or fertilize or spray for insects. How many winter nights had he walked the rows, checking the irrigation systems that would protect the trees from frost? It was work he loved, work he was born to do, but if Justine had her way, he might as well have spent his life shoveling shit in a pig sty.

At last his throat cleared.

"You cannot sell what rightfully belongs to me. I'll fight you on this, Justine. And you'll lose."

Anger flared in the wide blue eyes he'd have called pretty...if they hadn't been shooting daggers at him.

"I don't think so."

The harsh retort flew from the lips he'd once considered soft and kissable. Justine's hand sought purchase on her slim hip and anchored there.

"I plan to finalize the sale by the end of the harvest."

"It ain't gonna happen," he said flatly. Sizing her up the way he'd carefully scrutinized his opponents on the football field, he noted the nips and tucks in a skirt that probably came from a designer showroom. No gold glinted at her neck. No diamonds sparkled from her ears or fingers. So, she'd dressed down for the locals, had she? Her condescension assured him that she'd underestimated him. He could take the leggy blonde down in a fair fight.

Problem was, *fair* didn't seem to have anything to do with their situation.

It wasn't fair that he had to fight for land he already owned. Nor was it fair that he was standing here in work-stained clothes as ripe as yesterday's table scraps while the woman who'd trampled his heart stood, cool as an ice sculpture, not ten feet away. Looking for some advantage, he drew himself up to his full height and stared down at her. "No matter what Royce told you, rest assured, I'll contest Jimmy's will. And I'll win."

Her long blond hair shimmied when Justine shook

her head. "There wasn't one word in the paperwork filed with the courts to indicate you have any claim on Castle Grove whatsoever."

She folded slim arms across her chest, but not before Nate saw her hands tremble. For a moment, he almost felt sorry that she'd come all this way for nothing. Until her biting tone sank its claws into his heart. He gave himself a stern reminder that Justine had dumped him in favor of a career path that would take her to law school, where, no doubt, she'd excelled. She was a big, hotshot attorney by now and had most likely gone over every line of Jimmy's will with a magnifying glass.

"Our agreement was a handshake," he admitted, "but you can ask anyone in town. They'll tell you the grove belongs to me."

"A verbal agreement?" Justine scoffed. "That's the basis of your claim?"

As if she sensed victory, she leaned so close he caught a whiff of her cologne.

"Hasn't anyone told you an oral contract isn't worth the paper it's written on?"

"Oh, I don't know." The confident pose he struck allowed him to pull away from the faint scent of jasmine she wore. "I think once the judge hears my side of the story, he'll give me what should have been mine to begin with."

At Justine's "I wouldn't bet on it," Nate stopped to reconsider. In the citrus industry, a slight shift in the upper atmosphere was all it took to change a predicted light frost into a ruinous hard freeze. He'd learned early not to trust a year's worth of hard work and effort to a single weather report, the same way his breakup with Justine had taught him not to trust his heart to a girl who might bolt the minute she got a better offer.

"I've lined up witnesses. Half the town will show up in court on my behalf."

More than anything, he hated the way sympathy clouded her blue eyes, as if she'd already won and he'd lost. Things were far from over. To protect the town and the land he'd worked for, he'd see that things stayed the way they were, no matter who he had to fight to do it.

He eyed Justine. She'd always been a worthy opponent, even when they were kids. Back then, he'd enjoyed sparring with her. He might now, except there was too much at stake to let the grove pass from her hands to some large corporation that wouldn't give a damn about the town or its people.

He couldn't let that happen. The time had come to try another tactic, and he forced himself to take a much-needed breath. The scent of honest sweat, the smell of citrus, of dirt, of the flowers that grew nearby filled his head. As a reminder of what he was fighting for, it did the job. Dialing his anger back a notch, he marshaled the same congenial tone he used on the rare occasions when city council meetings grew tense.

"For the moment, let's agree to disagree. I have no doubt I'll win. It appears you feel the same, but the courts will sort it all out." When full lips smoothed into a straight line and the tension between Justine's eyes eased, Nate gathered his courage for the next part.

"Whatever the final outcome, you can't sell to Fresh Picked Citrus."

He watched her bristle with indignation, but he held out one hand, his open palm a conciliatory gesture. "Castle Grove is the only family-owned and - operated grove around these parts. The last of its kind. Orange Blossom won't survive without it."

He watched, silent, as she weighed the information. Certain he'd made his case and that she'd change her mind, he chewed the inside of his mouth in frustration when slim shoulders squared and her fine features firmed.

"I'm sorry, Nate. But it all comes down to the best offer. I don't have any other choice."

"You always have a choice," he countered. "Problem is, you're making the wrong one." Despite the way he'd bit down to cut himself off, the word *again* hung in the air between them. Without another word, Justine turned on one heel and headed back the way she'd come.

Much as he didn't want to, he watched her go.

She moved so quickly he almost missed the shimmer of tears on cheeks that had lost some of their rosy fullness in the years they'd been apart. He swallowed, knowing he'd make her cry again if he had to. He'd do anything, hound her until she wept buckets, if that's what it took to make her change her mind.

Silently, he swore a curse that featured Royce Enid's name. The next time they ran into each other, the lawyer was gonna get an earful for not letting him know about Justine's arrival. As it turned out, he'd barely had a second to strengthen his defenses before she'd stepped out from beneath the trees, her straight blond hair hanging like sheaves of wheat, shoes dangling from the tips of long fingers. The slim-fitting skirt and the sleeveless blouse had been guaranteed to draw a man's eye to long legs and full breasts. They'd done their job well. Too well. In less than a minute, she'd almost gotten under his skin, tempted him to let his guard down.

He hadn't, and he vowed he never would.

What was left except to fight?

He watched Justine duck beneath a final branch and disappear. He hoped she was ready for battle, because no matter what they'd once meant to each other, he refused to let her jeopardize the future of Orange Blossom.

How dare he?

Certain steam all but curled from her ears, Justine marched into the grove. She stared straight ahead, refusing to look back until a wall of trees shielded her from Nate's sight. The man had a lot of nerve. He thought he could simply assert a claim on Castle Grove and she'd hand over her family's heritage? *Her* family's, not his. Through the lean years and the fat ones, Uncle Jimmy had held on to the land. He never would have given it away. Not even to Nate.

Maybe when she'd been a star-struck teenager, head over heels in love with the caretaker's son, she might have at least considered his demand. But she'd changed in the last decade. A lot. She was no longer the naive little girl Nate had known back then. She was a mother whose child deserved the kind of life the sale of Castle Grove could provide. So, no. Even if he had a legal leg to stand on—which he didn't—Nate couldn't have the land.

She glanced over one shoulder, disappointed that the reunion with her old boyfriend hadn't gone better.

Not that she'd flown all the way from Virginia to Florida expecting they would simply put that last, awful fight behind them and pick up the threads of their past together. It was time to let go of all that and move on.

She had. Or at least, she'd tried. Was still trying.

But Nate... Nate was stuck in exactly the same place, doing the same things he'd been doing the last time she'd seen him. Okay, maybe his shirt had been a chambray straight out of the LL Bean catalog. And so what if he wore Dr. Martens instead of knock-offs from the local Walmart. Boots were still boots, weren't they? He still lived in the same small town where he'd been born and raised. Still resented her. Still blamed her for leaving.

Even though it had been his choice to stay behind.

Where the grass ended and the dirt road opened into a parking area, she dropped the sandals she'd dug out of a seconds bin at the outlet mall. She eyed the toes and reminded herself that no one—especially not Nate—would ever notice the crooked slant of one bow. Sliding her feet into the shoes, she had to wonder whether he was still trying to punish her for their breakup. If so, he was blaming the wrong person. Her parents had been the ones who'd refused to pay her college tuition unless she complied with their demands. They'd left her no other option but to go to Europe. Yet, she'd asked Nate to come with her, and he'd turned her down flat.

Huge mistake, Nate. Huge.

A cold tendril of well-aged pain reached for her. She slapped it, forcing it back into the darkened section of her heart reserved for really bad choices. When it came to world-class errors in judgment, she'd made a few. Thanks to her uncle, though, she had a chance to fix things. To make a better life—for herself, for Gracie.

And it all hinged on the sale of Castle Grove.

With or without Nate's support, she'd make it happen. Starting with the meeting she'd scheduled with a representative from Fresh Picked Citrus tomorrow morning.

Gaining the porch, she followed the instructions she'd been given and put her shoulder to the door. She stumbled forward when it flew open with a squeal of rusty hinges. Her determination to spend the weekend in the house weakened a bit when heat and a fetid smell wrapped her in a suffocating blanket. Coughing, she groped the wall for the switch. Bright light brought a hint of relief when it blazed from the bare bulb that dangled over a familiar scarred table. Her tension ratcheted up again when she sensed movement in a far corner. She blinked and peered into the shadows. There were bound to be bugs, this being Florida and all.

But what had skittered across the sideboard?

She braced herself for the worst. Searching for the source of the smell, and half afraid she'd find it, she explored the bedrooms and hallways that branched off from the living and dining rooms. Humidity and disuse had all but glued windows shut. She gritted her teeth and pried them open. A soft breeze fluttered spider webs that dotted the screens, but nothing else moved. She sighed and crossed her fingers, hoping she wouldn't have to spend the weekend with critters that had more legs than her own somewhat shaky pair.

In the living room, she traced one finger over a tear in the sofa's faded upholstery. So much mildew stained the grout in the bathroom that she wondered whether she'd need a sander or a blowtorch to remove the gunk. In the room she'd once shared with Penny and Sarah, dust lay in thick drifts across chenille bedspreads. Sleeping beneath one of those was out of the question.

She took a breath as washing sheets and linens moved to the top of her priority list, a plan that unraveled the minute she twisted the tap in the kitchen and got...nothing. Not so much as a single drop splashed into the rust-stained sink. There was no rumble of water in the pipes. The box of matches beside the stove looked promising, but nothing happened when she twisted the knob for a burner.

No gas. No water. A house long overdue for a cleaning.

To make matters worse, something reeked, and she hadn't been able to find it.

Determined, she circled back to the dining room where a current of slightly sweeter air stirred one corner of the sheet draped over the long, trestle table. She lifted an edge of the cloth, frowning at a cascade of what looked suspiciously like the droppings of a tiny animal.

Okay, so Nate was right about one thing—she couldn't spend the night here. Sleeping in the backseat of her rental car sounded better every minute, but she couldn't give up. Wouldn't cancel tomorrow's meeting.

A knock at the door interrupted her before she'd settled on her next move. Knowing it had to be Nate, she slowly shook her head. One run-in with her old boyfriend had been enough for the day, thank you very much. Another, louder knock sounded through the house, and she gave in, crossing the room to open the door for the one man she didn't want to see.

"Hey." Wearing a scowl that said he had better things to do than stand on her porch all night, Nate held out a foil-covered package. "I figured you didn't have time to make it to the store before it closed."

She glanced down. "Dinner? You brought dinner? You didn't have to do that." Despite her protest, she felt her resistance melt.

"I wouldn't be much of a neighbor if I left you to starve, would I?" Nate thrust the dish closer.

She'd forgotten about the local customs of the close-knit community. When she was younger, there'd always been a casserole or two tucked away in her aunt's freezer, ready to pull out and deliver at a moment's notice. Tentatively, she reached for the dish. A welcome aroma filled the air when she peeled back one corner of the foil. Her tummy growled a reminder that she hadn't fed it since breakfast.

"You cook now?" she asked in an effort to make polite conversation. Try as she might, she couldn't picture the man who filled her doorway in an apron.

"I reheat," Nate corrected with a wry grin. "Let's just say, my freezer is well-stocked." At her perplexed look, he patted a stomach that was flat as a board. "The women in town are constantly trying to fatten me up."

Imagining long lines of casserole-toting, marriage-minded singles, she fended off a curl of pea-green jealousy with a firm reminder that she and Nate had gone their separate ways long ago. He toed a loose board with his tennis shoe. "You get everything figured out inside?"

"Not exactly," she admitted. "There's no water. No gas. I guess Jimmy wasn't much for housework."

An insect buzzed Nate's head. He swatted at it. "Mind if I come in? The skeeters are fierce this time of year." He didn't wait for an answer but stepped across the threshold, forcing her to step back while the screen door slapped shut in his wake. "The house has been closed up since the funeral. If I'd known you were coming, I'd have opened it up for you."

The rebuke—no matter how gentle—stung. The frustration she'd been holding back ever since she parked her car surged forward. She fought it the only way she knew how, by holding the person accountable responsible.

"Don't tell me things got this bad in just three months. Wasn't it part of your job to take care of all this?" The words came out sharper than she'd intended, and she bit her tongue.

Instead of ducking the blame, Nate met her gaze and held it. "As manager of Castle Grove, it's my job to take care of the trees. I've done that—planted in the spring, fertilized and mowed through the summer, stood guard over the smudge pots on nights when the temperature dropped below freezing."

Somewhere in the house, a board creaked. Conflicting emotions played across Nate's face. "I loved your uncle. He was family. I kept tabs on him as best I could. We used to play checkers of an evening, but after he fell and broke his hip—"

"He fell?" Regret stirred in her chest. She wished she'd known. "You'd think Sarah would have mentioned it. We talk at least once a month."

"Here in Orange Blossom, we take care of our own." Nate paused, giving her time to mull over the fact that she was an outsider. With a nod, he continued. "Uncle Jimmy, he was in the hospital close to a week, rehab for a couple more. He always was a stubborn cuss, but after that, he changed. Stopped inviting me over for our nightly game of checkers. Said his responsibilities as mayor wore him out, and all he wanted to do at night was sleep. I used to pick up his mail for him every day, but he claimed he needed the exercise and said he'd walk to the mailbox on his own." A smile tugged at Nate's lips. "Most times, though, he drove the truck."

Justine spared a quick glance through the window to the dark beyond it. Every kid who spent the summer at Castle Grove had had their own chores. Getting the mail had been one of hers. Terrified of snakes, she'd hated making the trip from one end of the driveway to the main road by herself, but Nate had understood and taken pity on her. With him at her side, they'd turned the mile-long trek into a race. Back then, Nate had been a friend, a companion. A part of her had hoped to rekindle that friendship, something that no longer seemed possible, and she sighed. "I poked my head into his office. It didn't look like he was opening his mail."

"All his bills were on auto-pay. He never was one for much shopping."

"Don't remind me." She smiled, thinking of the ruckus her uncle had raised one summer when Aunt Margaret had insisted on buying a new couch. Her expression froze at the realization that the same sofa still sat, faded and torn, in the living room. She peered up at Nate. "You *never* checked up on him?"

"Did you?" he shot back. "Did any of your family?"

She raised her hands in a sign of surrender. "Point taken."

In the silence that followed, Nate cleared his throat. "Okay, then. I turned on the water on my way in. The cutoff is 'round back, at the base of the porch steps, in case you ever need it. The water heater is in that closet on the back porch. Thought I'd best light the pilot for you."

"I'd appreciate that," she answered, aware that he'd declared a truce...for now. She set the plate he'd brought on the table and watched as he slipped a wrench and a screwdriver from his back pocket. He brushed by, passing so close that she sucked in a breath. She drank in the musky scent of a man who'd spent the better part of a day outdoors and was surprised when a quiver of desire shimmied through her. She shook it off. She wasn't here to stir up old feelings. In control again, she trailed Nate toward the back of the house where a pair of ancient appliances sat side-by-side on the screened-in porch.

"Something stinks," he declared. His nose wrinkled.

"You think?" The smell had all but knocked her flat when she first opened the front door. Whether the air that now whispered through the windows had dispersed the odor, or she'd simply gotten used to it, she couldn't say. But it was definitely worse where they were standing.

Nate lifted the lid to the washing machine. Two parts rotten eggs, one part skunk, odor boiled up at them. He slammed the lid closed.

"Wouldn't use that," he suggested, as if she needed his advice.

"Wouldn't think of it." Not before she divested the machine of its three-month-old load of moldy, disintegrating clothes and cycled several gallons of bleach through the system.

"Or the dryer either." He folded his arms across a wide chest. "Least ways, not till I get a chance to check the exhaust and make sure nothing's built a nest in the tube."

Another place where critters can hide?

"Great, just great," she muttered. She shook aside a shudder. So conditions weren't ideal. It wasn't like she intended to move in. She tossed a handful of hair over one shoulder. She was staying only for the weekend. Just long enough to meet with the Fresh Picked Citrus rep and her uncle's attorney. Until then, she'd pretend she was on a camping trip. Only this time, she'd be surrounded by walls instead of tent canvas.

Nate opened the door to a closet where an ancient furnace stood beside an equally antiquated water heater. "This should be okay once I—" He pried open a panel in the wall and flipped a switch. Water gurgled in the pipes above the heater. "I drained it when I closed up the house. It'll take a few hours to fill and heat. By morning, though, you should have all the hot water you need."

Morning.

She hiked a questioning brow as a trickle of sweat rolled between her breasts. "Do you know what Uncle Jimmy did with the air conditioner?" At Nate's perplexed look, she added, "The one he used to keep in the living room." Late in the summer, when temperatures had hovered in the mid-nineties and there hadn't been a breath of air stirring, her uncle had hauled the boxy unit in from the barn.

"Jimmy, he never liked that thing. He tossed it on the trash heap when no one came to visit the year after Margaret died."

Guilt stabbed her midsection, and she swallowed the urge to defend herself. The summer between her freshman and sophomore years at Georgetown, she'd doubled up on class work in order to get a leg up on the stiff competition. She hadn't taken a break since.

"Okay," Nate said at last. He tapped his screwdriver against the pipes. "That takes care of the electricity and the water. Let me light the stove, and you should be good to go."

Moving into the kitchen, he jerked the oven door open and shone a light inside. Dark stains dotted the bottom and sides. Grease clung to the racks. "Could use a good scrubbing," he announced. "I think Jimmy kept a can of oven cleaner in the pantry."

Justine let her nose crinkle. "Maybe I'll stick to ready-made from the grocery store."

The remark earned her a throaty chuckle. "The General's still the only store in town. They don't stock much in the way of prepared foods. A couple of sandwiches is all."

Memories of riding their bikes into town on hot summer afternoons for ice cream flooded back. What had happened to the young man who'd been her champion throughout the long summer months? He'd probably grown a foot since she'd seen him last, making him somewhere near six-two to her five-ten. Thanks to long afternoons on the football field, Nate had been muscular, even as a teen. His shoulders were much wider now than she remembered, his tummy flat enough that his jeans hung on well-defined hips.

She swallowed, pulling her thoughts away from washboard abs and shifting her focus to the thin scar over his right eye. "Well, thanks for, well, everything."

"Yeah, sure." Moving toward the door, Nate stuck his tools in his back pocket. "Let me know if you need anything else. I'll be right across the way."

"So you're living in the caretaker's cottage?" The

two-bedroom house stood a stone's throw away from Uncle Jimmy's front porch.

"Dad's arthritis got so bad he moved out west. The cottage might seem too big for a bachelor like me, but I manage to use most of the space. If you'll excuse me, my own supper is waiting for me there now," Nate answered with an easy grin.

She led the way from the kitchen into the dining room, aiming for the front door beyond. But one step into the dining room, she halted, her mouth, like her feet, frozen. She flipped on the light switch. Several enormous bugs darted off the table, scuttled across the floor and disappeared into the baseboards. A shudder worked its way from the top of her head to her toes.

"Oh my," she whispered.

"They're just palmetto bugs." Nate's hand on her shoulder offered support. "You remember them."

"Yeah, sure, but..." Her throat closed. As kids, they'd made a game of searching for the hard-bodied roaches in the grass. But finding them outdoors was one thing. Seeing them scurry across the table, across her food, was something else entirely.

"So much for your dinner."

Acting as if palmetto bugs didn't give him a bad case of the heebie-jeebies, Nate crossed to the plate Justine had left, unguarded, on the dining table. He pried back the loose foil. Antennae bristling, the granddaddy of all roaches stared up at him. He shoved the foil back in place. Just for good measure, he crimped the edges. A frantic rustling threatened to loosen his grip, but aware of the wide blue eyes that tracked his every move, he managed to hang on long enough to carry the dish through the house and out the back door. A fifty-gallon barrel stood near the fire pit. He tossed the plate, bug and all, into the soot-coated can. Goose bumps rippled across his shoulders. He slapped his hands together, ridding them of the imagined prickle of six legs on bare skin. Empty-handed, he retraced his steps to the dining room, where he leaned one shoulder against the doorframe.

Justine stood, her arms akimbo, staring at the table. The disillusionment in her eyes said she couldn't see beyond the dirt and grime to the good times, the good meals, they'd once shared there. She'd probably forgotten the mornings he'd folded himself onto the porch outside her window while she'd read aloud from *Red Badge of Courage*, *Of Mice and Men*, *A Tale of Two Cities* or any of the books on her reading list for the summer. The rainy afternoons they'd all played cards at this very table, laughing and telling jokes. The plans they'd made for the future, a future they'd meant to spend together.

His long exhale took with it what little hope he'd had that she'd hang on to the house, the grove, them. This wasn't the skinny towhead who'd slit her thumb on a sharp knife grafting sweet stock to the roots of hardier, bitter orange trees. Not the same girl who'd swum with him in the creek that meandered through the back half of the property. This harsher, far more worldly version of the teen he'd once loved would never rest her head in the hollow space below his shoulder. Despite some impressive curves, she was rail-thin in that citified way of women who turned each lettuce leaf into an entire meal. The woman standing in front of him threatened everything he'd spent his entire life working for. She had ignored Jimmy for ten years, only to swoop down and claim the land that had been rightfully his the minute the old geezer kicked the bucket.

Still...

He couldn't leave her here. Not in a bug-infested house. Without so much as a bed to sleep on or a quart of milk in the fridge. Anyone, even his worst enemy—even Justine—deserved better treatment than that. And, hitching up his jeans, he guessed it was up to him to provide it.

"There's nothing else for it, I guess. You're gonna have to spend the night with me."

"What?" Justine's head jerked up. "No," she said, as if he'd propositioned her instead of merely offering a reprieve. "I don't think so."

"Relax. I have a guest room. With a lock on the door. Not that you'll need it." He might not be as polished and sophisticated as his former sweetheart, but he was pretty sure getting involved again was the last thing either of them wanted.

When she still hesitated, he pointed to the inch of dust on the sideboard. "I wish I could say this will all look better in the light of day. Fact is, it won't. I'll admit the place needed work before Jimmy passed. Sitting vacant all this time hasn't improved things one whit. Tomorrow, you can come back, armed with buckets and brooms, mops and"—he tilted a smile at her—"bug spray. But sleeping here tonight isn't a good idea. The closest motel is thirty miles away, and this time of year, they're probably booked solid. So, unless you want to spend one very long night in your car swattin' at skeeters, you don't have much choice."

Justine stared at her feet, her shoulders rounding. "I can't," she protested weakly. "People will talk."

His laugh startled a lone palmetto bug that had crept over the edge of the table on the hunt for crumbs. In a town the size of Orange Blossom, people always talked. He'd bet, even now, rumors of her arrival were spreading like wildfire from one house to the next. In this case, though, he could put her mind at ease.

"Everett Grimes is the nearest neighbor, and his place is more than two miles down the road." He made a sweeping gesture. "I won't tell him, or his wife, if you don't."

Justine's gaze drifted from a bare spot in the rug to the door and beyond. Her features softened. "I guess I don't really have much choice. Let me grab my bag."

That was fine with him, and he walked her to her car. At her trunk, he insisted on getting her luggage. "You packed light," he said, hefting the well-worn duffel bag.

"Just for the weekend. I'll see Royce and meet with some other people before I catch the red-eye back to DC on Sunday." She paused the way someone did when they'd said more than they'd intended. "I appreciate the invitation," she finished in a rush.

Nate's pulse throbbed. She still intended to meet with buyers, despite his objections? His footsteps across the grassy stretch between the houses slowed as he reconsidered offering hospitality to the enemy. But he wasn't the kind of guy who reneged on a promise. She could stay one night. After that, she was on her own.

Food, though, was another matter. He couldn't very well eat in front of his guest, no matter how far wrong she'd gone. But his stomach had that empty, hollow feeling it got after a long day of hard work. Drawing on the manners his mom had drilled into him before she died, he offered to fix them both a plate as he held the door to his cottage open.

"There's plenty of Dottie Carruthers's enchilada casserole left," he assured Justine. Lucky for both of them, the spinster had fixed enough to feed an entire family, with some to spare.

For one long moment, Justine ignored him while she silently observed the house he'd spent his spare time renovating.

"You've made quite a few changes," she said, just when he thought the moment would stretch out forever.

Nate hiked an eyebrow. "You mean, besides the obvious? Yeah."

"This area looks bigger somehow. Which is strange, considering how much smaller everything else seems."

"Hey." He clutched his chest. "You wound me."

She turned to give him a sly smile. "Exception duly noted. You're not the scrawny kid I used to know."

"Scrawny? I played football in high school. I worked out." Her searching look practically made his toes curl, but pulling himself erect, he dropped a heavy curtain over an unwanted spark of interest.

"For a teenager, you were okay." A hint of the Justine he'd once loved teased her lips. As if she was afraid he'd spot it, she spun away. "What'd you do with the dining room?"

"Noticed it was missing, did you?" Setting aside a whole room just for eating seemed like a waste of space for a guy with no family and no prospects. He'd taken a sledgehammer to the walls. Gone, too, were the kitschy, wall-eyed cats his mother had collected. After she ran off, his dad hadn't been able to part with them, but Nate had boxed them up and toted the crate to the barn. To banish the smell of his dad's pipe tobacco, he'd replaced twenty-year-old carpet with hardwood floors and tile, stripped wallpaper and repainted...everything. Tearing out the breakfast bar that had once separated the kitchen from the living room had given the place an open flow he liked. Granite counters had replaced the old butcher-block top. Modern, stainless steel appliances finished the update.

"Is that the new Keurig?" Justine crossed to the single-cup coffeemaker. "I've had my eye on one, but I'm waiting till the prices drop a bit."

Nate shrugged. "I got tired of making a whole pot every morning and pouring half of it down the sink. Figured as long as I was making changes, I might as well get the top of the line. Like it?" He waited a beat, aware that he wanted her opinion and not sure why it mattered.

"It's..." Justine's gaze took in the seating area filled with leather sofas and chairs, an oversized ottoman and electronic gadgetry. "It suits you."

It did. Which was another reason he had to prevent the sale of Castle Grove. With no claim on the property, he'd lose the only home he'd ever known. Fear that she'd win poked its head through the dirt. He chopped the idea off at its roots. He'd prove his case in court. He'd keep the land that was rightfully his. Till then, it would pay to keep in mind that knowledge was power. Dishing up their plates, he set about learning as much as he could about the woman who opposed him.

"Jimmy didn't talk about you, or your folks, much." Not that there was any news to share. The old man hadn't gotten much more than a Christmas card from her side of the family in ten years. "What have you been up to? I was sorry to hear about your dad. Sarah said your mom remarried. You like her new husband?"

"I hardly know him. They live in Arizona, and he never comes east with her when she visits. Mom's the same as she always was. Not willing to settle for anything less than perfection."

In the second before Justine looked down at her food, Nate followed an odd shadow as it passed over her features. And no wonder, he thought. Large-boned and plain, Margaret Castle must have inherited all the warmth and kindness in her family, 'cause Nola Gale didn't have a lick of it. He'd always wondered how Justine's mom had packed so much harsh criticism in a body he'd towered over even as a teen. He guessed time hadn't changed her much.

Once again reminded of the gulf between the life of the girl who'd been raised with every advantage and his own hardscrabble life, Nate swallowed. "And you? Are you enjoying the view from a corner office while minions bob and weave at your beck and call?" He tipped his chair back, prepared to listen to an account of her rapid climb to the top.

"That was the plan, wasn't it? Law school at Georgetown. Sign with one of the big firms. Make partner by thirty." Sadness clouded her eyes despite her smile. "No. No. And no."

Nate arched an eyebrow. He'd never known anyone as driven to succeed as Justine. Wondering what had let the air out of her dreams, he didn't bother to hide his curiosity. "I always figured you'd take the express elevator to Executive Row."

"Oh, you know how it is." She stabbed her food with her fork. "A baby can upset even the best-laid plans."

The odd look he'd noticed earlier put in a return appearance. Distracted by what she wasn't telling him, he nearly missed what she'd said. His own fork clattered to the tabletop.

"You have a kid?" At Justine's confirming smile, he demanded, "How old? Boy or girl?"

"A girl," she answered, her eyes brightening at last. "Margaret Grace. After Aunt Margaret. She goes by Gracie. She's five."

There'd been a day when he and Justine had dreamed of marriage and children of their own. Deliberately, he squelched a temptation to revisit that part of their past. He held out his hand. "Let me see."

Justine's eyebrows knotted. "See what?"

"Pictures. I want to see pictures." He'd dated a few single moms over the years. Their phones were always filled to overflowing with snapshots of their kids.

Almost reluctantly, Justine reached for the purse she'd hung on the back of her chair. Seconds later, he scrolled through images that brought back a flood of early childhood memories. "She looks like you," he said, using the chance to study features that, long ago, had been nearly as familiar as his own.

"Her hair's darker. And curly." She tapped a picture with an unpolished fingernail.

"But she has your coloring. Your nose. Your mouth." He took a second look at the little girl's impish grin. "I'll bet she's a handful."

"She keeps me on my toes." Justine slipped the

phone from his grasp and returned it to her bag. "Sometimes I wish I had half her energy. Speaking of which, I'm beat. If it's okay, I think I'll turn in."

If she expected him to sympathize with the long hours and heavy caseload of an up-and-coming attorney, she was barking up the wrong tree. He'd offered her a quieter life, a slower-paced one. She'd chosen to reject it—to reject him—in favor of the hustle and bustle of a big-city law firm. Standing, he lifted his empty plate and her half-full one from the table.

Justine remained seated, her fingers drumming the placemat. "There is one more thing, Nate."

A dozen topics—none of them good—flashed through his mind. Buying time to bolster his defenses, he scraped what was left of her dinner into the garbage and lowered the plates into the wide farm sink. His back braced against the counter, he faced her. "What is it?"

"Royce mentioned the Orange Fest when we spoke last week. You're involved with that?"

Involved was putting it mildly. As acting mayor of Orange Blossom, he was the guy in charge. The one people would blame if they had to cancel the event. Wondering what else Royce had told her, he ran a hand through his hair. "Yeah. I know a bit about it."

"From what I hear, Uncle Jimmy always helped out with the start-up costs. I don't see any reason that should change as long as we expect a good harvest." She pinned him with another long, searching look.

Offering the reassurance she wanted was easy— ripening fruit dangled from every limb in the grove. But with so much riding on her offer, he had to be sure he could count on her.

"It would mean a lot to the entire town," he acknowledged. Not only did the event provide college money for the town's teens, it boosted the bottom line of every small business for miles around. "It'll go a long way towards building goodwill. Which you'll want if there's any chance you might change your mind and make Orange Blossom your home."

Justine's lips firmed. "I'm going to sell, Nate. Make no mistake about it. But let me talk to Royce tomorrow, and I'll get back to you about the Orange Fest. Long as Uncle Jimmy left enough money for it, I'll see that you get what you need."

"A lot of folks'll be mighty glad to hear that." He clamped down on the urge to argue about the sale of Castle Grove. It had been a long day, and he had no desire to end it by going another round with the woman who was as determined to sell her birthright as he was to stop her.

"Well, good night, then." Justine pushed away from the table. "Thanks again for putting me up. I'll fix up a room at Uncle Jimmy's for the rest of the weekend and be out of your hair first thing."

"No rush. I'm up and at it before the sun most days. The pods for the coffeemaker are in that drawer over there." He hooked a thumb over his shoulder. "Sugar's on the counter. Milk in the fridge. There's a fair assortment of cleaning supplies in the hall closet. Help yourself to whatever you want. I'll stop by the house later, in case you need anything." Unless things had changed over the years, Justine was a late sleeper. He'd probably put in a good day's work and be on his way into town by the time she poured her first cup of coffee.

After stacking their dishes in the dishwasher, he trailed Justine's footsteps down the hall. Passing her room, he hesitated outside her door. Should he check on her? See if she wanted fresh towels? A softer pillow? Him? He shook his head. He wasn't kidding anyone, least of all himself. Sleeping with the enemy, even if her room was down the hall from his, had to rank among his top ten bad ideas. After all these years, Justine still drew him like a honey bee to a blossom. But he'd get stung if he came too close. He had to keep his distance. Orange Blossom, Castle Grove—and his heart—depended on it.

Soft as silk, butterflies kissed her cheeks. Yellow wings gently stirred the air. At her side, Gracie gave a nervous giggle at the tickle of tiny, thin legs on her bare arm. Offering reassurance, Justine started to run her fingers through her daughter's hair. Her laughter died when, instead of Gracie's curls, she touched a firm surface.

The dream winked out, replaced by confusion. Daylight played against the eyes she refused to open. She shifted, aware that nothing felt familiar. The mattress beneath her was far too comfortable, the pillow firmer than her own. She pulled the sheet up to her chin and caught a whiff of fresh air and sunshine.

Where...?

The memory of collapsing into the bed in Nate's guest room returned, and her disorientation cleared. She snuggled farther into the inviting covers. A long exhale turned into a sigh. There'd been a time when she'd wanted nothing more than to spend the night with the caretaker's son. Although, in those dreams she hadn't slept alone. Hadn't, in fact, actually slept.

Of course, that was before. Before their breakup. Before she lost control...of her life, her future. Before she found herself opposing Nate in a fight she couldn't afford to lose.

Rising, she padded through the house. As if reminding her to preserve the peace, the hems of her pajamas made slight, shushing noises against the hardwood floors. She spied a pair of suede slippers peeking out from beneath one edge of the couch and fought a smile. The grown-up Nate apparently liked his creature comforts far more than the boy who'd chased her barefoot through the groves. She gave another sigh, this one less about a walk down memory lane and more a determination to turn her life around. By leaving Castle Grove to her, Uncle Jimmy had given her a second chance. She wouldn't let anyone—not even Nate—stand in her way.

In the kitchen, she trailed her fingers across the glossy granite countertops to a note in Nate's strong, masculine handwriting. He'd left early, didn't expect to return before late afternoon. Straightening, she smiled as a mild tension eased from her shoulders. The representative from Fresh Picked Citrus was due at eleven for a meeting that would certainly go a lot smoother with Nate off doing whatever grove managers did all day and not around to interfere.

Coffee in hand, she hustled to the bedroom where she slipped into shorts and a faded T-shirt. Minutes later, dew from the neatly trimmed grass dampened her sneakers as she hurried across the open space between the houses. She wiped a trickle of early morning sweat from her temple. By the time she'd finish getting things ready for the meeting, she'd be drenched.

She stopped to ask herself why she was bothering with the house at all. It wasn't like FPC wanted the property for its buildings. In all likelihood, the company would knock the old homestead to the ground. Hands on her hips, she surveyed the messy interior. If she hadn't asked the FPC rep to meet her here, she'd probably leave things as they were.

But it was one thing to discuss business in a soon-to-be-razed house. Quite another if a platoon of bugs marched across the table in the middle of negotiations. Armed with cleaning supplies she unearthed from a closet, she tackled the dining room. She kept her shrieks to a minimum as she brushed away cobwebs and dodged the debris that fell from the corners. She worked without stopping until sweat soaked her shirt, every speck of dust had been banished and the floorboards shone wetly. For good measure, she circled the room, emptying a can of bug spray into corners and crevices.

Leaving the kitchen untouched for the time being, she moved on to her old room. Though she questioned her sanity for even thinking of sleeping in a room where who-knew-what had built a nest in the closet, coming back to Castle Grove had awakened too many memories. It had stirred a longing she'd ignored for far too long. But spending another night down the hall from the man she'd once thought hung the moon simply wasn't a good idea. There was too much at stake. So she plunged into the room, determined to set things right. When she finished, she eyed the bare mattress. Borrowing sheets that smelled of sunshine and fresh air—and reminded her of Nate—wouldn't do, and she jotted down a mental note to pick up a new set when she went into town that afternoon.

She dashed to the caretaker's cottage. A short time later, freshly showered and wearing a dress she'd pulled from a rack in a consignment shop—not that anyone ever need learn that little secret—she returned to Jimmy's house where, unable to sit still, she paced the dining room. Five minutes ahead of schedule, a black Lincoln Town Car braked in front of the house. A cloud of dust settled in its wake as a tall figure emerged. An extra jolt of nervousness shot through her as she studied the slicked-back hair and pale skin of a man so smoothly polished he could have stepped from one of the conglomerate's advertising flyers. His grin, though, was all boyish charm, and she caught herself wondering how often he'd practiced it in front of the mirror. Summoning a sunny smile of her own, she squared her shoulders, prepared to greet her guest.

"Ms. Gale?" he asked, mounting the steps. "Ken Thomas, vice president of acquisitions for Fresh Picked Citrus. We spoke on the phone."

"Several times. Welcome to Castle Grove, Mr. Thomas." She extended one hand while her visitor did the same. "I appreciate your coming out here today. I'm only in town a few days, and as you can imagine, I have a lot to do before I leave."

"My pleasure. Call me Ken. Please." His hand fell away after the obligatory two pumps.

"And I'm Justine." It took a conscious effort, but she suppressed the urge to wipe her hand on her skirt. For a corporate bigwig, Ken's grip had been surprisingly damp and weak. She cast an appraising glance from the polo bearing an FPC logo to summer-weight dress pants and Gucci loafers that must have cost more than she made in a week. Dressed as he was, Ken probably didn't intend to walk through the grove her uncle and Nate had spent their lives maintaining, and she stopped to consider what that said about FPC's plans for the property.

Would the company support Orange Blossom the way her uncle had? The question burned a hole in her stomach, and she pressed one hand to her midsection. She couldn't, wouldn't think of that now. No, she had to stay focused. She had her daughter's future to secure. For now, that was all that mattered.

Holding the door open, she asked, "Won't you come in?"

Considering how the dining room had looked only hours before, she gave herself a mental pat on the back. True, they weren't meeting in one of Jacoby & Sons's richly appointed conference rooms, but chilled bottles of water she'd borrowed from Nate's fridge glistened on the freshly polished surface. Her pen and notepad sat, precisely aligned with the edge of the table, just the way she liked them. Thanks to the pounding she'd given the chairs, only a few dust motes rose into the air when she slid onto hers. With a wave of one hand, she motioned Ken toward the seat closest to the window.

He settled a gleaming briefcase on the table and snapped it open with a flourish. "Ms. Gale—Justine. I hope you don't mind if I get right down to business." He flashed another grin, this one a mix of humble pride, and launched into a corporate summary. "You may not realize it, but FPC is the largest citrus conglomerate in the state. We've been in the industry for twenty-four years. Currently, we're looking to expand our operations in Seminole County. We're particularly interested in the area around Orange Blossom, where we intend to develop a major presence over the next few years."

"That certainly sounds impressive," she said into the silence that followed. "But I do have a couple of conditions before we talk facts and figures." She shifted in her seat. "As I'm sure you know, the Rhodes family has worked alongside mine for several generations. Whatever else happens, I want Nate Rhodes to keep the caretaker's cottage for as long as he chooses to live there." She studied Ken's face, and when the rep didn't flinch, she added, "I'd also expect the new owners to offer Nate a commensurate job in their company."

"Oh, now, I don't think we can guarantee that." A troubled frown creased the representative's brow. "FPC makes it a practice to promote from within."

As much as it pained her to do so, she pushed back her chair. "I'm afraid we don't have anything further to discuss, then. Nate's employment is nonnegotiable."

A tremble forced its way through her. What would she do if Ken called her bluff?

"Hold on now." Ken held up a hand. "I didn't say we couldn't make it happen. Let me see what I can do."

He whipped out a cell phone. His fingers flew over the keys while she held her breath. Seconds later, he lifted a smiling face. "All set," he announced. "Assuming we reach an agreement on the land itself, FPC would be happy to keep your foreman on. Is there anything else?"

Stunned by FPC's quick change of heart, she drummed her fingers against the table. "Well, I know how much businesses in Orange Blossom depend on the income they receive from Castle Grove. Before I can consider selling, I'd want some kind of assurance that your company would continue to support the local economy."

A genuine smile spread across Ken's face. "I'm happy to say that FPC has a track record of supporting the community," the man boasted. "Why, wherever we've been fortunate enough to establish a presence, the job market has boomed and local businesses have reaped the benefits." He took a breath. "Believe me, we have no intention of buying this property just to let it set fallow."

"Then I think we can move forward," she said, pleased with what she was hearing.

Despite the breeze that ruffled the curtains, Ken swiped a hand across his brow. "Let's get right down to it, shall we?"

From his briefcase, the representative withdrew two thick stacks of paper. He slid one across the table. "If you'll turn to page five, you'll see that FPC is prepared to make a very attractive offer on your property."

As Ken's chest expanded the tiniest bit and he laced his fingers atop his copy of the offer, alarms sounded in Justine's head. She gave the rep a second look. Cool confidence practically oozed from the man. A hint of smugness tainted the smile that graced his lips. Was he trying to pull one over on her?

For the moment, she let the papers lie, untouched, in the center of the table. She'd done her homework, knew the value of every one of Castle Grove's two hundred acres. When it came right down to it, she could quote the book value on every piece of equipment on the property.

Her breathing steadied. Drawing the paperwork toward her, she flipped to page five. She glanced at the figure, counted the zeroes and came up one short. Disappointment zinged through her chest, but she hadn't spent ten years at Jacoby & Sons without picking up a few tricks in an office filled with high-powered litigators. Aware that in spite of his nonchalant attitude, Ken remained alert, watching for any sign of weakness he might use as a bargaining chip, she kept her face an impassive mask.

"I might not be from around these parts, Ken, but I've read up on the area. I know how much my uncle's land is worth. Frankly, your offer isn't even close." She closed the document and pushed it aside.

Behind the blinding smile, annoyance flashed in Ken's dark eyes. His fingers curled over the edge of his papers. He blinked, his anger fading so quickly Justine might have missed it if she hadn't been carefully watching from behind lowered lashes. She drew in a thready breath and reminded herself that this wasn't her first rodeo. Marco, too, had been all smooth, easygoing charm...until he hadn't gotten his own way. She braced herself in case Ken was cut from the same cloth.

"That might be true for a fully functioning grove. Maybe." As if calling attention to an error in her math homework, he adopted a patronizing tone. "But half your trees are just now reaching their first harvest. You have no idea how well they'll yield."

Justine arched one eyebrow. She didn't need a degree in botany to see the hundreds of green balls hanging from every limb on the property. She might not know citrus as well as Ken, but she knew Nate. Or she used to. He'd poured his life's blood into the land, the trees, and if he said Castle Grove would have a bumper crop, it would.

She gazed steadily at the man seated across the table. "I'm aware of how much can go wrong between now and this winter's harvest." She ticked off a few of the biggest threats. "Too much rain. Or not enough. An unexpected freeze. Citrus greening. In the end, though, you have to admit that healthy, young trees on fertile land like Castle Grove will turn a profit more often than not."

"I suppose that's true." He shifted uneasily. "But it doesn't necessarily follow that FPC will meet your asking price."

Suddenly, she wanted nothing more than to bypass the whole negotiation process. Wanted to go home to Gracie. Wanted to put the past behind her and move forward. Knowing the time had come to play her ace, she straightened.

"I'm also aware that FPC has been buying up abandoned groves throughout the area. Your company already owns land on either side of Castle Grove. Adding my acreage would give you unfettered access from one end of the county to the other." Without it, every time FPC wanted to move equipment from one grove to another, they'd have to load it on trucks, apply for permits and haul it on county roads. Which, alone, made her property a valuable commodity.

"How did you..."

Justine favored the man with a quiet smile. As a paralegal in one of the country's largest law firms, she knew her way around property records. She gave FPC's representative a moment to gather his thoughts before she put it all on the line.

"Ordinarily, we could go round and round, but

several other buyers have expressed their interest." None of them had as much to gain as FPC, but if Ken didn't know that already, shame on him. She tapped her pencil against his stack of papers. "Yours is not the only meeting I'm taking while I'm here, so if you intend to counter, you'd best do it before you leave today. Otherwise..." She let the possibility of cutting a deal with another buyer hang between them. Finished with all she had to say—for now—she leaned back and waited.

"You drive a hard bargain, Ms. Gale." Ken straightened the collar of his polo while he gave her a respectful sidelong glance. He tore a sheet of paper from his notebook, scribbled a number on it and handed it across. "I appreciate your desire to save time. If this figure is acceptable, I'm prepared to place a hundred thousand dollars in equity today."

This was it. The moment she'd been preparing for ever since the courier knocked on her door. Below the table's edge, she crossed two fingers while, with her other hand, she lifted the scrap of paper. She fought lips that tried to gape open as she studied a number that exceeded her expectations by a wide margin.

Tears stung the back of her throat. Cicadas buzzed in the grove beyond the house. A puff of air swirled into the quiet room. Across the table, Ken cleared his throat.

"That's for the land and improvements. Any farm equipment, vehicles and personal items are yours to do with as you see fit."

Satisfied with everything she'd heard, she stuck out a hand. "Then I think we have a deal, Ken."

No sooner did she say the words than a truck roared into the front yard. While Justine and Ken watched, dust and dirt pelted the windows as the driver slammed on the brakes. Seconds later, a heavy tread pounded up the front steps and thudded across the porch. Without knocking, Nate burst through the screen door.

Justine flinched when he pinned her with an angry glare. But if she expected him to rail at her, she was mistaken. His face set in rigid lines, Nate wrenched his gaze from hers. He stared at Ken and refused to look away.

"I don't know what she's told you," Nate announced, "but Castle Grove is mine, and I have no intention of selling it."

Nate toed one work boot against the floorboards. Disappointment flooded his chest, crowding out the air until his breathing stuttered. He stared at Justine, unable to believe his eyes any more than he could explain her betrayal.

When she'd shown up unannounced yesterday, he'd believed that maybe—just maybe—she'd take him at his word and do the right thing. Over dinner last night, he'd sworn he was making progress. And why not? He and Justine had been friends once. Fact was, they'd been more than that. She'd nearly been his first. With so much history between them, surely they ought to be able to forge some kind of alliance.

But finding her knee-deep in discussions with a representative from one of the big juicing conglomerates—yeah, that brought reality crashing down around him. He'd expected so much more from the girl whose family had taken their livelihood from this ground going back four generations. Jimmy's will hadn't even been through probate, and here she was, trying to sell the place.

Didn't she have any idea how much she stood to lose by selling out to FPC? How much everyone counted on her to maintain the grove?

Not that he had any intention of relinquishing his own claim. Not that. Never that. But he'd clung to the thin hope that they could resolve things, same as he'd held on to the rope when they'd played tug-o-war when they were kids. He didn't want to waste his resources—or hers—on court costs and expensive lawyers. Not if he could avoid it.

But he should have known better. And from the moment he'd spotted the black car kicking up dust on the drive to the main house, he'd known Justine hadn't listened to a word he'd said about hanging on to the land. As he'd sloshed his way from the middle of the irrigation pond to the sloping bank, he'd known she didn't give a damn about him, much less about Orange Blossom. That her thirst for the almighty dollar had driven her to sell Castle Grove, the same way it had ended their relationship the last time.

He rubbed his chest where anger burned. He couldn't begin to describe how it hurt to learn she'd been here less than one day, and already, she was trying to steal his inheritance right out from under him.

"Not gonna happen," he swore.

Staring at him, the tall blonde paled beneath skin that could benefit from more time in the sun. Unable to bear her shell-shocked face a moment longer, he broke the connection. The Fresh Picked Citrus exec sat by the window where he hogged what little breeze stirred in the August heat. Nate nailed the selfish pig with his darkest look.

Like a guy who'd been kicked when he least expected it, Justine's visitor slowly rose to his feet. "I'm not sure I understand, Mr. uh..."

The jerk has the audacity to pretend we haven't met?

"Nate. Nate Rhodes," he reminded. They'd taken drinks from the same serving tray at last year's Buckaroo Ball, butted heads more than once at town council meetings. He scrubbed a grimy hand on his jeans, studied it and let it fall to his side. If memory served, shaking hands with Ken Thomas was never a pleasure. "You're one of the head honchos over at FPC."

"VP of acquisitions," Ken answered as if Nate needed a refresher course. "I'm afraid Ms. Gale and I were in the middle of a business meeting. If you don't mind, we'd appreciate it if you'd leave us to finish up."

"I'm sure you would, but I have just as much right to be here as she does." He hooked a thumb over one shoulder to the chair where guilt froze Justine in place. "Ask her if you don't believe me."

Ken's head tilted slightly. "What's he talking about?" he asked, though, by now, any idiot would have figured things out.

"It's nothing. He...he—" Justine's breath hitched, and her words tumbled out in a rush. "He says he owns part of Castle Grove, but he has no proof."

Nate's stomach twisted at the treachery that etched deep lines in Justine's finely chiseled features. He held his ground.

"Seems like that's something you should have mentioned earlier," Ken mused.

Across the room, Justine drew herself erect. "Believe me, if there was any merit to his claim, I would have. I'm meeting with my attorney this afternoon. He'll take care of this issue."

How she'd managed to convince Royce Enid to waddle off his porch on a Saturday afternoon was something Nate wished he knew. Just as he wished he'd known a lot of things about Justine's weekend visit to Orange Blossom. He shifted his weight from one foot to the other while he considered crashing another of her meetings. In the end, he let it go. An emergency session of the town council was slated to start after lunch, and as interim mayor, his presence was required. Much as he wanted to, he couldn't be in two places at once.

Across the room, Justine turned earnest blue eyes his way. "Nate, you know I'm telling the truth. Uncle Jimmy left Castle Grove to me, not you."

Jimmy might have reneged on his promises, but what was done was done. Nate wouldn't lie, wouldn't say the entire grove was his. But he wouldn't hand over the land he'd worked so hard to earn either. He'd wanted a place to call his own his entire life. Now that he had it, he wasn't about to let it go.

"Jimmy and I struck a deal. In exchange for running the grove at a profit, he turned ten acres a year over to me. That makes eighty, all told. He swore he'd leave me the rest, but the courts'll sort that out. The important thing is, Ken, I'm not interested in selling." He'd already made that sentiment perfectly clear, but it bore repeating.

"This certainly puts things in a different light." Ken's eyes narrowed. "I assume you have proof?"

"I do." Nate met the man's gaze head on. "In

spades." He'd already lined up more than a dozen people who'd testify on his behalf. And he'd barely gotten started.

"Nothing that'll hold up in court," Justine sputtered.

The FPC rep held up one finger. "Hold on a minute, Ms. Gale. I'd like to hear more about this. What kind of proof are we talking about here?" Ken leaned against the table as if he expected Nate to call his first witness.

He gave the FPC rep a withering look. "I don't have to show you anything, 'cept maybe a smile and a clap on the back when you leave. You want evidence? Talk to my attorney. He'll present my side of things at the probate hearing in December. Till then, I'd thank you kindly if you got off *my* property."

He caught the hint of a smug smile just before Ken turned to face Justine and stiffened. What was with the pompous attitude? he wondered. Hadn't he just thrown a king-sized wrench into FPC's plan to buy Castle Grove? Why wasn't the man slinking out the back door like a whipped puppy?

"Justine, this claim, whether spurious or not, is something you should have disclosed. It'd be foolish for Fresh Picked Citrus to pay full price for Castle Grove when the ownership of the land is being contested. Once word gets out about this"—Ken's sly smile let everyone in the room know how eagerly he'd spread that word—"I doubt you'll find any buyer willing to invest in the property at all. Not until you have clear title."

Justine's bravado sprang a leak. Her shoulders slumped. The tiny crow's feet at the corners of her eyes deepened. Her mouth pulled down.

"But," she protested weakly, "but that'll take months."

116

Unmoved, Ken lifted one shoulder in a careless shrug. "Maybe longer. I've seen cases like this drag through the courts for years."

Justine gave her head a firm shake that loosed some of the hair around her face. It trailed down over her shoulders, giving her a waifish look that, despite all that was at stake, stirred every protective nerve in Nate's body. He curled his fingers inward as he summoned the strength to refuse to reach out to her. She'd brought the situation on herself.

"What do I do now?" she whispered more to herself than anyone else.

"Because FPC's position is unique, we are still interested in buying. Not at the price we negotiated, of course, but I can probably convince the home office to stand by their original offer as long as you agree to the sale today." Ken rapped his knuckles against a stack of papers on the table. A patently false grin on his face, the big man held up a hand. "However, absolutely no money can change hands before probate is completed and we know for sure that the land is indeed yours."

The VP cupped his chin in one hand. With the other, he thumbed the corner of the document on the table. "Let's sign these papers and get this over with."

Does she see how Ken is toying with her? Figuring it was time to add his two cents into the mix, Nate stepped forward. His voice dropped to its lowest register. "Make no mistake. I know exactly what's going on here."

FPC was trying an end run, that's what. Once Justine made a formal commitment to sell Castle Grove, the company would gain legal standing in the courts. With its deep pockets, the big conglomerate could bury Nate in delays and legal maneuvering until he died of old age. In the meantime, the grove would be left unattended, and from there, the dominos would fall. One after the other, local businesses would shutter their doors until Orange Blossom became a ghost town. His gaze dropped to the pen resting on the papers closest to Justine. He had to stop her before she made the biggest mistake of her life.

As if she'd read his mind, Justine issued a warning. "Nate, stay out of this."

Not a chance.

"Just give me five minutes. Five minutes alone"— he shot Ken a meaningful glance—"before you sign anything. If I can't convince you, I'll leave." He sucked in a fortifying breath. Walking out that door would be the hardest thing he'd ever do, but he'd keep his word. He called on every memory, every vestige of their time together, and shoved it all into one plea. "Please."

The longest thirty seconds of his life passed before, with a lift of her chin, she signaled Ken onto the porch. Nate held his breath when the representative argued, but Justine held firm. When the door closed behind the retreating figure, she touched her watch. "Okay, you have five minutes," she ordered. "Start talking."

She'd given him a chance. One chance. For the sake of Orange Blossom, as well as his own future, he wouldn't blow it. He marshaled his best arguments. Showing her the palms of his hands, he began.

"The grapefruit and oranges we raise on Castle Grove are shipped all over the country. Shiny, big, juicy. They're meant for the table, and they're damn near perfect," he said, letting his pride show.

"FPC, though..." He shook his head. "FPC is a juicing conglomerate. They don't care how the oranges look, how easily they peel, how they fall apart in sections. All they care about is the juice. We don't grow juice oranges here, Justine," he said, intent on making her understand. "FPC will come in here with bulldozers and tear out every tree for miles around."

Determined their first harvest wouldn't be their last, he pointed out the window toward the heavily laden branches. Encouraged when a pair of big blue eyes tracked his movement, he appealed to her sense of continuity.

"You saw the grapefruit on the other side of the drive?" At her nod, he let nostalgia fill him. "Those trees were planted before you were born. We played tag beneath them when we were kids. But if you sell to FPC, they'll disappear in a matter of days. The lemons that went into Aunt Margaret's lemonade, too."

He saw her eyes flicker, and certain he had her attention, he continued. "FPC will plant new. Only this time, instead of big, heavy navels, they'll plant thin-skinned Valencias. Trees that can't be harvested for fifteen, maybe twenty years. When they finally are mature enough, FPC won't handpick their fruit the old-fashioned way. Won't give a second thought to the pickers they're putting out of work. They'll bring in machines to do the job. Not that it'll matter. By then, it'll be too late."

Nate's flickering hope became a steady flame when Justine's forehead furrowed. Concern showed in her knitted eyebrows. Had he gotten through to her?

"Too late for all the people around here." He pressed the point home. "The ones who depend on Castle Grove—on us—to make their living. The migrant workers who flood our area each harvest will go elsewhere. At the Ham Hut, Sam won't hire the extra help he puts on that time of year. Think what'll happen if Castle Grove stops buying fertilizer from the hardware store in town. What we spend there in a year keeps Bill and Karen Smalley afloat. Without our business, they'll have to close. Take away the local citrus she's built her reputation on, and Miss Bertie will shut off the ovens and turn out the lights at the pie shop." His voice dropped to its most solemn tone. "And that's just a start. Once Orange Blossom starts to die, there's no reviving it."

"I think I've heard enough." Justine held up a hand, stopping him. "You can let Ken back inside now."

Wishing she'd given him another thirty seconds, Nate pressed his lips into a thin line. He wasn't surprised when he opened the door and found the FPC representative lingering on the other side. If he'd been in the same situation, he'd have had his ear pressed against the wood, splinters or no splinters. Nate's heart hammered as Justine made quick work of filling in any gaps in what Ken had overheard. When she finished, she searched the rep's face.

"Is this true? Is this what you have planned for Castle Grove?"

Despite his confident air, sweat dampened Ken's collar. He shrugged. "I'm in acquisitions, not planning. I leave those decisions up to the experts on that side of the house."

"As I mentioned before," Justine cut in, "I'm going to need certain assurances from FPC. Nate, here, has called those promises into question. I think it's best for both of us if I postpone any decision until after I speak with my attorney. I'm going to have to think about all this." She swept a hand through air heavy with the smell of Ken's aftershave.

A muscle along Ken's jawline twitched. "Think fast, Ms. Gale. I can extend our offer for twenty-four hours, but my people won't wait any longer for your decision. After that, we'll withdraw our offer."

Nate pulled himself another inch taller as Ken glared at him.

"At least, until the true ownership of the land has been determined."

Pure, unadulterated relief shot through him as Nate watched the FPC rep sweep papers into a leather briefcase. The instant the door closed behind Ken, he turned, eager to wrap his arms around Justine and thank her properly for making the right decision. A move that faltered the moment he spotted the daggers in her eyes.

"What?" he asked.

"You," she breathed. "You've ruined everything. Why couldn't you just leave everything the way it was?"

Keeping things the way they were was exactly what he was trying to do, wasn't it?

Out of words and out of patience, he executed a one-eighty. Last night, Justine had agreed to fund the Orange Fest. Today, she'd postponed the sale of Castle Grove. Given more time, he was certain he'd convince her to do right by him, by the town. But just this minute, putting some time and distance between them sounded like a good idea, although he was beginning to doubt there were enough hours in a day or miles on the globe to erase the ache in his heart.

The screen door slapped shut behind Nate. Justine gritted her teeth as he stomped across the porch and down the stairs. She rubbed her midsection where acid threatened to burn a hole in her stomach while she swept the paperwork from the table into her briefcase. "Thanks for nothing, Nate," she muttered.

What was wrong with him? He acted as if she'd come to Orange Blossom intent on destroying the town and the lives of everyone in it, when nothing could be further from the truth. Hadn't she gone out of her way to protect his job? Hadn't she insisted on FPC's continued support of the local economy? Didn't their past mean anything to him?

It hadn't been all that long ago that they'd been friends. Almost lovers. Yet he'd stormed in on a private meeting and deliberately sabotaged her hopes of reaching a quick and satisfactory agreement with FPC. As if that weren't bad enough, his refusal to drop the matter had delayed her, making her late for her meeting with Royce Enid.

The handle of her briefcase clenched tightly, she marched through the house, her heels beating out an adage against the worn wooden planks.

You can't go home again!

It had been foolish to think she could relive the good times on Castle Grove, if only for a day or two. Aunt Margaret and Uncle Jimmy were gone. Her friends were off living lives of their own. As for Nate and her, they'd changed too much to reclaim what they'd once had.

She was a different person from the naive young woman she'd been back then.

She'd made mistakes back then. Sure she had. But at least she'd known better than to slide behind the wheel of a car that had been baking in the hot summer sun, she told herself moments later. Pretty sure her bare thighs were going to fry like a hamburger patty in a hot skillet, she shifted on the hot leather seat. She regretted the move immediately when another swatch of exposed skin sizzled. Biting down on a protest, she flipped the air conditioner to high. Heat blasted through the vents, making her wish for the days when she'd gone to town with her friends.

Sarah and Penny usually complained about the five-mile trek, but she'd never minded riding in the back of a pickup truck, her feet dangling inches above the roadway while her hair blew in twenty different directions. Hadn't thought twice about pedaling through the muggy heat on borrowed bikes. Not really. Not with Nate leading the way.

Despite the clouds of bugs and the occasional dive-bombing bumblebee, Nate had had a knack for turning every trip into an adventure. Tilting his head to the sky, he'd laugh out loud whenever a shower caught them halfway into town. She'd scream along with the other girls, but while the rain had dripped into her eyes, it had also washed the sticky heat from her sun-parched skin. Afterward, they'd splash through oily, rainbow-colored puddles, pedaling so fast her clothes would dry before she'd reached the welcome sign at the outskirts of Orange Blossom. But the best part—the absolute best—that had always come about midway home. When, with her handlebars wobbling fiercely, she and the others had followed Nate as he veered off the road. Ditching their bikes in the grass, they'd hop a fence and gorge on sweet, wet fruit from a neighbor's strawberry or watermelon patch. At a time when Nate had held all the answers to life's thorniest problems, he'd been her best friend, her closest ally.

She missed having someone like that in her life. Missed the way Nate's laughter used to send shivers up her spine. Missed the kisses they'd shared the summer she turned eighteen, the plans they'd made.

But what had she expected?

That she'd come back to Castle Grove and things would be the same? Well, they weren't, and the sooner she accepted it, the better. Nate, the old Nate, the one who'd always had her back, was as much a thing of the past as the orange trees that had once crowded both sides of the road, dappling the asphalt with shade. Nor was he the only one who'd changed. Becoming a mother had taught her to take whatever life dished out and stay on her feet, unlike the roadside stands which, under the onslaught of thick, twisting kudzu, had collapsed into misshapen piles of weathered boards.

Halfway to town, the air blowing through the vents finally cooled. She aimed the flow at her face and pushed harder on the accelerator, as eager to leave her memories of the past behind as she was to settle things with Royce and head back to Virginia.

As she neared the heart of Orange Blossom, she slowed enough to take a good look at a town that hadn't changed much since her last visit. The saplings that lined the streets had matured into leafy trees. Nodding, she bet most folks appreciated the shade as they walked from the First Baptist Church at one end of the square to the Ham Hut at the other for Sunday dinner. Through the windows of the Book Nook, she caught a quick glimpse of shoppers and smiled, glad she could tell Penny that her dad's store seemed to be doing well. Pulling into a vacant slot in front of the hardware store, she glanced at the same worn sign that dangled from a hook on the door. Mr. Smalley's hours hadn't changed, and for that, she was grateful. If she was going to sleep at the house tonight, she needed to pick up a few things.

Stepping from her car, she drank in a tart, citrusy smell. She eyed the entrance to Miss June's while her stomach grumbled about the breakfast and lunch she'd skipped. She patted her tummy. She'd planned to meet Sarah at the bakery, but her friend was on the tail end of a summer cold. If she was over it by then, they'd catch up tomorrow. Grabbing her briefcase, she hurried up the steps to Royce's office.

Seconds later, she stepped into a reception area far less intimidating than Jacoby & Sons's. Cool air dried the light sheen of perspiration from her skin, and she shivered, her gaze traveling from a cozy seating arrangement to a desk piled with open boxes. Seated behind them, her full cheeks dominating her features, a petite brunette seemed to be waking from a nap.

"Mary Beth?" Justine ventured after a beat.

"Oh, my goodness, Justine!" One hand cupping her swollen abdomen, the pregnant woman rose with a grunt. She edged from behind her desk. "Look at you. You haven't changed a bit."

Enveloped in a fleshy hug, Justine managed, "It's so good to see you. I didn't know you worked for Royce."

"I've been with him for, oh, gosh, going on eight years now. But today's my last day. For a while, at least." Mary Beth stepped far enough away to rub her tummy.

"I am seriously going to have to have a talk with Sarah. There's far too much going on in Orange Blossom that she isn't telling me. I didn't even know you were expecting."

"Ooof." Mary Beth bent slightly. She slipped one hand around to her lower back. "I won't be for long. I'm due any day now. It's a boy. A little Jack Junior." Straightening, she asked, "You don't mind if I sit down, do you?"

"Sit. Sit." Justine made shooing motions. "You and Jack Sparling?" she asked, recalling a tall boy with blond hair who'd rarely left Mary Beth's side when they were teens.

"Who else?" Mary Beth collapsed into her chair with a groan. "We've been together since high school. He finally popped the question two years ago, right after he made deputy sheriff. I'd show you my rings, but my fingers are too swollen to wear them right now." Her left hand inched around to her back, while a small frown played across her features.

"Well, congratulations on both counts. You'll have to let me know where you're registered so I can get something for the baby."

126

"That's sweet, but you don't need to bother. Jack Junior will be the first grandchild on either side of the family. His grandparents have bought enough diapers, clothes and toys to fill three nurseries." Mary Beth's frown deepened, then smoothed. "What have you been up to?"

"Oh, you know." In all likelihood, Mary Beth already knew everything there was to know about her past. She opted to gloss over most of it with a vague, "The usual," before steering the conversation to the highlight of her life. "I have a little girl. Gracie. She's five."

"Oooh, a girl!" Mary Beth gasped. "I wanted a girl in the worst way."

Justine had barely nodded when Mary Beth switched to another subject.

"I was sorry to hear about your dad," she announced, absently patting her stomach. "Your mom doing okay? You have *got* to bring your daughter down here for a visit sometime soon. I'd love to meet her."

Mary Beth's scattershot delivery hadn't changed one little bit, Justine mused, while the idea of bringing Gracie to Castle Grove stirred a fresh wave of nostalgia. Imagining the two of them sharing an ice cream soda at the luncheonette in the five-and-dime or walking hand in hand down the now tree-lined streets of Orange Blossom, she blinked. Slowly, she pushed the images away. As much as she might enjoy exploring the old haunts with her daughter, another trip to Orange Blossom didn't factor into the game plan any more than exposing Gracie to the dust and dirt—and germs—in the old farmhouse.

"We'll see," she answered at last, using the phrase

her five-year-old had already pegged as her mom's version of *it ain't gonna happen.*

"Penny says you're working in a law firm in DC?"

"Jacoby & Sons," she murmured, bracing for the kinds of questions she didn't want to answer. Like, why she hadn't followed through with her plans to become an attorney herself.

"I bet you run the place. You always were the smart one. Always studying, even on summer vacation. Does your daughter take after you? Your mom probably dotes on her. My mom and dad are so looking forward to becoming grandparents."

For once, Mary Beth's disjointed conversation worked in her favor. Spared the need to wax poetic over her amazing view of the gray-walled cubicle next to hers or her mother's decided lack of interest in her only grandchild, Justine smiled. "Enough about me. What about you? Shouldn't you be home with your feet propped up, eating bonbons?" She would be. In fact, that was how she'd planned to spend the last few weeks before her own due date. Plans that had changed—along with everything else—when, twenty-seven weeks into her pregnancy, the doctors hadn't been able to stop her premature labor.

"I will be, starting tomorrow. I came in today to pack up my things, but"—another frown dented Mary Beth's full cheeks—"there was a message from the temp we hired to fill in while I'm gone. She took a better offer in Orlando. Now, instead of packing, I'm trying to find someone to replace her. The way my luck is running, I'll probably have this baby first. You don't happen to know anybody, do you?"

"I'll keep my ears open." Considering Mary Beth hadn't recognized the name of the country's largest law firm, Justine bet the job wasn't too taxing. "Is the pay decent?"

The receptionist rolled her eyes. "Peanuts, but there's health insurance. Plus, Royce is a dream to work for." The intercom emitted a low buzz. "That's him now. He must be ready for you." Mary Beth tipped her head toward a short hallway and a door at the end of it. "You don't mind seeing yourself in, do you?"

"Not at all. Maybe we can grab a cup of coffee when I'm finished," she offered, though she was pretty sure they'd covered all the basics.

Wiping her forehead with the back of her hand, Mary Beth said, "Some other time, maybe. I'm going to finish up here and call it a day."

Not a problem. She wasn't planning on sticking around town for very long herself. Once she had Royce's assurance that her uncle's will was valid, she'd schedule another chat with Ken Thomas. It might take some effort, but as much as Fresh Picked Citrus wanted Castle Grove, she'd untangle the mess Nate had made of their deal. With luck, she could wrap everything up and still make her flight home tomorrow night. Her arms ached to hold Gracie before she reported for work on Monday.

Straightening, she smoothed a hand over her skirt, then tapped on the closed door at the end of the hall. At the gravelly voice she recognized from their talks over the phone, she let herself inside.

"Mr. Enid? I'm Justine Gale."

"Come in, come in." Propping his hands on his chair's armrests, the portly senior citizen behind the desk rose halfway to his feet.

"Oh, don't get up on my account," she said when he

appeared to struggle. She gave the room a cursory look, her tension easing as she scanned a wall dotted with more framed certificates and diplomas than she'd expected of a small-town lawyer.

"Thanks. Much obliged. Summer. I swear it gets hotter every year." Easing his bulk onto his seat, Royce motioned her into a chair while he blotted his forehead with a monogrammed handkerchief. "My, my, my. The last time I saw you, you were just a little mite of a thing. And now look at you. All grown up. It's a pleasure to see you again."

"I wish it could be under better circumstances." Justine took a notebook and pen from her briefcase.

Royce's face fell. "I'm so sorry about your uncle. His loss is a blow to the whole town. He was a staunch supporter of Orange Blossom. He'll be sorely missed."

Keeping the conversation on point, she said, "Although we hadn't kept in touch, I'll always be grateful for the summers I spent on Castle Grove."

"Yes, well. It appears you share your uncle's love for Orange Blossom. I can't tell you how happy everyone will be when they learn you've agreed to fund the Orange Fest." At Justine's puzzled look, he explained, "Nate stopped by a little while ago with the news."

Is there no end to his interference?

"I'm afraid he misunderstood," she corrected. "What I said was that I'd discuss the matter with you. While I'm not opposed to continuing Uncle Jimmy's sponsorship, I need to understand where things stand before I can commit. So..." She flexed her fingers. She needed more details about the estate, and Royce was the person to provide them. "What can you tell me?"

The lawyer's chair emitted a protest as he leaned

forward. "Like most of the folks around here, your uncle Jimmy didn't keep a lot of money on hand. Most of his reserves he poured back into the grove or the community. Last year, citrus prices bottomed out. Which means there's enough left in his bank account to cover the operating expenses for the rest of the year. Not much more than that."

Justine nodded. She'd lived through a few lean summers on Castle Grove. Times when Aunt Margaret would spend the day shopping with friends and come home empty-handed. When dish soap replaced shampoo in the bathroom. When dinner was nothing more than lima beans and sliced tomatoes straight from the vegetable garden.

"And Nate's claim that he owns half the estate, how will that affect things?"

Twin white brows came together over Royce's eyes. "I'll tell you, same as I told him—he doesn't have legal standing."

"Apparently, he didn't believe you, 'cause he barged into my meeting with Fresh Picked Citrus this morning. He created quite a stir. Tell me, Mr. Enid—"

"Royce, please."

"Royce. How did we end up in this mess?"

"Depends on who you ask. To understand Nate's version, you have to go back a ways." Royce leaned back in his chair, fingers intertwined over a belly that rivaled Mary Beth's. "When the canker hit in the nineties, it devastated the citrus industry. Pesticides won't kill it, and the stuff spreads like wildfire. Before the grove owners hardly knew what was happening, the federal government had stepped in. They sent inspection teams door-to-door throughout the state. Wherever they found so much as one infected tree, they torched every bit of citrus within a quarter mile. Whole groves went up in smoke. Meanwhile, the rest of the country banned fruit shipments from Florida. Not long after that, the processing plants closed. People lost their jobs, their homes. Things were looking pretty grim. Most of the family-owned groves defaulted on their mortgages or sold out to big conglomerates for next to nothing."

"Like Fresh Picked Citrus," she noted. "They haven't done much with all that land." All along the drive from Orlando to Castle Grove, skeletons of dead trees had stretched to the horizon, their sooty, black limbs poking through nearly two decades' worth of undergrowth.

"I've heard rumors lately that they're interested in expanding their operations."

Justine recrossed her legs. None of this explained Nate's so-called claim on the land Uncle Jimmy left her. "So how does Nate figure into all this?"

"Some say you'd get orange juice instead of blood if you'd tapped Jimmy Castle's veins. His family owned that land free and clear for a hundred years or more. With no mortgage, he didn't have to sell out like the others. Would have killed him if he had."

Despite Royce's roundabout way of answering a question, Justine let the corners of her mouth curve upward. Much as her uncle loved his trees, he loved his family even more.

"If memory serves me correctly, only one of Jimmy's trees caught the canker, and it was on the very edge of his property. The inspectors, they only torched half his grove. Which meant, once the embargo on Florida citrus was lifted, Jimmy still had money coming in. Nate, he swears he and Jimmy struck a deal soon after that, and he's been taking his bonus in land instead of cash ever since."

She stifled a groan.

"On top of that, he swears Jimmy promised to leave him the rest of the land in his will."

She'd heard the same version of the story from Nate. Her stomach souring, she leaned forward. "What are your thoughts on that?"

"Other than a few people who saw Jimmy raise a toast to Nate at The Crush at the end of the season, there's not a single shred of corroborating evidence. Your uncle never transferred the deed for so much as a single acre. Never changed his will. Never contacted me about any intent to do so. From a purely legal standpoint, that's the end of it. Castle Grove remains intact and is passed along to Jimmy's heir. In this case, you."

"You're sure the Testator's Family Maintenance Law doesn't apply?" Justine crossed her fingers. She'd dropped out of law school before her second year when most students studied trusts and estates, but she'd heard that, in some cases, a caretaker or loved one could bring suit if they felt they'd been unjustly overlooked. Did the rule have merit in this case?

The older man's hands slipped down the sides of his belly. He pinned her with an owlish stare. "Know a little something about the law, do you?"

"Not as much as I'd like to," she answered honestly. "I work as a paralegal at Jacoby & Sons."

Royce nodded, his bushy eyebrows wagging. "Rest assured. Your uncle Jimmy's will is just as valid today as it was when he wrote it out. No matter what he said, or didn't say, in the interim."

For the first time since her run-in with Nate yesterday, Justine took an easy breath.

"That being said..." Royce's gaze drifted out the window.

"Yes?" Wondering if she'd been too hasty in letting down her guard, she tapped one finger against the notebook.

The older man cleared his throat. His focus drifted about the room. Finally, it settled on her. "That being said," he continued, "I've seen courts overturn a will— a perfectly good and valid will—on far less grounds. But that's not the real problem. The problem here is, if Nate files suit, the courts can tie up the estate for years."

Justine stiffened. A protracted court battle would require both time and money she intended to devote to Gracie.

"As executor, you'll fight him?" Royce might not look like much, but he'd been her uncle's lawyer since before she was born. Uncle Jimmy had trusted Royce to make sure his estate was handled according to his wishes.

"Not me. The fact of the matter is, whoever takes your side in this case is going to get run out of town on a rail."

Say what?

She straightened. "I'm not sure I follow."

Royce pinched the bridge of his nose and breathed a heavy breath. "A case like this can have a polarizing effect on a small town. Everyone in Orange Blossom loved your uncle Jimmy. But Nate, he's well respected around these parts, too. Your lawyer—whoever it is— will have to prove either that Jimmy made promises he never intended to keep, or Nate did something so despicable that Jimmy changed his mind. I can't be the man who makes everyone choose sides. Not if I hope to have any peace in my retirement." Royce tipped his chair upright and spread his beefy fingers on the desk blotter.

"Then there's the little matter of Mary Beth."

Justine felt her eyebrows climb higher. What did his administrative assistant have to do with her case?

"Mary Beth swears she's coming back after her maternity leave, but my wife said the same thing before our first was born." Royce swiped his cheeks with his handkerchief. "Mary Beth's been with me so long, I'll be lost without her. I certainly can't take on a big case like yours without her."

He glanced toward the door as if he feared Mary Beth might barrel through it at any second, doubled over with labor pains, a situation Justine considered well within the realm of possibilities. "Hopefully, you'll find someone to fill in for her," she offered.

"Yes, well." Royce peered across the desk at her. "You interested in the job?"

"Me?" Justine shook her head. "I'm not sticking around. I just came down for the weekend."

Royce shrugged a well-padded shoulder. "Figured as much, but I had to ask."

"About Nate," she said, drawing the conversation back to the topic at hand while the muscles along her jawline tensed. There had to be a way to avoid a lawsuit in which the lawyers, with their fat retainers and stiff legal fees, would be the only winners. Her best chance at finding a solution sat in front of her. "What would you suggest?"

"That's easy." As if he had the answer to one of the world's thorniest problems, Royce's cheeks dimpled.

"Search the house from top to bottom. Look for anything that supports the will. A canceled check showing Jimmy paid Nate his bonuses. A note, a scrap of paper detailing ways in which Nate failed to hold up his end of the bargain. The more you can find to support the will and negate Nate's claim, the better."

She fought the urge to squirm as protests rose in her throat. She didn't have the resources for a long stay in Orange Blossom. She needed to get home, to Gracie, to her own job. "Have you been to Castle Grove lately?" she asked, trying to keep hide her skepticism. Cleaning off her uncle's desk alone would take longer than the day she had left in Orange Blossom.

"No." Royce pursed fleshy lips. "Can't say as I've had a need."

"It's a disaster," she said sadly. "The front porch is so rickety, I'm surprised it hasn't collapsed. The inside has been, well, neglected." She gave an unladylike shudder.

Royce frowned. "I don't think you have another option. It's either that or plunk down a healthy retainer for another attorney. If you want, I can give you the name of some lawyers in Orlando." He spun the cards in an old-fashioned Rolodex on one corner of his desk.

The feeling that she was forgetting something nagged at her, and she took a minute to run through the conversation. As she replayed Royce's opening remarks, it hit her—the Orange Fest. Her eyes narrowed, and she fixed the attorney with a hard stare. All but certain she had her facts straight, she said, "There isn't enough money in Uncle Jimmy's accounts to cover a retainer and the Orange Fest, too, is there?"

The dismay etched on Royce's face gave her the answer she sought before his apologetic "No" whispered into the room. "Truth is, underwriting the Orange Fest will cause the estate's reserves to dip pretty low. But the harvest is just around the corner—another couple of months. That'll replenish the coffers."

Unless there's a hurricane. Or an early freeze. Or a host of other catastrophes.

She couldn't take that chance. "I guess that settles it. I won't be able to fund the Orange Fest, after all."

The lawyer ran a hand over his face. "Man, I'm going to hate telling Nate."

The fact was, Nate had no one to blame but himself. With his claim hanging over her head, she couldn't sell Castle Grove. If she couldn't sell, she wouldn't be able to give Gracie the life her daughter deserved. Determined to let nothing stand in the way of meeting that goal, she sipped air. Nate might tower over her, all broad shoulders and slim hips, dark hair falling just so over a pair of the dreamiest eyes she'd ever seen, but he was also a constant reminder of what they'd once had and lost. She swallowed.

"I'll take care of Nate." It was, after all, her decision, her responsibility.

They spent another half hour going over paperwork before Royce heaved himself to his feet. With a final reminder to let him know if she uncovered a shred of evidence to negate Nate's claim, he guided her to the door. Justine said a quick good-bye to Mary Beth and retraced her steps down the stairs. Reaching the sidewalk, she spotted Nate across the street and adjusted her purse at her shoulder. Her mother had always insisted that bad news, like a dose of vile-tasting medicine, was best delivered quickly. Prepared to give Nate exactly what he deserved, she followed him across Main Street.

His stride a mite jauntier than it had been during his last visit, Nate stepped into the offices of the town hall. Karen Smalley sprang from her seat the instant his feet crossed the threshold. He halted, his foot hanging in midair. Slowly, he lowered it.

"They're waiting for you in the chambers." Karen's voice carried a shrill note that was totally out of character. Color stained her cheeks. "Everyone's a little antsy."

"They won't be for long." Nate gave the secretary his most reassuring smile. He hadn't planned on sharing the good news until he took his place behind the podium, but what the heck? Karen—and everyone else—would find out soon enough. He quickly explained the recent set of developments.

"That's wonderful news, Mr. Mayor," she gushed as worry lines melted from her face.

Pretending he didn't see Karen give her eyes a quick wipe, he held one finger to his lips. "Shhh," he whispered. "Mum's the word."

Not that Karen had been the only one on tenterhooks about the Orange Fest and what it meant for the town. To be honest, he'd spent more than one long night mulling over alternative ways to fund the event and came up empty. He hooked one thumb in the corner of a pants pocket and took a sec to savor the moment. Thanks to Justine's offer, he could probably run for a second term when elections rolled around. Though, if he wanted to cement his victory, he'd have to preserve Orange Blossom by blocking the sale of Castle Grove...permanently. Which was exactly what he intended to do.

"Are you ready to join the others, then?" Karen plucked a spiral notebook from her desk and snatched a pen from behind her ear.

He slapped his hands together. "Let's get this party started."

With Karen leading the way, they moved into the oversized conference room where the Orange Blossom seal hung on a wall between two flags. She moved toward her spot at the end of the long, curved desk, joining the other five members of the town council who had already taken their assigned seats. Nate nodded at a chorus of "Mr. Mayors" and made his way between the rows of folding chairs filled with curious citizens. Shaking hands with local business owners, he commiserated with Sam, the owner of the Ham Hut, who'd been battling indigestion over his son's college expenses. On the next row, Bertie Bowen brushed a smudge of flour from her apron while she fretted aloud about the lead time needed to prepare for the Orange Fest.

"I have to order my supplies, Mr. Mayor. I can't afford to do that if there's a chance we might cancel."

Nate patted Bertie's plump arm. "Don't you worry," he soothed before heading for the hard wooden chair he'd occupied for the past three months.

He'd once asked Jimmy why the town council didn't spring for padded cushions. The old man had laughed and said, "To keep the meetings short." Nate had laughed right along with him then, but he didn't feel much like laughing now. Considering what had come to light recently, he wondered whether he and his friend and mentor would still be on speaking terms if Jimmy was around today. He brushed the question aside as he took his seat and rapped the gavel on the table.

"I call this emergency meeting of the town council to order. Karen"—Nate aimed a confident look toward the secretary—"this being a Saturday, let's dispense with the roll call and such."

The folks of Orange Blossom didn't normally stand on such ceremony. But a couple of months ago, Karen had unearthed an ancient copy of Robert's Rules of Order. She'd been doing her best to formalize their meetings ever since. When the secretary's lips pinched shut over a protest, Nate breathed a grateful sigh and faced the crowded room.

"Thank you all for interrupting your busy weekend to be here. I know many of you want to get back to your stores and businesses, so I'll get right to the point."

An uneasy murmur rippled through the crowd. Knowing how much the winter festival meant to everyone, Nate waited for things to quiet down before he acknowledged the elephant in the room.

"We've all been concerned about funding for the Orange Fest. Especially now that it looks like the Castle estate is going to be tied up for a while longer." He paused while several heads bobbed. There wasn't any need to reiterate the details. By the time he'd hit the sidewalk outside of Royce's office three weeks ago, word of Jimmy's will had already been racing along the town's grapevine.

Nate swallowed and shook aside his doubts. The

problems with the Castle estate were an oversight, pure and simple. They'd get corrected soon enough.

"Jimmy's niece, Justine Gale, is in town this weekend. Some of you might remember her, though it's been a few years since she's visited. I've had a chance to speak with her and..."

A noise at the back of the room derailed his train of thought. Whispers rose when the door opened to admit the last person he'd expected to see in the middle of a town council meeting. He took a moment to get his bearings.

"Well, what do you know?" he said when Justine lingered at the door. "Here she is now."

At her end of the table, Karen spun toward the new arrival, her brown eyes widening into ovals the size of a pheasant's eggs. "Oh, Ms. Gale," she called. "I can't tell you how glad we are that you're going to sponsor the Orange Fest this year. We're all so relieved."

Rather than smile and accept the tribute, Justine froze as the news Karen hadn't been able to contain rippled through the room. Within seconds, every person had risen to their feet. Someone clapped, then another and another, until applause echoed off the walls.

Earlier, Nate hadn't given Justine more than a cursory glance. He did now, though, and barely suppressed a whistle at the sundress that flared in all the right places. Shapely legs emerged from beneath the full skirt. They arrowed down into a pair of heels that made his heart pound. She'd swept her hair into a no-nonsense bun that emphasized high cheekbones and expressive blue eyes. Eyes that, if he hadn't known better, had filled with ice.

Across the room, someone coughed. Nate

straightened, aware he'd been ogling the enemy in full view of the very people who counted on him to win the war over Jimmy's estate. He ran a hand through his hair, waited for the general hubbub to die down and tapped his gavel lightly on the table.

"If we could all come to order…" When the room quieted, he picked up from where he'd left off.

"As I started to say earlier, Ms. Gale has graciously consented to—"

"Excuse me, Nate, but could I have a word?" Justine's voice trembled the tiniest bit as she broke into the middle of his announcement for the second time.

Karen looked up from her notepad. "Will you yield the floor, Mr. Mayor?"

"Mr. Mayor?" Eyes widening, Justine swept the room again, this time her gaze taking in the assembly and Nate's position on the dais. Her lips rounded. "You're the mayor," she breathed.

"That's right." Nate squared his shoulders. Ignoring the rules of order, he addressed Justine directly. "Is there something we can help you with?"

From her chair in the corner, Karen tsked at the breach in protocol. Nate ignored her. This was Orange Blossom, for crying out loud. Where the desire to preserve the town's heritage was important to every person on the council, every person in the room.

"The floor yields to Ms. Gale," Karen announced.

The mix of dismay on Justine's fine features gave way to resolve as her gaze lifted from the gathered assembly to meet his eyes. "There isn't enough money in the Castle Grove accounts to cover the operating expenses, plus make a substantial donation to Orange Blossom. Not when there's a protracted legal fight on the horizon. I'm sorry. I know I said I'd help support the Orange Fest, but I can't. Not unless you drop your claim."

Having said her piece, Justine turned on one kitten heel and marched back the way she'd come, leaving him to deal with the stick of dynamite she'd tossed into the meeting. His stomach plummeted as a collective gasp rose from the crowd.

Suddenly, everyone was talking at once, and from the sounds of things, no one was happy. Where was Karen now that he needed help? He glanced at the secretary, who sat with a blank look on her face, tears trickling down her lined cheeks. And no wonder. With two boys headed to college in the fall, she'd probably been counting on the town's grants to help with expenses. Two rows down, Miss Bertie wrung her hands. Sam's face took on an oily sheen, a sure sign that his indigestion had kicked up in earnest.

"Order. Let's have some order." Nate rapped again. He pinched the bridge of his nose, striving for patience until the hubbub subsided. At last, a hand rose in the back. Recognizing someone who was privy to all the details of the estate, Nate took a slow, even breath.

"The chair recognizes Deputy Sheriff Jack Sparling," he said.

Jack slowly rose to his feet. "Mr. Mayor, esteemed council members, I—"

A klaxon alarm sounded, the noise loud enough to break Karen out of her trance. The secretary's lips pursed.

"Jack, you know the rule about turning off your cell phone during a council meeting."

Jack held up one finger while he pressed the phone to his ear. "Yes? Her what?" The tall deputy paled.

Words stuttered over his shoulder as he moved toward the door. "I make a motion to postpone discussion of the Orange Fest till our next regular town council meeting. Gotta go. Mary Beth's water broke."

"Second!" someone shouted.

"So noted." Nate brought the gavel down in an economy of motion. "Meeting adjourned."

Under any other circumstances, he imagined most of the townsfolk would have stayed to pepper him with questions. But the prospect of a new baby took precedence over all but the most dire of emergencies. Those without an official need to stick around followed Jack out the door.

"It's just us in here now, Nate." George, the interim vice mayor, leaned over the desk. "You can't drop the suit?"

Nate rubbed his temples. "I might if it was just me, but this involves all of us. Justine plans to sell Castle Grove to the highest bidder. In fact, she met with Ken Thomas, the rep from Fresh Picked, today."

Pleading expressions turned to shock as the threat of a big juicing conglomerate takeover sank in. Someone cleared his throat.

"We can't let her do that, son."

"Tell me something I don't already know," Nate shot back. "That's why I can't drop my claim to the land—not that I would. Not only would it mean I've wasted the last ten years of my life on land that'll never be mine. But right now, I'm the only thing standing between Justine and Fresh Picked's efforts to put an end to Castle Grove. This is a fight I can't afford to lose. Not for me or for our town."

A firm hand gave his shoulder a squeeze. "We're behind you, Nate."

They were now. But would his fellow council members still feel the same way when the town could no longer afford to do all the things that made Orange Blossom special?

"I'm so glad you're feeling better. Thanks for coming all the way out here," Justine said as she ushered Sarah into the dining room. "I wanted to swing by Miss June's and see you before I left town yesterday, but after the council meeting, I got the distinct impression that I'd worn out my welcome in Orange Blossom." How else could she explain the clerk's grumpy attitude as he'd rung up her purchases at the hardware store? Or how the Ham Hut had fallen silent the moment she'd walked into the restaurant?

"You might not win the Miss Popularity Award right now, but that's because people don't know you like I do. Once they do, they'll figure out you're not an ogre and find someone else to talk about. I reckon twenty years ought to do the trick." Paper crackled as Sarah slid a tall shopping bag onto the table.

"Twenty years, huh? Too bad I'm only here for the weekend." Sarah's infectious grin drained most of the tension of the last twenty-four hours from Justine's shoulders. Glad there was at least one person in Orange Blossom who had her back, she took a cardboard coffee tray from the brunette's outstretched hand and set it aside. Then, leaning in, she wrapped her arms around her friend.

"How's it possible that you haven't aged a day since the last time we saw each other? You have to tell me your secret," she said when they pulled apart.

"It's all in the padding." Sarah patted her barely rounded backside. "I'm only five-two. On me, every extra ounce shows. And working in the bakery doesn't help, let me tell you. If I hadn't added a couple of extra miles to my daily run, I'd be as big as a barn."

Justine eyed Sarah's white shorts and loose T-shirt. If anything, her friend looked trimmer, healthier than ever, but some things never changed. Sarah had been concerned about her weight for as long as they'd known each other. During the long, hot summers they'd spent at Castle Grove, when she and Penny had wanted nothing more than to curl up with a good book, it was always Sarah who'd cajoled them into motion, insisting they join her on a walk or for a swim in the spring-fed creek. As an adult, the brunette ran half-marathons for fun.

Wondering at her friend's definition of *fun*, Justine peered into the paper bag and gasped. "Is that what I think it is?"

"Orange meringue." The pie was a staple in Miss June's Pie Shop.

"Oh, I could just kiss you!" Justine pretended to swoon. Her mouth watering, she grabbed the box and stared through the clear cellophane at a sprinkling of crystallized sugar across a perfectly browned topping. "I can almost taste it already."

"Have at it." Sarah grabbed one of the coffees and took a swig.

"Later. If I start now, I'll eat the whole thing." Giving the pie a wistful glance, she hefted the box. On her way to the kitchen, she asked, "How's your mom?"

"So far, so good." Relief radiated from Sarah's voice. "She's finished with chemo and doing radiation now. She says she'll be back to work by the first of the year, but, well..." Sarah shrugged. "We'll see."

"I pray for her every night." Justine slid the uncut pie into the fridge. "I haven't done any shopping since I've been here. I can't offer you much more than bottled water. Want some?"

"No, I'm good. I have my coffee. If you still take yours with cream, no sugar, there's a cup here with your name on it." Sarah's voice echoed over the hardwood floors. "This place doesn't look so bad. From the way you described it, I expected much worse."

"Hold that thought," Justine answered, shutting the fridge. "You should have been here yesterday morning," she said as she returned to the room she'd scrubbed clean the day before. "It took hours just to make this room presentable. I haven't touched the rest. Want to see?"

At Sarah's nod, she crossed to a tiny room that had served as Uncle Jimmy's office for as long as she could remember. When they were kids, the space had been pin neat and dust-free. Now, a jumble of mail littered the desk. Against one wall, shelves sagged beneath the weight of tools and equipment that, with no apparent rhyme or reason, Jimmy had stored in the bookcase. A lone leaf clung to an otherwise bare twig in a pot. Beside it, clods of dried mud spattered the floor around a pair of well-worn boots. Justine plucked a circular from the table and studied a sales flyer from last March while stacks of unopened envelopes shifted at her touch.

"Aunt Margaret would've skinned Uncle Jimmy alive for letting things get so out of hand," Sarah breathed. "This is beyond beyond."

"You can say that again." Her aunt had been a stickler for cleanliness. Every one of the Castle Grove campers had been required to make her bed and tuck her pajamas under the pillow before she ventured out for breakfast each morning. Dirty clothes had gone in the hamper, never on the floor. A chart in the kitchen had kept track of daily chores, like sweeping and taking out the trash. On Saturdays, all the girls had pitched in, dusting and mopping until the house gleamed. And, thanks to Aunt Margaret's cardinal rule that shoes were taken off at the door and lined up in a neat row on the porch, it had mostly stayed that way from week to week. But without Aunt Margaret here to keep tabs on him, Uncle Jimmy had obviously let things slide. "It's a good thing I didn't bring Gracie with me this trip. There's no telling what she'd come down with while she was here."

Sarah arched an eyebrow. "Penny said you'd turned into a germaphobe. When did that happen? The Justine I remember never let a little dirt bother her."

"Once you have a child, it changes you." Justine shrugged. She hadn't even considered sharing the news of Gracie's condition with her friend, not while

Sarah was still dealing with her mother's diagnosis. But hadn't they all changed over the years? Penny had once been vivacious and fun, the life of the party, but at some point, she'd traded in her pom-poms for dark-rimmed glasses and long skirts. "The rest of the house is pretty much in the same shape."

"The bedrooms, too?"

"They aren't quite as bad, as long as you don't mind dust an inch thick. But the roaches..." She shuddered. "I put a plate down on the dining room table the other night and came back five minutes later. Palmetto bugs had swarmed it."

"Even Gram's lumpy couch would be better than this," tsked the girl who'd offered it for as long as Justine was in town. "I can't believe you're staying here."

"I'm not that brave." Justine's cheeks warmed at the hesitant admission. Her plan to spend the night in her old room had collapsed when, at dusk, mosquitoes had swarmed through the torn screens. In desperation, she'd banged on Nate's door. To his credit, he'd let her in without a word. "Nate insisted on putting me up. I spent the last couple of nights in his guest room."

"Awk-ward," Sarah trilled, her eyes widening. "How did that work out for you?"

"I'm sure he regretted inviting me, but he was too much of a gentleman to kick me out." Not that they'd been spending any time together. By the time she'd wandered out for a cup of coffee this morning, a windbreaker draped across one of the chairs had been the only sign that Nate had been there and gone. With luck, she wouldn't run into her host again before she headed to the airport later this evening.

Across the room, paper rustled in the still air. "Royce Enid said I should comb through all of Uncle Jimmy's records to find statements, notes or whatever to support the will. To tell you the truth, everything's such a mess that I don't know where to start."

"We ought to at least put these outside." Sarah bent to pick up the boots.

An instant later, her shrill screech rent the air when a saucer-sized spider realized his hiding place had been disturbed and skittered across the floor. The boots slipped from Sarah's grasp and thudded down in a shower of dirt. By the time they'd hit the floor, she'd retreated to the hall. Though she didn't share her friend's phobia, Justine was right on her heels.

"So much for working in there for now," she gasped, trying to catch her breath. Bugs or no bugs, she still needed to sort through Jimmy's papers if she had any hope of disproving Nate's claim. "I had planned to box up all those papers and sort through them at home, but I'll have to fumigate the room first."

"Know anyone with a flamethrower?" Brushing and slapping, Sarah ran her hands over her chest and hair like someone who had just walked into a web.

"Don't tempt me." Justine gingerly grasped the door handle and pulled it shut. "After a scare like that, we deserve a treat. Pie is just what the doctor ordered."

She headed for the kitchen where she dished generous slices onto paper plates and toted the plates to the dining room table. As the first taste of tart-sweet orange burst across her tongue, Justine moaned. "Ahhh. That's sinfully good."

"Made from scratch using oranges grown on those trees right out there." Sarah pointed out the window to the grove surrounding the house.

"Honest?" Justine broke off a piece of flaky crust. "I thought your grandmother bought from Fresh Picked or one of the other big distributors."

"Yeah, right." Sarah sneered. "The only thing fresh about Fresh Picked is their name. They freeze or concentrate all their juice. If we used that crap in our pies, we'd go out of business."

"Well, whatever you do, don't change a thing. This is the best pie I've tasted in ages. Too bad Penny isn't here to share it with us. She'd swear she'd died and gone to heaven." She glanced across the table when Sarah pushed her plate aside after taking only one bite. Noting the tiny divot that had deepened between her friend's eyebrows, she asked, "What's wrong?"

"It's...nothing." Sarah let out a long breath.

"There's obviously something. What's up?" Did Sarah have man troubles? Was her mom worse off than everyone thought? The possibilities were endless.

"It's just..." Sarah's gaze drifted toward the screen door. "Looks like you have company," she said. "Are you expecting anyone?"

"Not that I know of." Justine twisted around in time to spot a white sedan stirring the dust on the road to the house.

"I think that's Royce Enid's car," Sarah offered.

"Odd. Must be important to make him drive all the way out here." Turning to her friend again, she tilted her head. "Don't think this lets you off the hook. Whatever's on your mind, I want to hear all about it after Royce leaves."

Sarah's blank stare promised nothing, but Justine vowed not to give up until she'd wormed the truth from her friend. A white Caddy pulled to a stop in front of the house. A door thudded shut. Soon after, a weary groan accompanied heavy footsteps on the porch.

"Guard the rest of my pie," Justine told Sarah as she rose to greet the new arrival. At the door, she held the screen door open. "Afternoon, Royce," she said without trying to hide her curiosity. "We didn't have an appointment or anything, did we?"

"No, no. I'm just stopping by." Wiping his forehead with the handkerchief he'd pulled from a pocket inside a wrinkled seersucker jacket, Royce stepped from the heat of the porch into the relative cool of the house. "It's too hot out there for man or beast, but what else can you expect in August? Am I right?"

"It is that," Justine agreed, wondering why the man chose to wear a three-piece suit in ninety-degree weather. "Can I get you some water or anything?"

Spotting Sarah seated at the dining room table, the lawyer pursed his lips. "Sorry for the interruption."

"It's fine. Sarah and I were just catching up over a slice of orange meringue. There's plenty more. Would you like a piece?"

"Much as I 'preciate the offer, I just ate dinner at the Ham Hut. Today's special was fried chicken. My favorite. I couldn't eat another bite." While Royce patted his belly, he surveyed the room. "I see what you mean about Jimmy letting the place go, Justine. Those stairs out front need some work. In fact, the whole place could use some sprucing up."

Justine smiled tightly while she wondered how the lawyer would react if he peeked into any of the rooms she hadn't spent hours cleaning. "Have a seat, Royce. Tell us what brings you out here on a Sunday afternoon."

"No, thanks. I can't stay." He lingered at the door

as if he feared getting a smudge of dirt on his pale suit. "I wanted to let you know that Mary Beth had her baby this morning. A boy, just like she expected. Six pounds, two ounces."

Whatever Royce intended to say next, it was drowned out by Sarah's squeal. "That's terrific news, Mr. Enid. I bet Jack's thrilled."

Instead of the expected broad smile, the lawyer's face fell. "Well, now, he would be, 'cepting for a few problems. They had to do a C-section, and I guess things got rough, 'cause Mary Beth ended up needin' two pints of blood."

Justine gasped at the news and guessed Sarah did the same, because Royce waved his hand.

"Now, now. Everything's going to be all right. It's just that Mary Beth won't be returning to work as soon as she thought she would. Her doctor says she'll need to take it easy for a while. Two, maybe three months."

The hairs on Justine's neck prickled as Royce's gaze landed on her and tightened.

"Her being out that long leaves me in the lurch. I have a couple of cases on the court docket this fall, and I don't have anyone to fill in for her. I've come, with my hat in my hand so to speak, to ask you if there's any chance at all that you could come to work for me in the interim. I'd match your current salary, of course, and provide the usual benefits. You'd really be helping me out."

Justine sucked in a steadying breath. Royce's proposal was ridiculous. Her job, her home, her daughter were in Virginia. The airline ticket in her purse would get her there in time to see Gracie off to day care in the morning. Intending to politely decline, she started to respond. Royce's fleshy fingers on her wrist stopped her before she could say a word.

"Now, before you say no, just think about it. I'd be lying if I told you I had a busy practice. Truth be told, I'm mostly biding my time till I retire next year. Which means I still can't sign up for a long, drawn-out battle if Nate challenges your uncle's will. But if you were to, say, see your way clear to helping me out of this jam, it'd only be fair for me to return the favor. Between the two of us, we might be able to convince Nate it's not worth his while to file suit at all."

Torn, Justine shook her head. "Three months is a long time," she whispered.

She couldn't be away from Gracie that long. She already missed her daughter's little-girl hugs so much her arms ached. And judging from the number of phone calls she'd received this weekend, Gracie was feeling just as lost as she was.

On the other hand, wasn't Royce offering her the very thing she'd been praying for, the chance to prove Nate wrong so she could move forward with the sale of Castle Grove? She rocked back on her heels, considering. Somewhere among the stacks of papers in her uncle's spider-infested office, she knew she'd find the proof she needed to defend her inheritance. From there, the dominoes would fall in a straight line to the pot of gold that would ensure Gracie's future. The vein in the center of her forehead throbbed while she wrestled with the decision.

"You've given me a lot to think about," she said at last. "I'll need some time."

The older gentleman's head bobbed. "I expected as much. Talk it over with Sarah here. Think about my offer tonight. Give me a call in the morning and let me know what you decide. But I have to tell you, this could really work in your favor."

Executing an about-face that was oddly graceful for a man his size, Royce left as quickly as he'd arrived. Less than a minute later, Justine stared through the screen door at the dust that rose in his wake. Her head reeling, she returned to the table.

"Wow. I didn't see that coming. Did you?" she asked, collapsing onto her chair. Her mouth parched, she downed half her coffee.

"Ah, no." Sarah's forehead wrinkled. "It's not like Mary Beth to leave Royce in the lurch like that. She loves that man like a father."

"She'd hired someone to fill in for her. When I stopped by the office yesterday, whoever it was had just called to let her know they'd accepted another offer. Mary Beth went into labor right after I left." Tension held her in a viselike grip while memories of the harrowing day she'd given birth to Gracie played in an endless loop through her mind. Giving herself a stern reminder that Mary Beth and her baby were fine—just fine!—Justine rolled her shoulders and forced herself to relax.

Across the table, Sarah shook her head. "Everyone in town knows how much Royce depends on Mary Beth. Do you think you could handle the job?"

"No doubt." At Jacoby & Sons, she wrote legal briefs and handled filings for a dozen attorneys. "It's not like Mary Beth left the country. I could always call her if I needed her to walk me through her filing system, or if I ran across something I couldn't figure out."

"What about your job? Would your boss let you take that much time away from work?"

"I'm only one of a hundred paralegals in the firm." The truth hurt, but she wasn't going to lie about it. "It's not like I'm irreplaceable or anything." Though it wouldn't look good on her resume if she quit without giving notice.

Sarah leaned back in her chair while she drummed her fingers on the table. "You know, taking Royce up on his offer has a lot going for it."

"How so?" Determined to examine the idea from all angles, Justine waited.

"You wouldn't have to pay an attorney, for one thing. At least, not for a while. Maybe not until after the harvest. This year's citrus crop will put Castle Grove in the black again. Which..." Sarah drew in a thready breath. "Which means you could afford to underwrite the Orange Fest. Doing that would go a long way towards getting some of the people in Orange Blossom on your side."

Justine studied her friend through narrowed eyes. For someone who dreamed of escaping the small town where she'd grown up, Sarah seemed awfully invested in the winter festival. "And you think that's what I should do?"

Sarah held up both hands in a gesture of surrender. "As your friend, I'll support you, no matter what. But you should probably know how much people in Orange Blossom depend on the Orange Fest for their livelihood. To be honest, Miss June's Pie Shop is one of them."

Justine shook her head to clear her muddled thoughts. When that didn't work, she stared into her friend's dark eyes. "Okay, now you've got me. What does a craft fair have to do with pies?"

"It's a simple matter of mathematics," said the

woman who could double or triple a recipe without thinking about it. "Honestly, how many pies do you think a town the size of Orange Blossom can use in an average week? Four, five dozen tops. Contracts with local restaurants are good for another dozen or two. For a mom-and-pop place like ours, that barely covers the overhead. But during the Orange Fest, we'll go through a thousand pies at four-fifty a slice. That bump, plus the business we do at Christmas, is enough to keep the lights on for the rest of the year."

"I had no idea." Because she'd only spent summers on Castle Grove, she'd never attended the winter event. Even so, she'd have never guessed it made such a huge impact on the local economy. "That explains why everyone was so tense at the town council meeting. They must have thought I was pretty heartless." She paused for a moment, letting the new information sink in. "If it was just up to me, I'd give Orange Blossom whatever it needs. You know I would. Uncle Jimmy would be disappointed if I didn't."

Sarah leaned back in her chair. "I hear a *but* coming."

"Yeah," Justine admitted with a sigh. "*But*...I have Gracie to consider—what's best for her. I can't possibly be away from her for three months. And I can't bring her here." She sent a deliberate glance into a kitchen where stains and splatters swirled across the countertops like some parody of modern art. Cockroaches and palmetto bugs had long since eaten their way into the boxes of dry goods in the pantry. They'd left their droppings on the cans and bottles. The rest of the house was in even worse shape. Even if she didn't have Gracie's health issues to consider, she couldn't bring her daughter here.

"I get it," Sarah said slowly. "You're between a rock and a hard place. But what if we could turn things around here and make the house livable? Would you stay then? Or at least consider it?"

The idea was too farfetched to even think about. "What you're suggesting is impossible. Royce clearly needs me to hit the ground running, and I can't do that and get this place cleaned up enough for Gracie to come down."

Faint lines around Sarah's eyes crinkled as a slow grin spread across her lips. "You obviously don't remember how things work in Orange Blossom. There's not a woman within fifty miles who hasn't heard how much Uncle Jimmy let things go. They've all been itching for a chance to set things right again. Partly because people loved your uncle. And partly 'cause they feel guilty about not doing more while he was still here. You say the word, and I guarantee that by the time you can get Gracie down here, this house will be so spotless you could eat off the floors."

"I'd settle for not having to wrestle the bugs for my dinner." Justine darted a look into the kitchen while memories of the days they'd spent cooking and canning with Aunt Margaret rushed back. Was it even possible to return the house to that pristine state?

"Oh, don't you worry." Sarah's eyes gleamed. "Those roaches won't know what hit 'em."

"I don't know." Justine bit her lip, her head spinning. "There's still the little matter of Gracie's school. She starts kindergarten next month. It might be too late to get her registered down here."

"I've got you covered on that one," Sarah said, brightening. "You remember my sister Mandy, don't you?"

Recalling a lively strawberry blonde who'd roasted marshmallows beside her at countless Friday-night bonfires, Justine nodded.

"She has a daughter the same age as Gracie. Mandy was just telling me last night that there are still a few openings in SueEllen's class. We can get Gracie registered on Monday, and she'll be all set for when school opens the week after next."

"Wow," Justine said, sinking into her chair. "You're moving so fast I'm not sure I can keep up."

"Does Gracie eat peanut butter?"

Justine blinked at the odd question. "It's not her favorite, but yeah."

Sarah tapped one finger to her chin. "I'm asking 'cause one of the boys in SueEllen's class has a bad peanut allergy. The school is being extra cautious about the whole thing. Not only have they banned peanut products, they've assigned an aide to wash the students' hands and faces with antibacterial wipes before they step foot in the kindergarten classroom each day. It's supposed to minimize the chance of cross contamination."

"That's..." Justine sagged against her chair's back. "I can totally go along with that." So far, she'd managed to stave off the usual colds and flu by diligently monitoring her daughter's exposure to germs, but she'd been worried sick about sending Gracie to public school. But if the kindergarten was already taking extra precautions...

"I'm not promising anything, but if you and your friends can whip this house into shape—"

"We can and we will." Sarah traced her finger over her chest, making a cross.

"And if we can get Gracie into the class and a few

other things"—things like finding the right doctors to monitor her daughter's health—"then I'm in. But I'm going to need another piece of that pie."

"You get it while I make a couple of calls." Sarah hit a speed-dial number on her phone and lifted it to her ear.

In the kitchen, Justine held her empty plate over the sink and stared through a filthy window at trees loaded with fruit. Was she doing the right thing? Now that she knew how much it meant to the town, she felt compelled to help out with the Orange Fest. And it'd be foolish to walk away from Royce's offer to help defend her claim to Castle Grove. But it would take a miracle to make her uncle's house livable again. Could Sarah and her friends really pull it off? She tossed her empty plate into the trash can. With so much riding on the outcome, she had to let them try. Besides, it wasn't as if she'd promised to stay, no matter what. She'd roll up her sleeves and give Sarah a day or two, but if they couldn't make it work, she'd head back to Virginia.

She tugged her own phone from the back pocket of her cutoffs. By the time she'd enlisted Penny's help and changed her travel itinerary, the house bustled with women who'd shown up carrying mops, dustrags and enough bleach to eradicate every germ within four counties. After introductions so brief they made Justine's head spin, she donned a pair of heavy rubber gloves and joined the team assigned to her bedroom. Like an army waging a war, they attacked the years' worth of dirt and grime. Vacuums whirred. Dust stirred. The mattress and box springs from her bed made a round trip outside, where it was thoroughly aired.

Throughout the house, other teams tackled their

assignments. By sunset, the kitchen shelves had been completely emptied and scrubbed to the point, in some cases, where the paint had worn off. Every dish and serving utensil had been treated to a hot, soapy bath. The thorough application of countless steel-wool pads had removed every trace of cooked-on grease from the pots and pans. Not so much as a crumb remained in the drawers. As for the refrigerator, it had been hauled into the backyard, scrubbed down, aired out and hauled back across scarred, but noticeably cleaner, linoleum.

The sun sank below the tree line as, promising to tackle more of the house in the morning, the last of the crew packed up their gear. In their wake, floors had been mopped until they gleamed. The whole house smelled faintly of disinfectant and pesticides, but there was nary a speck of dust—or a bug—to be seen. Watching the last of the women climb into cars and trucks, Justine lowered her weary body onto the porch swing, which, thanks to the application of a stiff broom and a can of spray, no longer offered a haven to wasps.

"I can see why people come to Orange Blossom and never leave." Freshly oiled chains squeaked softly as she rocked back and forth. "This kind of turnout is unheard of in the city. If I hadn't had Penny to turn to after Gracie was born, we'd have landed in a shelter."

Sarah studied her from a sparkling-clean metal chair. "Does this mean you'll stick around for a while?"

"Assuming we get the rest into shape before Penny flies down with Gracie next Saturday, yeah." The spare bedrooms and her uncle's office remained untouched. "I spoke with my boss in Virginia. He's giving me a leave of absence so I can stay till Mary Beth comes back to work."

"And the Orange Fest?"

Justine ran a hand through her hair. "I'm still on the fence, but I promise to talk it over with Royce."

"What about staying on permanently? Holding on to Castle Grove?"

At the suggestion, Justine shook her head. With so much of the town's economy dependent on her uncle's citrus groves, people were bound to hope she'd change her mind about selling out. But with Gracie's future hanging in the balance, she gave the only answer she could give. "I'm sorry. It's just not possible."

Justine hefted two of the heavy grocery sacks off the backseat of her uncle's pickup truck and toted them up the rickety stairs to the front porch. Retracing her steps, she repeated the process twice before the results of her shopping foray were piled near the front door. She eyed the bags of groceries that included all of Gracie's favorites, plus enough staples to get them through the next couple of months. A happy tune hummed past her lips.

Imagining a joyous reunion, she closed her eyes. Penny and Gracie were due to arrive in Orlando at noon tomorrow. She added another half hour for them to take the tram to the main terminal where she'd be waiting, her arms open and the world's silliest grin on her face.

Was Gracie half as excited as she was?

Probably not, she admitted, as she swept her surroundings with a wry glance. While Justine had spent the last week rushing to prepare their temporary home for her daughter's arrival, Penny had pulled out all the stops in her attempts to keep the five-year-old entertained. Gracie had filled their daily phone calls with gushing reports of having tea parties—"with real tea, Mommy"—and getting to watch two whole hours of her favorite shows. By now, her daughter was probably so used to being the center of attention that she might not appreciate Castle Grove's slower pace.

Justine brushed aside the moment of self-doubt. There were plenty of activities Gracie would enjoy at Castle Grove. When she was her daughter's age, hadn't she'd loved playing tag among the trees, wading in the spring-fed creek that ran through the grove, making wildflower wreaths with her friends?

She had, but things were different for Gracie. The song she'd been humming died out as she forgot the next few notes. How could she risk letting her daughter play outdoors when every pool of stagnant water harbored a fresh crop of mosquitoes? When the high grass was home to chiggers and ticks and all sorts of biting insects? Hadn't she read somewhere that parasites lurked in ponds and lakes? One bite, one infection could prompt a cascade of health problems and cause even more damage to Gracie's kidneys.

She sighed and clenched her fists. There'd be no dashing among the orange trees for her daughter. No wreaths made of wildflowers. As for wading or, worse, swimming in the creek that meandered through the property, that was definitely out.

Safeguarding Gracie's health had to be her number one priority, but once she ruled out all the dangers, there wasn't a whole lot for a five-year-old to do at Castle Grove. Living so far from town, they didn't even have cable TV. Thank goodness, she'd invited Sarah and Penny for dinner tomorrow night—Gracie always loved having company. And the new school year started on Tuesday. That was something they could both look forward to. In the meantime, they'd spend a day together, visiting all her old haunts in Orange Blossom. They'd have lunch at the Ham Hut, shop for school supplies and maybe even stop in for a treat at Miss June's.

A long, slow breath escaped Justine's lips. At least she had a plan, even if it wasn't filled with exciting adventures.

Propping the screen door open with one of the bags, she hauled the groceries from the porch into the kitchen. Once she had everything inside, she made quick work of storing the dairy products, meats and vegetables in the now-spotless refrigerator. At last, carrying an armload of cereal and pasta boxes, she headed for the pantry.

She paused on the threshold as something hissed from the far corner of the closet. Justine nudged the light switch with her elbow. She scanned empty shelves and the floor that had been bare the last time she checked. Whatever she'd been expecting to find, a large black snake certainly wasn't it. Especially not one curled into striking position, its head bobbing and swaying for all it was worth not five feet from where she stood.

She screamed. The boxes she'd been holding hit the floor and scattered. Lightning fast, the snake struck at the closest one.

Stumbling back, she groped for the door and slammed it so hard, the noise echoed through the house like a shotgun blast. Something—the snake or one of the boxes—bumped against the wood. A dark shape blocked the light that seeped through a half-inch space between the floor and the door.

"Oh, Lord!" she gasped.

Her eyes locked on to the gap and refused to let go. Backpedaling as far and as fast as her feet would take her, she grunted when her hip hit the edge of the counter. Desperate to stay beyond the snake's reach if it slithered out of the closet, she shoved the remaining groceries aside and scrambled onto the Formica surface of the counter. Cans spilled from one of the bags. They thudded onto the floor and rolled across the room. She drew her knees up to her chin and wrapped her arms around her legs.

Nate tipped his beer to Jack's. The aluminum cans clinked softly, the sound breaking the stillness of the backyard. "Congratulations, man. You did it."

"Mary Beth gets all the credit. She's the one who did all the heavy lifting." In spite of the humble words, Jack nearly beamed with pride.

"A son, though. Before you know it, you'll be coaching peewee football." Propping his forearms on the railing of the deck, Nate pretended to study the hostas clustered in a leafy circle beneath a tall oak. "Think he'll be a wide receiver like his old man?"

"Let's get him out of diapers first." But if the gleam in his eyes was any indication, Jack was already dreaming of the day he'd hear his son's name echo from the bleachers while the boy led his high school football team onto the field.

"I don't know. He's such a little guy." Nate nudged

the deputy's elbow. "Maybe he should stick to soccer."

"Yeah, right." Jack snorted. "He can chase a round white ball as much as he wants. Long as he puts all that fancy footwork to use on the football field." He took a long pull from his can, the lines in his face smoothing. "Seriously? He can do anything he wants. Tennis. Ballet. Hell, even video games. I'm just thankful they're okay—both of them. It was a close thing. I don't know what I would have done if…"

"Hey, don't even go there. Everything turned out fine." Nate slapped his friend on the back as the thin wail of a newborn came from the house. "You need to get that?"

"Nah. Mary Beth's mom got here a little while ago. She's gonna stay and help out for the next couple of weeks. They told me to get lost so they can have some mother-daughter bonding time." Jack passed his beer from one hand to the next and back again. "I've been so wrapped up with Mary Beth and the baby that I never asked you what happened after the town council meeting. Any news?"

Nate expelled a heavy breath. "I imagine you heard Justine's going to stick around for a bit."

"So I gathered from Royce when he stopped by to drop off a gift for Jack Junior. A blanket his wife had crocheted. Mary Beth got all weepy over it." As if he realized he'd veered off track, Jack straightened slightly. "Anyways. I thought Justine was in a hurry to get back up north to her kid."

"Penny's bringing the little girl down here. The two of them are due in sometime tomorrow. They're staying at Jimmy's." He didn't see any need to mention that for the first couple of nights she'd been in town, Justine had slept down the hall in his guest room.

"In that mess?" Jack pushed away from the railing. "How on earth..."

"The way I hear it, Sarah rounded up a crew to clean the place." Though he'd done his very best to keep his distance in the six days since the council meeting, it hadn't been possible to ignore all the work taking place a stone's throw from his front door. So much junk had accumulated on the burn pile that he'd taken to lighting a fire in a fifty-gallon drum each night and feeding as much of the trash as he could to the flames. Someone must have dumped five gallons of bleach into the washer and scrubbed it down, because every time he looked across the way, the breeze sent a different set of sheets or towels flapping on the ancient clothesline that stretched across Jimmy's backyard. One day, Justine's rental car had disappeared. Soon after, he'd spotted the slim blonde behind the wheel of Jimmy's old pickup truck on her way into town.

"After the way she withdrew her support for the Orange Fest, I woulda thought folks'd sooner run her out of town on a rail than lend her a hand," Jack said as he worked the pull tab on his can back and forth.

"That's another thing. She evidently had second thoughts about the Orange Fest, 'cause somebody dropped an envelope through the town hall's mail chute on Monday. Inside was a Castle Grove check made out for the same amount Jimmy always gave to cover the start-up costs. Just the check. No note or nothing." He'd checked.

Jack whistled, long and low. "You've got to be kidding."

"Nope. I have to admit, knowing we can move forward with the festival has taken a load off my mind.

And word's already spread. Miss Bertie called to thank me personally for, as she put it, 'talking some sense into that bull-headed girl.' I had to tell her I didn't have anything to do with it." Nate polished off the last of his beer. "But I can't stop wondering what made Justine decide to help out."

A pair of blue jays landed in the oak. Calling to each other, they flitted among the branches for several minutes.

"You think she's trying to get on the town's good side?" Jack asked when the birds continued their journey.

"To what end?"

"Maybe she hopes to sway public opinion against you. You know, in case you contest Jimmy's will."

"You think that's a possibility?" The burger and fries he'd eaten for lunch rolled uneasily in Nate's stomach.

"Do I think she could bribe her way into Orange Blossom's good graces?" Jack crushed his beer can in one hand. "Nah, man. That ain't gonna happen. Loyalty runs deep in this town."

Nate wished he shared his friend's confidence. And why would he? Seemed like the very people he was supposed to be able to trust the most in his life had developed a nasty habit of turning their backs on him. His mother had. Hadn't she packed her bags and run off the morning after his seventh birthday? His dad had already gone to work, so he'd been the one who'd found the note she'd left propped against the coffee can. A note that said she'd stuck it out for as long as she could, but she'd never been in it for the long haul and wouldn't be tied down anymore. When they were teens, Justine had done practically the same thing, choosing a bigger life, a bigger future than the one he had offered her. In her own way, she'd done him a favor. He understood himself well enough to know that the fear of rejection drove him to work harder, be a better person than he would have otherwise. It was part of the reason he'd worked so hard to gain Jimmy's trust and approval. And it probably explained why Jimmy's ultimate betrayal had cut him so deeply.

So, did he trust the good people of Orange Blossom to stand behind him when he needed their support? Not entirely. But that didn't mean he'd let Justine, or anyone else, take what was rightfully his.

"Make no mistake. I'm going to contest the will. And I'll win." He pitched his can into the recycling bin by the door. "Matter of fact, I've already spoken to an estate attorney in Orlando. I have an appointment with him next week."

"If there's anything I can do to help out—and I mean anything—you know all you have to do is ask." Jack shaped the crushed can into a ball, tossed it into the air and caught it. "You want another one?"

"Thanks, but no. One's my limit."

"Mine, too, now that Jack Junior's keeping us up nights." The deputy rubbed his eyes. "He's got his days and nights all turned around. Mom says that's normal, and he'll figure it out if we let him. She says we ought to shut his door and let him cry. That eventually he'll get tired enough to go to sleep." Jack shot a glance toward the far end of the house where Nate had spent an afternoon helping him assemble a baby crib in the nursery. "Like that's going to happen. I can't listen to him cry and not pick him up. Could you?"

Nate chuckled. "I thought girls were the ones who were supposed to have their daddies wrapped around their little fingers. Sounds like boys can do the same thing."

"You can say that again."

Jack's head lifted as the sliding glass door onto the porch rattled in its tracks. Mary Beth's pale face appeared in the gap. "Jack, honey, could you get Mom and me a little something to eat?"

"Sure thing."

While Nate watched in amused silence, his friend immediately shifted into motion. Jack was halfway across the deck, his beer can sailing into the recycling bin where it rattled among the other empties, before his footsteps slowed. "You sticking around?" he asked over one shoulder.

"Nah, you go ahead. Give my best to Mary Beth and hug that little one for me. I'll see myself out."

"Okay. I'll catch you later, then."

Three more steps took Jack across the threshold and into the house where he disappeared from view. Left alone on the deck, Nate ran a hand through his hair while he shoved down a jealous twinge. There'd been a time when he'd thought he'd have a wife and children of his own by now. It hadn't worked out quite the way he'd planned, and he wondered where he'd gone wrong.

Oh, he'd had a few women in his life, but none he'd really loved. Certainly no one he'd seen himself still being in love with twenty or thirty years down the road. Truth be told, Justine had been the only girl he'd ever considered spending his whole life with, and after they broke up, he'd been reluctant to risk getting his heart trampled again. But now that his best friend had settled down, now that Jack and Mary Beth had a baby, maybe he ought to work a little harder at finding someone to do more than share his bed. Maybe he ought to find someone to share his life. Otherwise, one day he'd end up like Jimmy, with no immediate family to inherit the fruits of all his hard labor. Fruits that included Castle Grove.

With that thought, he headed down the wooden steps from the deck to the flagstone pathway that led around to the front of the house Jack and Mary Beth called home. After climbing into his truck, Nate drove through the deepening twilight toward Castle Grove. There, sure enough, the burn pile had grown another foot taller. He went to work, layering old catalogs and empty cereal boxes into the drum. Orange flames licked at the curled edges of the cardboard when a woman's scream split the evening air.

Justine!

Nate spun away from the fire. A loud report cut through the air, piercing his heart. Paralysis clawed at him. He shook it off and got moving. Time slowed to a crawl. The ground sucked at him like quicksand, so he flew over it, his feet barely touching the dirt. At the back porch of Jimmy's house, he mounted the stairs two at a time and shoved the screen door aside. Bursting into the kitchen, he prayed that whatever had happened he'd reach her side in time.

"Justine!"

Someone shouted her name over the rush of blood in her ears, the hammering of her heart.

She flinched as the door to the back porch burst open with enough force to send it crashing into the wall and rattle the glassware in the cupboards. All broad shoulders and muscular legs, the man she'd have voted least likely to ever race to her rescue appeared in the doorway. She'd never been so happy to see him.

"Careful, there's a—"

"Are you hurt?" Nate raked his gaze over the floors and counters until it reached her. His gray-blue eyes pinned her with a demanding stare.

Justine shrank into herself. "Snake." She aimed a shaky finger at the pantry. "In there."

Nate's gaze lingered on her a moment longer before he slid a sidelong look at the closed door. "Did you shoot it?" He scanned the room. "Where's the gun?"

Gun?

Her eyebrows slammed together with such energy, they actually stung. She forced herself to relive the past few seconds. "No. I banged the door shut. Hard."

Some of the strain melted from Nate's posture. "When I heard you scream and the noise, I thought..." He coughed. His attention dropped from her face to the bare legs she'd drawn up to her chin. "It didn't bite you, did it? Do you know what kind it is?"

"B-big. Black," she managed. Drawing in a breath, she relinquished the death grip she'd held on her knees. "I didn't exactly take the time to get acquainted."

"Okay, then." He nodded as if he might have done the same himself. "Let's see what we've got here. You have a broom handy?"

She bit her lower lip. "There's one on the back porch."

Nate ducked around the corner, returning seconds later carrying the object in question. Easing the pantry door open, he wedged the broom into the space and peered inside. "Uh-huh."

"What? It's still in there, isn't it? It didn't escape?" She searched the floor, her breath coming in fits and starts. When nothing moved among the cans and paper bags that littered the linoleum, her chest loosened marginally.

"I need to get something from out back. Are you okay where you are for a few minutes?"

Blindly, she nodded. She wasn't going anywhere. She certainly wasn't getting down off the counter as long as a snake—any snake—hid in her kitchen. Frozen in place, she spent the next few minutes alternating between staring at the closed pantry door and taking furtive glances at the spilled groceries. Just when she'd decided Nate had gone off to have a quiet laugh at her expense, she heard his boots strike the steps. Seconds later, he carried a cardboard box across the room, his legs eating up the distance in long strides. Armed with nothing more than the broom and the box, he disappeared into the closet.

She flinched when something heavy thudded against a wall. A few dull thuds followed. She caught muffled words that might have been curses. At last, the door opened. The muscles along Nate's forearm flexed as he pressed his hand firmly over the closed lid of the box. Slithery sounds emanated from within. "Hang tight," he called and was gone again.

Time stretched out for an eternity or two. Her bottom firmly glued to the counter, she sat while pins and needles prickled her legs.

"You can relax now." Nate marched into the kitchen empty-handed. "It's gone."

"Gone?" She cupped her fingers over her knees. "You didn't kill it?"

A muscle twitched along Nate's jawline. "It was a

175

black racer," he said, as if that explained anything.

It didn't, and she refused to budge from her perch.

The corners of Nate's mouth arrowed down. "Racers help keep the rodent population under control. They're good snakes."

"There's no such thing as a good snake in the house," she corrected. She stared at a small tear in one of the window screens. "Did it get in through there?" Envisioning cold-blooded reptiles slithering up the outside of the house and plopping onto the floors, she shuddered. She studied Nate's unruffled brow as she silently begged for him to laugh and tell her she was being ridiculous.

Nate hooked one thumb on the pocket of his jeans. "With all the work that's been done around here of late, I imagine someone left a door open. That snake was probably looking for someplace cool, somewheres he could get out of the heat. Once he got in, he couldn't find his way out. Black racers usually avoid people. Which explains why he wasn't very happy to see you."

"Not half as unhappy as I was to see him." An uneasy feeling rolled through her gut. Hadn't she just left the front door open while she brought in the groceries? A shiver ran down her spine. That was one mistake she'd never make again.

"You're sure he's gone now?" She gave the paper bags lying about another quick study while she flexed her toes. The prickly feeling had subsided.

"Yeah." A smile tugged at the corner of Nate's mouth. "He's gone. You shouldn't have any more problems." He bent to retrieve a couple of cans.

Gingerly, she dropped her feet to the floor. "Crap," she muttered the moment her weight shifted from her butt to her feet. The pins and needles had faded all right, but only because her legs were completely numb. She froze, unable to move.

"You okay?" Nate straightened, concern marching across his face. "You're sure he didn't bite you? Racers aren't poisonous, but a bite still hurts."

Refusing to let him fawn over her, she waved his attention aside. "My legs went to sleep. Give me a minute. I'll be all right." Stamping her feet, she grimaced as the circulation painfully returned to her limbs.

"Yeah. Hate that feeling." Cans in hand, Nate turned toward the pantry.

"Don't put those in there." Strident, demanding, her tone stopped Nate in his tracks.

Confusion wrinkled the big man's brow and drew his lips together. "I was just putting them away for you," he said, sounding defensive.

"Sorry. I know you're only trying to help. It's just that, now I have to bleach the floor." She paused, mentally mapping the snake's probable path. Oh, hell. She had no idea which door or window the reptile had slithered through. She'd have to douse all the floors with germ-killing disinfectant. Otherwise, she'd never rest easy.

"Because?" Nate's eyebrows hiked halfway up his forehead.

"Because of the snake. Who knows what it slithered through outside? Gracie will be here tomorrow. I can't risk her coming in contact with whatever germs he might have brought in with him." She nodded to the cans Nate still held. "Just set those on the counter by the sink. I'll wipe them off and put them away later."

Nate just stood there, staring at her like she'd lost

her marbles. Brushing past him, she headed for the cleaning supplies that were kept in a closet on the back porch. Her hand shook as she grabbed the key that hung from a hook beyond the reach of little fingers. Air hissed over her lips when her first attempt to unlock the cabinet failed. Surprised that she was still upset over the encounter with the snake, she took a calming breath. But instead of settling, her nerves thrummed as doubts crowded her head.

No matter how many hours she and Sarah's friends had spent cleaning the dirt and grime from her uncle's house, the fact remained that she was moving her daughter into a one-hundred-year-old house that had more openings than a wheel of Swiss cheese. Until she had the time and money to repair them, mosquitoes and flies would continue to find their way inside through torn screens on the windows.

She'd set off a bug bomb in Jimmy's office and wedged towels into the gap at the bottom of the door to make sure nothing crawled out. And while she was reasonably certain that anything trapped inside was eight legs up, she hadn't given any thought to snakes.

Did she have to add them to her list of worries, too?

She leaned her head against the cool metal cabinet. What if Gracie got sick? What if she couldn't find the proof she needed to negate Nate's claim on Castle Grove? What if...

"Mind if I get myself a glass of water?"

And then there's Nate.

She'd gotten so lost in thought about Gracie that she'd almost forgotten her knight in tarnished armor still waited for her in the kitchen. But the man who'd run to her rescue had already seen her weak and defenseless enough for one day. Refusing to give him any more ammunition, she stuck a five-gallon bucket in the deep sink. Water thundered into the pail, along with a liberal helping of bleach and cleansers. Minutes later, she lugged her cleaning supplies into the kitchen.

In her absence, Nate had retrieved all the boxes and cans from the floor and neatly lined them up beside the sink. He stood, one shoulder propped against the refrigerator as though he intended to stay awhile. Not sure it was a good idea to hang out with the man who had once loved her but now wanted to take everything from her, she eyed him.

"Thanks for helping with the snake and all, but I can take it from here."

"I'll be out of your hair soon as I finish this." Ice cubes clinked in the tall glass Nate lifted.

"Suit yourself." Suddenly more aware of the masculine presence in her kitchen than she had any right to be, she deliberately turned aside to don a pair of rubber gloves. Getting down on her hands and knees, she sloshed cleaning solution onto the pantry floor and chased it into the corners with a scrub brush. The task didn't take long—only a few minutes—but by the time she finished the confined space, the pungent smell of bleach made her head spin. Eager to escape the fumes, she scrambled to her feet the moment the last square of linoleum glistened wetly.

Black spots danced before her eyes as she ripped the gloves from her hands. Her knees buckled. She pitched forward, helpless to stop herself.

"Whoa, there." Nate's firm grip caught her shoulders. He hauled her upright.

She clung to him, unable to trust her legs. Suddenly, she wasn't able to trust the rest of her either as her body reacted in a decidedly feminine fashion to Nate's firm grip. The command to pull away from him got lost somewhere between her brain and her feet. Meanwhile, every other part of her body sprang to life with awareness of Nate's presence.

Great.

Goose bumps broke out on her arms as Nate's icy breath caressed her skin through the openings of her cold-shoulder shirt. At the brush of his stubbled chin against her cheek, warmth pooled low in her belly. Unable to do anything else, she clung to Nate's upper arm with one hand while she braced the other against his broad chest.

Beneath her open palm, Nate's heart shifted into overdrive. His arm tightened around her waist. His free hand cupped her elbow, his fingers tracing lazy circles over sensitive skin. Bending down, he buried his face in her hair and inhaled so deeply his chest expanded.

"Christ," he whispered.

"I—we—this isn't right." Justine drew in a breath. The faint scent of chlorine seared her lungs and shocked her into action. She jerked her fingers into a tight fist and stumbled out of Nate's arms. Reeling to the counter, she gripped the edge with both hands and shook her head to clear it.

What had she been thinking? Only an idiot would allow even the glimmer of attraction for the man who threatened to steal her inheritance. The very inheritance that meant everything for her daughter.

For that matter, what was she doing here in the first place? She should never have agreed to fill in for Mary Beth. Never have agreed to stay on at Castle Grove. Never, ever, have thought it was a good idea to bring Gracie to a place where each morning she had to sweep a fresh batch of cobwebs from the porch. Where snakes crawled willy-nilly into the house. What kind of mother dragged her little girl away from all the friends she'd ever known to attend a new school?

She couldn't do it. Couldn't stay here. Yet she couldn't go. She'd invested every spare dime she owned in fixing up the house for Gracie's arrival. But it wasn't enough. It would never be enough.

Her arms propped on the counter, she leaned forward. Tears filled her eyes and spilled onto her cheeks. Others followed, splashing onto the counter while she stood, her back to Nate, unable and unwilling to dam them.

Nate's hand on her shoulder broke through her thoughts.

"Hey now. What's all this?"

More tears showered the counter as she shook her head in denial. She drew in an unsteady breath. "I shouldn't have come here. It was a stupid idea to think I could stay here. In this house. To bring Gracie here. I should have known better."

"Because of one snake? When we were kids—"

"—They scared me to death, but I never wanted you to know." She sniffed, wiped her tears with the back of her hand. "It's worse when you have a child. Gracie..."

She shouldn't say any more. She didn't owe anyone an explanation for her fears. Nate, least of all. "It's everything," she said, unable to stop herself. "I don't think I can do this. My daughter needs me to be strong for her. But I'm not. I'm falling apart."

"Who says you aren't strong? You're one of the strongest women I know."

A sad smile shaped her lips. If he only knew how

scared she was of the future, he wouldn't think she was brave at all.

"Look at all you've accomplished," he continued. "You brought a little girl into this world. You've raised her as a single mom. That can't have been easy."

"I had help," she said, aware of those she'd leaned on. "Penny gave me a place to stay when I had nowhere else to go. Sarah and I have remained close."

"You put yourself through school. You're working to make a good home for Gracie. Even coming here, I get the impression this isn't for you as much as it is for her."

If he only knew.

She forced herself to face the facts. "But I can't give her all the things she needs."

A kidney.

"No, but you love her. That makes up for everything else."

She blotted her tears. She should have known Nate would be the one to calm her fears. Even when they were kids, he'd always been the voice of reason. The one she could trust...until she couldn't.

"Besides," he continued, "it's not like you planned on sticking around. You'll only be here for a couple of months. Once the courts settle Jimmy's estate and Mary Beth gets back on her feet, you'll be moving on. Then things can go back to the way they've always been."

Unless I prove that the land he wants is mine alone.

Stepping out of his embrace, she hardened her heart. Nate was the enemy. If he had his way, she'd soon be headed back to Virginia with no hope of ever providing a better life, a better future, for her daughter. She couldn't let that happen. Straightening, she squared her shoulders.

"Thanks for the pep talk. I appreciate it. I really do. But I have a lot to do tonight if I'm going to be at the airport on time to pick up Gracie and Penny tomorrow." She took another step away from him. "I have to make sure everything here is perfect before I leave."

"Life isn't perfect." Running a hand through his hair, Nate backed away. "What time's her flight get in?"

"Just before noon. I'll leave here at ten." Although the international airport was only thirty miles away on the outskirts of Orlando, traffic never slowed in the big city. Thinking aloud, she added, "We'll probably stop for lunch. Then I have to drop Penny off at her dad's. It'll probably be four before we get back."

He nodded as if mulling something over. "Sounds like you have everything under control. If I don't see her tomorrow, say hi to Gracie for me."

As Nate headed out the door, Justine stared after him. As a teen, she'd dreamed of spending her life with the man whose shoulders had once seemed broad enough and sturdy enough to withstand any threat. She'd been wrong about that, and he'd broken her heart. Eventually, she'd gotten over him. Moved on to the point where, a decade later, she'd hoped they could at least be friends. But that wasn't likely to happen either as long as they stood toe-to-toe over the ownership of Castle Grove.

"Morning, Bill." Nate dumped an armload of supplies on the counter of the hardware store.

"You're in mighty early." Bill swept a calculating gaze over the array of patching compounds, tubs of wood putty and tubes of caulk. "I thought you'd finished remodeling your house. Decide to tear out another wall?"

"Nah." Nate studied hammers and wrenches that hung from hooks near the cash register. He had all the tools he needed, but a gleaming putty knife caught his attention. Figuring there was no such thing as too many of those, he added one to his stack.

"You sure you need caulk in every color? You went with eggshell and bone throughout, if I remember right."

"You know my house better than I do." No surprise there. Even though the prices were lower at the Home Depot in Orlando, convenience drew people to Bill's Hardware. Good, old-fashioned customer service turned them into loyal customers.

Nate gave his purchases a second glance. Okay, maybe he'd gone a little overboard, he thought as he counted not less than six long tubes of caulk, ranging in color from clear to pure white. But he wouldn't know exactly what the job called for until it was underway, and he sure as heck didn't want to stop in the middle for a supply run.

"Jimmy's place could use some work," he said, sticking to facts that wouldn't betray his sudden interest in fixing up the house next to his. "I wasn't exactly sure what I'd need, so I grabbed a little bit of everything."

"You don't say?"

"It's a matter of self-preservation," he explained, offering the answer he'd decided to give anyone who needed all the particulars. "A snake got into Jimmy's pantry last night. Justine found it. Her screams 'bout gave me a heart attack." The fear that she'd been injured—or worse—had sent a chill straight through him. It wasn't something he wanted to repeat on a regular basis. Though he hadn't minded that last bit, when she'd clung to him like she'd never let him go.

That part had been nice, he admitted.

Bill's guffaws rang through the store, though he didn't make a move toward ringing up Nate's supplies.

The man would probably hold his purchases hostage until he confessed the real reason behind the shopping foray, Nate realized as he waited for the laughter to die down. "Turned out it was nothing more than a black racer that had lost its way, but I can't be running to the rescue every time a palmetto bug flies in through the window."

Not that Justine had a problem with winged roaches the size of small cars. He suppressed a shudder. Truth be told, she handled those better than he did himself.

"It's probably time and money well spent. Sooner or later, that place'll be yours. Any effort you pour into it now will see you in good stead when the time comes." Apparently in no hurry to turn a profit, Bill crossed his arms and leaned against a nearby filing cabinet. "However, it seems to me like your timin's off. I'm not sure you want to encourage Ms. Gale to stick around, do you?"

"There is that." Once Justine gave up on her pointless attempt to steal his land out from under him, he'd definitely sleep easier at night. As would the people of Orange Blossom whose livelihoods were somehow connected to the grove. Bill was a prime example. Castle Grove accounted for a large chunk of the hardware store's annual sales. If Justine somehow won the battle and carried through with her plan to sell the grove to Fresh Picked, this store and others like it would go out of business.

So, yeah, he probably should mind his own business and let Justine suffer. If she'd been the only one involved, he might have been tempted to do just that. But the arrival of her little girl changed things. He hadn't even met the child, but he already felt protective toward her. He couldn't be part of subjecting a five-year-old to the worst part of Florida living.

"I'll need some of your best window screen and enough spline for"—he paused to count windows and doors—"let's say twenty-five openings." He scuffed one boot against the spot where countless customers had carved a shallow dip in the wood floor.

"These supplies will set you back a pretty penny."

Bill nodded as if he'd given the sagest advice in the world.

"Like you said, eventually, it'll be money well spent." Especially once his lawyer proved that he was the rightful owner of Castle Grove. Soon after, Justine and her child would return to wherever they'd come from, leaving the larger house to him. Though why he'd need five bedrooms and an office, he'd never know. It wasn't like there was a Mrs. Rhodes in his future. Or likely ever would be.

"Anything else I can get you, seeing's as you're in a spendin' mood?"

Nate rocked back on his heels. "Didn't you have a sale on air conditioners a while back?"

"I did. There's a nice window unit that'll cool the living daylights out of a couple of rooms."

"Throw a couple of those in at the sale price, and I'll pay cash."

"You got 'em." Bill hastily jotted notes on a spiral pad of paper. "Come back in an hour, and I'll have everything ready for you."

"Sounds good. I need to stop in at the town hall anyway. I want to see how the plans are shaping up for the Orange Fest now that we have the funding to kick things off." He didn't have to explain Justine's change of heart. That news had been passed across back fences throughout the county faster than a storm warning.

"Clara was in here yesterday. She pulled enough lumber to build the check-in booths for the 5K. I've started a running tab for her, same as I always do."

"I know I don't have to tell you to keep a close eye on her expenses." Plans for the race that kicked off the Orange Fest had grown a little more elaborate—and a lot more expensive—each year. Time and again, Jimmy had reeled Clara in a bit. Nate squared his shoulders. He supposed that, as mayor, the task would fall to him for as long as he had the job.

His back to Nate, Bill gripped one end of a roll of dark screen that hung from the ceiling on long chains. "As long as you're going across the street, tell my wife Coach Martin wants to see us in his office tomorrow morning."

Nate rubbed his stubbled chin. Getting called to the coach's office set off all kinds of alarms. "The boys aren't in any trouble, are they?" Co-captains of the football team, the scholar athletes rarely gave their parents anything to fret over.

"They're teenagers. They're always up to something."

"I'll give her the message, but I'm sure it's nothing to worry about. You and Karen have raised two of the levelest-headed young men to come out of Orange Blossom High since I was a student there."

"Yeah, well, I seem to recall you getting into hot water with the coach more than once."

The bell over the front door tinkled, announcing the arrival of another early-morning customer. Nate said his good-byes and headed across the street to the town hall, where everything appeared to be under control. After Karen updated him on the latest gossip, he delivered Bill's message. Nate frowned at the dark shadow that passed across the secretary's features at the mention of Coach Martin's name.

"Anything I should know about?" he asked.

"Are you asking as the mayor or my friend?" Karen heaved a sigh worthy of the worst kind of trouble. Without waiting for an answer, she said, "It's the football team. The players TP'd Coach's house last night. Rumor has it, he's holding the team captains responsible and plans to make an example of them."

Nate's hand slid over his midsection where, despite the years that had passed since he'd last walked onto a football field, a hard knot formed in his stomach. Getting on the coach's bad side was something every boy on the team did his damnedest to avoid. And with good reason. Coach Martin held his players' futures in his hands. One good word from him was all it took to land a tryout at a top university. On the flip side, any prospect of getting scholarship money would splatter like a bug on a windshield if the coach benched a player for the season.

"Did they trample his plants? Break a window?" Toilet-papering the coach's house the week before school started was a team tradition that stretched back several decades.

"I think it's that new wife of his." Over folded arms, Karen nodded knowingly. "Someone needs to sit her down, explain to her how things are done in Orange Blossom."

Nate winced at another example of how poorly outsiders fit into the scheme of small-town life. Hadn't Justine made a similar mistake when she'd bucked Castle Grove's traditional support of the Orange Fest? In her case, though, she'd realized her error in time to correct it.

"If she does anything that hurts my sons' chances at a scholarship, there'll be hell to pay." Unshed tears glistened in the secretary's eyes.

"Now, don't you fret." Nate patted Karen's shoulder. "I'll swing by the school and see if we can't straighten this out before it comes to all that." His days of glory on the football field might not carry much weight with the coach, but surely his position as mayor would count for something.

He checked his watch. He had just enough time to answer a few emails and sign the checks Karen had lined up on his desk before the morning practice ended. Sure enough, by the time he'd loaded his purchases from the hardware store into the back of the pickup truck and driven to the high school at the edge of town, blades of grass were the only things moving on the football field.

Inside the red-brick building, Nate's footsteps echoed in an empty corridor where the smell of fresh floor wax competed with thirty years' worth of lunches left too long in metal lockers, teen hormones and sweat. He strode past the display case where his name topped the list for the most touchdowns in a single season. In all likelihood, one of Bill's sons would shatter that record this year. He was okay with that, he decided. He'd had his fifteen minutes of fame. It was high time someone new stepped into the limelight. Squaring his shoulders, he headed down the hall to make sure Bill and Karen's boys had their chance.

Nate skirted the team logo painted on the floor outside Coach Martin's office. Current player or alumni, no one stepped on the Orange Blossom eagle. He paused respectfully at the threshold of the office of the school's most-respected figure. "Hey, Coach," he said. "Got a minute?"

A pair of athletic shoes slid from the desk to the floor. Without Coach's size thirteens to block his view, Nate stared at a lined face that had been browned by the sun until it was the color of burnished gold. A little more stooped, a little rounder in the belly than he'd been when Nate played for him, Coach Martin adjusted an ever-present baseball hat embroidered with the Orange Blossom insignia.

"Mr. Mayor." Coach Martin spoke with the gravelly voice of a man who'd spent the better part of his life either cheering his team on or berating the players for going left when they knew fool well he'd told them to go right.

"Still Nate, sir." His days of calling audibles and bootlegging his way down the field might be over, but Coach still commanded his respect. "How's the team shaping up this year? Any prospects?" He slid onto the same uncomfortable side chair he'd sat in when he was wet behind the ears and the man behind the desk was a god.

"You know how it is. We always start the season with high hopes. These boys are looking mighty good in practice, but a lot can happen between the first coin toss and the ref's final whistle."

Coach had been saying the same thing for as long as Nate had known the man.

"I heard talk you had some trouble over at your house last night," he said, not wanting to waste the coach's valuable time with dancing around the reason for his visit.

"Damned fool kids." At odds with his muscular chest and sinewy arms, the loose skin under the coach's chin jiggled when Martin shook his head. "I warn 'em every year. They never listen. It wasn't anything more than the usual high jinks, but the wife's got her feathers all ruffled this time 'cause somebody trampled her favorite hibiscus." His face fell. "Heads are gonna roll, I'm afraid."

"Any way to set things right before that happens?"

The knot in Nate's gut tightened. Plants had been damaged before, but no player had ever been cut from the team because of it.

"Well, now." Appearing to mull the idea over, Martin cupped his jaw in his hand. "I've had my eye on a couple of yellow hibiscus down at the Dixie Nursery. If one or two of those was to get planted in my front yard before I meet with the parents tomorrow morning, I sure don't see how the missus could stay mad."

"I guess we'll see what this team's made of." Nate swallowed a smile. Coach's yard ought to be positively overrun with flowering plants, considering how many years he'd been holding some version of this same conversation with the town's mayor. Playing his part in a tradition that stretched back to the school's beginning, Nate stood and extended his hand. Coach shook it without bothering to rise. A few minutes later, Nate cleared his throat at the doorway to the weight room.

"Gentlemen," he said.

Across the room crowded with equipment and soaking tubs, free weights clanked onto their racks. Spotters pivoted away from lifters. Two beefy young men doing squats in the far corner slowly came to attention. Treadmills and cross-trainers slowed as sweaty young men hit the pause buttons on their exercise routines.

"Coach Martin just told me about a bit of vandalism that took place at his house sometime after he turned in last night. He's identified the culprits."

"Ah, shit, man. I told you guys we should have steered clear of Coach's house. We've stepped in it for sure this time." Across the room, William, the older of Bill's twins by thirty minutes, threw a hand towel on the floor.

"Hold on now." Nate worked to keep his face from displaying any hint of humor. He'd had the same reaction as William in the days when he was team captain. "Coach seemed a tad disturbed about some damage to his prized yellow hibiscus."

"Eff that," came a voice from the back. "We was real careful 'bout them flowers."

"Shut your pie hole, Gunther." Jeffery, Bill's youngest, glared at one of his teammates. "Nobody argues with Coach."

"Not if they want to run out onto the field this season," Nate agreed. "William and Jeffery"—he nodded to the co-captains who'd face the coach's wrath if the job didn't get done—"you two need to shower off and come with me. We have a different job to take care of this afternoon."

Though Bill's boys traded confused glances, they moved swiftly to the exit. Nate lingered in the doorway until the co-captains had filed past. It seemed like only seconds before showers ran in the locker room. Once he heard the water, Nate addressed the rest of the team. "Gentlemen, the burden is on you to protect your captains. If I were you, I'd make sure the job is done before Coach gets home this evening."

Having said his piece using nearly the same words the mayor had said to him back when he'd been certain that absolutely nothing was more important than what happened on the football field on Friday nights, he left the leaderless team to figure out the next step. On his way to the truck, he wondered what Coach would do if the team didn't come through on their own. Would he carry out his threat to sack William and Jeffery?

Nate squared his shoulders. Testing the team's loyalty to their captain—or in this case, co-captains—was another time-honored tradition. In the twenty-two years Coach Martin had been at Orange Blossom High, not one team had failed the test. Sure, one or two of the kids on the team could be mouthy, but they'd live up to the challenge.

In his truck, Nate fiddled with the air conditioner and radio while he bided his time. He didn't have long to wait before, their hair still wet, Bill's boys climbed into the cab.

"Mr. Nate, if you don't mind, me and Jeffery would just as soon take care of them flowers ourselves," William began.

Jeffery finished, "Yeah, but we need to swing by our house so we can get some money to pay for 'em."

"Your hearts are in the right place, but it's not going to happen that way. This team needs to have your back. The time to find out whether they do or not is now. Not when you're fourth and long."

Having said all there was to be said on the subject, Nate put the truck in gear and headed for Castle Grove. There, he put the boys to work caulking animal-friendly holes, tightening window frames and replacing torn screens. With the help of two stronger, younger backs, he leveraged air conditioners into Justine's bedroom window and the small parlor beside the dining room. When they were finished, he plugged the units into nearby outlets and stood back to admire his handiwork.

While cool air blew through the vents, William gathered the tools they'd used. "Mr. Nate, I'm sorry, but we need to get back to the school."

"Yeah, Coach'll have our hides if we miss practice this afternoon." Jeffery dumped an armload of trash into a garbage bag.

"There's more to life than football, son," Nate said, feeling his age plus another fifty years or so. "You're looking out for one of Orange Blossom's own, and that's part of living in a small town." He squirted a thick bead of sealant around the edge of the air conditioner. "I can pretty much guarantee practice was canceled so Coach could take his wife out to dinner."

That was another tradition that led up to the start of the school year.

Finishing up, he checked his watch. "Miss Justine will be back from the airport soon. Let's wrap things up here, and I'll run you back into town. If you're hungry, we can stop for burgers on the way."

"Now you're talking." This time, William spoke for both boys.

Smiling, Nate shook his head. Growing men needed fuel, and Bill's young sons still had some growing to do.

Later, after dropping his helpers off at their home, he took a little detour on his way out of town. Silently, he counted not two, but four new plants among the hibiscus that dotted the acre of land surrounding the coach's house. His chest filled as he drew an easy breath. Knowing the traditions of their small town had survived another test, he aimed the truck for home.

The large table in the corner of the Ham Hut looked clean. Apologizing to her friends for the delay, Justine whipped a pack of hand wipes from her tote bag anyway. Shaking a damp sheet open, she proceeded to wash down every inch of the wood-grained Formica. When she was finished, she shook out a second wipe and gave the table another going-over. Where her daughter's health was concerned, it never hurt to be extra cautious.

"Where shall we sit, Gracie?" she asked, reaching into her bag again and eyeing the chairs.

"I want to sit with SueEllen." Her dark curls tumbling, Gracie grabbed the hand of the waifish child beside her.

"Me, too. Can we, Aunt Sarah?" SueEllen's braids flew as the two girls headed for chairs at the far end of the table.

Justine clamped down on a guilty twinge. This past week, she'd missed Gracie more than she'd thought possible. Every waking minute, she'd looked forward to the time when she'd have her daughter by her side again. She'd imagined the two of them snuggling on the couch together, playing board games and reading books out loud.

And yes, their initial reunion had been everything she'd dreamed of. The instant Gracie had spotted her at the end of the Jetway, she'd pulled away from Penny and raced into Justine's open arms. As other travelers from the plane streamed past—some smiling fondly, others oblivious—mother and daughter had hugged each other for all they were worth. But once the *I missed you mosts* had petered out and Gracie unlocked her arms from around Justine's neck, the five-year-old had turned decidedly mulish. Now, she wanted nothing to do with her mother.

What was that all about?

"Don't let it get to you," Sarah whispered. "SueEllen reacted the same way when my brother and his wife returned from their trip to Hawaii last year. It was almost like she was punishing them for going away and leaving her. Give her a day or two. She'll get over it."

"I hope you're right." Justine eyed the two girls who'd become instant best friends only moments before when they'd met on the sidewalk outside the restaurant. Sighing, she withdrew another wipe and gave one of the chairs a thorough going-over while a bouncy SueEllen described the pet rabbit she kept in a cage in her room.

"You want to come and see him at my house?"

"Does he have big teeth?"

Catching an oddly reticent note in the voice of a girl who, not so long ago, had begged for a guinea pig, Justine leaned a smidge closer.

"Really, really big." SueEllen giggled.

"Will he bite me like Brutus did?"

Justine froze in midswipe. "Brutus? Mrs. Morrison's dog?" Fighting a rising panic, she straightened. "He *bit* you?"

"Right here, Mommy."

Abandoning the chair, Justine peeled back Gracie's sleeve. Beneath the floral print, her daughter's pale pink skin didn't have so much as a mark, and she drew in a shaky breath. "I bet Aunt Penny gave you special kisses and made it better." She searched Penny's guilty face.

"It was an accident. They were tussling for a ball. He didn't even break the skin. And before you ask, yes, I checked. The dog was up-to-date on all his shots. I slathered her arm in antiseptic cream and bandaged it, just to be sure."

Justine deliberately flexed her shoulders. Brutus was as sweet-tempered as his owner, and Penny had done all the right things, taken all the right precautions. She waited a beat while her fears settled, then turned to the woman who'd done so much for her and her daughter.

"Thanks for taking such good care of her." She ruffled a hand through Gracie's curls. "I bet you were a very brave girl. I'm proud of you. Why don't you and SueEllen sit right here?"

She waved her daughter into the seat of the chair she'd just washed, then looked on in dismay when SueEllen climbed up instead. Shaking her head, she pulled yet another wipe from her bag and wiped down a second chair. But when she started to sit beside her daughter, Gracie pushed her away.

"No, Mommy. I want Aunt Penny to sit next to me," she insisted. "You can go over there." She pointed to a spot at the opposite end of the table.

"I think Aunt Penny might like some time to visit with Aunt Sarah," she suggested, looking to her friends for help and finding none. When Gracie's lips wobbled and storm clouds gathered in her big blue eyes, Penny edged around her. Mouthing, *I'm sorry*, she settled next to her godchild, leaving Justine no choice but to take the vacant spot beside Sarah.

Unwrapping her silverware, Sarah spoke out of the side of her mouth. "Relax, Mom. The girls'll be fine."

"Easy for you to say," Justine muttered in return. Sarah didn't have children. She didn't know what it was like to have to stand guard over a sick child every minute of every day.

"Hey, y'all." Thin enough that a stiff breeze would blow her across the street, a waitress wearing a uniform the color of ripe lemons stepped to the end of the table. "Welcome to the Ham Hut. I'm Zoe. What can I get to start y'all off? Tea? Coffee? We have a full selection of soft drinks for the little ones."

Justine's smile froze as the woman doled out paper placemats to the children, then plunked a plastic tub between them. A cold knot of fear unraveled in the pit of her stomach, sending chills straight up her back when she spotted the gnawed ends of several crayons sticking out over the rim of the basket. Before either girl could reach for their favorite color, she leaned across the table and snatched the cup.

"Thank you," she said aware that Sarah and SueEllen were looking on in stunned silence. She thrust the container at the waitress. "But we brought our own." Disaster averted, she reached into her bag of tricks where she kept a ready supply of well-scrubbed toys and fresh packs of pens, pencils and crayons.

"Here you go." Shaking waxy colored sticks in bright wrappers onto the table, Justine scanned the children's menu. "What's everyone want for lunch? How about some fresh fruit and chips, Gracie?"

"I'll have chicken nuggets and fries, Aunt Sarah," SueEllen blurted as she bounced in her seat. "Can I have lemonade?"

"Sounds good." Sarah nodded to the waitress. "I'll have the ham plate with coleslaw."

"I want chicken nuggets and fries like my friend." Gracie giggled at SueEllen.

"I'm not..." Justine braced for an argument with her testy daughter.

Before she could finish the thought, Sarah leaned in close. "If it's germs you're worried about, next to Miss June's, the Ham Hut has the cleanest kitchen in the county. But, as a general rule, I'd recommend freshly cooked foods like nuggets and fries over fruit that was probably cut up last night and has been sitting in a water bath ever since."

Justine swallowed. By feeding her daughter what she considered a safe and nutritious meal, had she been exposing Gracie to potentially harmful bacteria? She cast a worried glance at the child who jiggled in time with her friend, waiting for an answer with all the patience of a monkey.

"Okay," she said, giving in. In the not-too-distant future, she'd have to deal with dietary restrictions, but for now, Gracie's doctors had advised her to keep everything as normal as possible. For a five-year-old, nuggets and fries practically made up two of the basic food groups.

When Gracie rewarded her with a smile that almost made the disagreement worthwhile, she added her own order to the others. The girls colored while the adults swapped tidbits of information. Soon, though, Zoe returned with their drinks. Justine pulled wrapped straws from her bag, inserted one through the plastic lid on her daughter's cup of lemonade and handed it across.

"I have extras. Want some?" She offered a handful to Penny and Sarah.

As Penny took one, Sarah's eyebrows dipped low. "We're fine," she said, grabbing two of the unwrapped straws Zoe had dropped on the table. She stuck one in her glass of iced tea and the other in SueEllen's cup.

"Thanks, Aunt Sarah." Taking her drink, SueEllen looked up from the colorful scribbles she'd drawn on her placemat. She nudged Gracie's arm. "We're going to be in the same class in school. Our teacher's name is Ms. Porcher. She's really nice."

Uh oh, Justine thought as doubt flickered in Gracie's eyes. Her daughter's head swiveled.

"What about my old school?" Across Gracie's face the sheer joy of being in the same class as her new friend waged war with the unexpected change of plans.

Who could blame her?

Gracie's excitement about starting kindergarten had been building for months. Three weeks ago, the two of them had taken a tour of the elementary school in their neighborhood. They'd met her teacher and seen her classroom. But now the plans had changed.

"Wouldn't it be fun to see SueEllen every day?" she asked in an attempt to focus on the positives. An attempt that didn't exactly succeed, judging by the dark look Gracie threw her way.

"We'll eat lunch at school," SueEllen declared.

"There's a big room with a bunch of tables and benches, but we can't eat there 'cause Billy Marchal has lurgies."

"Allergies," Sarah corrected.

"We'll eat in our classroom. You and me can sit together."

Time and again, Justine had told herself, that when it came to children, she'd never resort to bribery. Never trade gifts or favors for good behavior. But that had been before. Before she'd landed the role of a single parent. Before she'd learned her only child faced an uncertain future. Given their current set of circumstances, what was wrong with giving Gracie what she wanted?

"Tomorrow, I'll take you shopping for school supplies and a new lunch box," she said, dangling a carrot she knew her daughter couldn't resist. Didn't she beg to go down the office-supply aisle at the grocery store? Certain the prospect of picking out notebooks and pencils would thrill Gracie, she sat in shocked silence when the center of her world ignored her to play with her friend. The girls put their heads together in a whispered conversation clearly not meant to be overheard by the adults.

Across the table, Penny cupped one hand over her mouth, laughter glinting from mirth-filled eyes. "She's a piece of work, that daughter of yours. She's kept me hopping this past week. I don't envy you the next couple of days."

Justine faked a groan and shook her head. "Don't I know it."

Motion beside her demanded her attention. She turned, catching Sarah just as the petite brunette tugged open Justine's tote bag. "Careful," Justine cautioned.

"You know what they say about cats and curiosity."

"Yeah. Yeah." Sarah sifted through the contents of a bag that contained as many medical supplies as a small clinic. "I get that you're a concerned parent, but do you seriously think all this is necessary?"

"Of course I do. Otherwise, why would I bother?"

"I'm just saying, you seem to have gone off the deep end," Sarah insisted. "Making us wait while you clean a table that was clean to begin with. Bringing your own crayons." She reached into the bag and pulled out a zippered case filled with Band-Aids, gauze pads and adhesive wrap. "Are you expecting Armageddon?" She dipped into the bag again, this time retrieving sealed packs of rubber gloves. "Who carries all this crap around with them everywhere they go?"

"Let it go, Sarah," Penny hissed with a meaningful glance at the two youngsters who were involved in a heated game of tic-tac-toe. "Little pitchers have big ears."

Justine shot the woman across the table a grateful look. As her roommate and closest friend, Penny understood her situation better than anyone.

"Well, it doesn't make any sense." Sarah locked eyes with Gracie's godmother. "She wasn't a germaphobe when we were kids. The last time I visited, she seemed perfectly normal." Angling her head toward Justine, she asked, "What turned you into such a health nut?"

Justine blinked. Sarah was acting as if there was nothing to be concerned about. Didn't she realize that a cold, one bout of the flu, or any number of childhood illnesses could cause Gracie's kidneys to fail completely?

She edged away from the woman she'd always counted among her best friends. Pitching her voice below the hearing range of the two girls at the opposite end of the table was a challenge, but she managed. "It probably happened the day my daughter was diagnosed with a life-threatening condition."

The smaller woman went ghostly white. "Wh-what?" Sarah's voice rose. Tears instantly filled her eyes. She tore her gaze from Justine's, swept it past Penny and draped it firmly over Gracie.

Confusion set up housekeeping in Justine's head as though it planned to stay for a while. Though she hadn't discussed Gracie's illness with Sarah, surely Penny had shared the news. The three of them never kept secrets from one another. Suspecting she'd been wrong about that, she aimed questioning glance at Penny. "You didn't tell her?"

Penny retreated into herself like a timid rabbit. "I couldn't. I tried, but I couldn't."

"Oh, sugar," Justine breathed. "I guess that explains a lot."

Not everyone knew, of course. But those who did were divided into two camps. There was the group that fawned over Gracie, treated her as if she was a china doll, as if they could somehow make up for her terrible diagnosis. One of Gracie's preschool teachers had been like that, nearly bursting into tears at the end of every day. At the other end of the spectrum were people like her own mother who, on hearing that her only grandchild might soon need a kidney transplant, responded, "Oh, posh. By the time she gets old enough to need one, they'll simply grow one for her." After that, she'd refused to so much as discuss the matter.

However, ever since the diagnosis, Sarah's reaction had been decidedly...neutral. She hadn't showered Gracie with gifts or called constantly to check up on her. But she hadn't withdrawn either. She'd sent cards on birthdays and holidays, occasional gifts, but nothing special. In short, Sarah had treated Gracie no worse or better than she'd treat any good friend's perfectly normal child.

Sarah's gaze slammed into her like a gale-force wind. Questions spun circles in her eyes. "What's wrong with her?" Sarah whispered. "Is it... Please tell me it's not cancer."

"No, not cancer." Justine's stomach clenched. At least they'd been spared that nightmare.

"We only found out two months ago that Gracie's kidneys are failing," she began. Her voice a mere whisper, she recounted the day in Dr. Lassiter's office when she'd studied the spreadsheet that scrolled across the screen of his laptop while the pediatrician pelted her with words made of stones.

By the time she finished, the waitress hovered, ready to clear the table of meals that had barely been touched.

"How can I help?" Sarah, rousing herself from stunned silence once Zoe had carted their dishes away and the girls headed across the restaurant to look at the fish tank.

Justine patted her friend's arm. "You've already done so much. Helping me get the house ready for her to come here. Being my friend. When the time comes, I'll need a shoulder or two to cry on. I—" She bit her lower lip. "You think I'm nuts now. I'll probably be certifiable when we get closer to the transplant."

"You could get tested like I plan to do." Penny's gaze never wavered from Gracie and SueEllen. "Justine won't ask, but somebody's going to have to donate a kidney to save Gracie's life."

"Donate." Sarah's lips firmed. "Count me in. And if I'm not a candidate, I'll organize a drive. We'll get the whole town of Orange Blossom involved. Someone around here has to be a match."

Tears stung the corners of Justine's eyes. Aware that the girls were apt to return at any second, she wiped her eyes. "With any luck, it'll be years before things get that bad. But I just have to say thanks. I don't know how I'd cope without you." Her gaze shifted between her friends. "Especially you, Penny. I'll never be able to repay you for all that you've done."

"That's what friends are for." Penny adjusted her glasses. "Here come the girls. Big smiles."

"The Three Musketeers, that's us," Sarah said with a grin that trembled only slightly at the edges.

"How 'bout some dessert?" Zoe circled the table, picking up glasses and refreshing drinks. "Our chocolate cake is the best in town. One piece is plenty big enough to share. What do you say?"

Justine hesitated. After the heavy discussion of the past hour, she could go for something decadently sweet, but the thought of five people—even five friends—digging into the same slice of cake was enough to loose a torrent of fresh worry in her chest.

"While that cake sounds terrific, Zoe," said Sarah, "I don't really like to share. Do you think you could wrestle up a bunch of those little sundae bowls, divvy up the cake and maybe add a scoop of ice cream for each of us? That'd be heavenly."

When Zoe sped off to fulfill the special request, Justine patted her friend on the arm.

"Thanks," she whispered, grateful for the support of her best friends.

Nate ran a finger over a glossy leaf. Thick, yet pliable, the vibrant green flexed beneath his fingers. He tore the leaf in two, relying on experience to tell him whether the tree was getting enough water and nutrients. It was, and he dropped the torn pieces to the ground where they'd eventually fertilize the tree they came from. Next, he ran a hand over one of hundreds of green globes that weighted the top branches until the tree bowed like a penitent before the king. His fingers traced the nubby surface of the fruit, probing for soft spots, feeling for any sign of disease or insects. Finding none, he gave the navel orange a quick twist. It broke cleanly away from the stem, just as it should.

Stepping into the grassy aisle between the rows, he pulled an aging Swiss Army knife from a back pocket. The blade sliced through the thick rind and into the fruit. So far, so good. He squeezed, smiling at the juice that wept from the cut. The heady scent of still-green citrus tickled his nose. Holding the orange higher, he tipped his head and caught a few tart droplets with his tongue. The bitter taste puckered his cheeks. He turned aside and spat.

By his estimation, the fruit needed another month or more of sweltering temperatures and near-daily rain showers before it'd be ready to pick. While it ripened, the crop of navels would swell to twice their current size. The skin would turn from dark emerald to orange. The scent would lose its sour tang, the juice sweeten. By the time workers swarmed the grove, filling boxes and crates with tree-ripened fruit, brightly colored juice would all but gush from freshly sliced citrus, but for now, satisfaction swelled his chest and eased his nagging fears about the coming harvest. Everything was exactly as it should be.

Everything, that was, except for the small child peering out at him from behind a low branch.

She was definitely not where she ought to be.

He'd been aware of her ever since she darted off Jimmy's porch a little while ago. She'd run through the field, her short legs pinioning as if she was playing tag with an invisible friend. When she'd come to the orange trees, she'd stopped, and he'd figured she'd turn around and go home. But she hadn't. Instead, she'd walked through several rows to where she stood now, her pale arms and face sticking out like sore thumbs amongst all the green.

Did her mother know she'd wandered off?

The blade of his knife slid into the case with a snap. His movements slow and cautious, he returned the tool to his back pocket. Whistling a cheery tune, Nate plucked a piece of grass from the aisle that grew between the rows of trees. He ran the thin leaves through his fingers while he wondered if he should do...something. The kid could probably find her own way home. All she had to do was walk back the way she'd come. Hoping she'd do that on her own, he moved deeper into the grove.

Damn.

The silent curse whispered across his lips when he realized she'd followed him. The little munchkin had no business wandering around alone. Left on her own, she was sure to get lost. Or have a run-in with one of the spiders that spun enormous webs between the trees. Snakes, some poisonous, slithered through the grass. Coyotes hunted the area. He'd even seen a Florida panther slinking around a few years ago.

Unable to leave her to her own devices and afraid she'd run off if he startled her, he stood where he was. Before long, Justine would come looking for her. Till then, he'd bide his time.

A plan that fell apart when the child bent down. The orange she picked up from the ground had to be one of the discards left behind at the end of last year's harvest. By now, it had to be rotten through and through. His chest tightened when she broke the soggy mass in two. Knowing what came next, he covered the ground between them in long strides.

"You don't want to eat that one. It's nasty," he said, gently lifting the pulpy mess from her hands. The orange landed on the ground with a soft splat. Taking a handkerchief from his back pocket, he squatted before the girl whose familiar blue eyes widened impossibly.

"Hey there." Trying his best not to scare her, he wiped her fingers on the cloth. "I'm Nate. I'm a friend of your mom's. I bet your name is Gracie. Am I right?"

"Mommy says I'm not apposed to talk to

strangers." She retreated as far as she could without snatching her hand away.

"That's a good rule. You should always listen to your mommy." He glanced over the top of her head to the thick foliage that hid the house from view. "I bet your mommy told you not to wander off, didn't she?"

Tiny little lips turned down at the edges. "She said I had to stay on the porch. But I didn't have anybody to play with. I saw a rabbit. I thought he'd want to play with me."

"You did?"

Her frown did a somersault. "He was brown and he went hop-hop-hop. I tried to catch him, but he ran away. Can you help me find him?"

"I think we need to ask your mom before we bring home a bunny."

"She won't let me have one." The girl gave a tremendous sigh. "She won't let me have any fun. I got sweaty on the porch."

"I imagine you did." Nate gave her clothes a once-over. He didn't know much about kids' fashions, but with temperatures hovering at the ninety-degree mark, he thought Gracie was dressed more for church than playing outside.

Her focus drifted to the tight clusters of fruit on a nearby tree. "I like it here in the shade. What are those?"

"They're oranges. These are orange trees. And this"—he waved an arm—"is an orange grove."

"You're tricking me."

Nate wasn't sure how Gracie managed to tilt her head up to see him and still look down her nose at him, but she did. He struggled against a smile while her expression all but accused him of telling a whopper.

"Sometimes my friend Timmy Burroughs, he tricks me. Timmy lives a long, long way away. You have to ride in a plane to get to his house. I rode on a plane." Two little arms folded across her chest. "I know my colors. These trees aren't orange. They're green."

Her solemn expression teased a laugh from him. "You're right. The leaves are green, but the trees are called orange trees 'cause oranges grow on them."

In a move that made him think of Justine, the child cocked her head and studied him. "Where?" she asked, her tone all challenge.

"There." He pointed to the round balls that dripped from the branches. "Those are oranges." Before she had a chance to argue, he added, "They aren't ripe yet. In another month or two, they'll turn bright orange and we'll pick them."

"I like oranges. I want to eat one."

"We have to wait awhile. We don't pick them till they're ripe."

"You did. You ate it, too. I saw."

"Yeah, but..." He stopped himself. Apparently, Gracie had inherited more than an aquiline nose and wide-set blue eyes from her mother. The child also had Justine's penchant for logic.

"I was testing them," he explained. "That's part of my job. I have to make sure they're growing just right."

"Are they?"

"I think so."

"You didn't test this tree. What if these oranges aren't growing right? Don't you need to pick one and try it?"

Nate shoved his fingers through his hair. It was starting to sound like he'd sooner win an argument with a brick wall than one with Justine's daughter. "I suppose we should. I'll need some help, though. Have you ever picked an orange before?"

Twin braids shimmied when Gracie shook her head.

"Well, there's a trick to it. First, you have to find the one you want to pick. Look it over closely. Don't reach for it till you know there aren't any spiders or bugs on it."

Taking her job very seriously, the little girl all but buried her head in the leaves. "No bugs," she announced.

"Okay. That's good. Next, you don't just yank it off the tree. If you do that, it'll break the branch and next year, the tree won't be able to make as many oranges. Gently, you take the orange in your fingers and you twist it till it comes off the tree. Think you can do that?"

"Uh-huh." A whisper of air passed through her tiny little rosebud lips.

"Go ahead. Give it a try."

She yanked. The branch snapped. Her lips parted as she stared down at a handful of leaves still attached to a hard green ball. "I did it," she breathed.

Nate's lips twitched. "You sure did. Your technique needs a little bit of work, but you did just fine."

Stubby little fingers pinched the skin. "I can't open it." She thrust the fruit toward him. "Will you open it for me? Please?"

The little heartbreaker stared up at him so sweetly, he couldn't resist. "Sure. I need to use my knife, though, so step back a little bit." Carefully, he unfolded his handkerchief and, using a clean corner, buffed the orange until it glowed. Then, after retrieving his pocketknife, he ran the blade in a circle around the fruit.

"Here you go." He separated the orange into two neatly split halves and tucked his knife out of sight.

"It's not orange inside."

"It will be. Or, the others will be. This one can't get ripe now that we've cut it."

Gracie stared at the fruit in her hand. "I'm sorry, orange."

"It's okay. Every tree loses a few oranges before we pick them."

Her nose wrinkling, she sniffed the open half. "How come?"

Pretty sure a five-year-old wouldn't know much about hurricanes and storms, he kept his answer simple. "Sometimes a big wind comes along and blows them off the tree. Sometimes they get too big or there's too many, and the tree can't hold them, so they fall off."

"You sure have a lot of them." A tiny frown worried the space between her eyebrows.

"Yep. We should have a bumper crop this year." He was getting used to the way her mind worked, so before she asked, he added, "It means we'll have a lot of fruit to sell."

"Oooh." She stared down at the fruit. "Can I eat it now?"

Nate shook his head. "You won't like it. It's pretty sour."

"You had some," she pointed out with all the persistence of a bulldog.

When they were kids, how many afternoons had he spent reading in the swing on Jimmy's front porch instead of riding his bike because that's what Justine wanted to do? He'd never been very good at telling her no, and it seemed like her daughter was going to have the same effect on him.

"If you watched me," he said, giving in, "you saw how I tilted my head back and squeezed the juice into my mouth. We'll do the same thing."

Obediently, the little girl tilted her head back. Nate raised the orange over her open mouth and dribbled a couple of drops onto her tongue.

"Eww. It's sour!" she squealed. Her tiny tongue darted in and out.

"I tried to warn you."

She sucked on her lips. "I like it. Can I have some more?"

Nate pitched the half aside. "Maybe later, when they ripen. You'll like it even better then. For now, I think we need to get you back to the house, don't you? Your mom's going to be plenty worried when she finds out you wandered off on your own."

As if on cue, a decidedly frantic voice cut through the still afternoon. "Gracie! Gracie, where are you?"

Nate hauled himself to his feet. "It's okay. I've got her." His voice boomed over the quiet sounds of cicadas and crickets. He looked down at the tiny child. It wasn't far to the edge of the grove, but considering how small Gracie was, it'd take at least five minutes to get there. From the fear that slid up the register of Justine's voice, that was about four minutes and thirty seconds too long.

"C'mon, kiddo. Up you go." He swung the child onto his shoulders, surprised at how light she felt in his arms. "You okay up there, Little Bit?" he asked.

"I'm up high! I can see everything."

"Okay. Well, hang on," he cautioned, taking her

two small hands in his. Keeping an eye out for spider webs, he lengthened his stride, emerging from the last row of trees just as Justine reached the same spot. Her pasty face twisted a knife in his gut. Without stopping for explanations, he swept the little girl from his shoulders and into her mother's waiting arms.

"Gracie! Oh my God, Gracie. You nearly gave me a heart attack." Justine smothered her daughter with kisses and hugs. "What were you thinking, going off on your own like that?"

"I saw a rabbit, Mommy. I thought it was SueEllen's rabbit. I tried to catch it, but it was too fast. Did you know these trees are orange trees? They aren't orange, though. They're green. I had some juice. It was orange juice, but not like yours. It was sour. Mr. Nate says the balls on the trees will change colors. Can we watch them turn colors?"

Nate rocked back on his heels, smiling at the rapid-fire delivery.

"Margaret Grace Gale, you are never to leave the house again unless I'm with you. Do you understand?" She pressed kisses to Gracie's tiny fingers. The faint lines across her forehead deepened. "What do you have all over your hands?"

"I don't know. It's from the oranges, I guess." Gracie pulled back her hands and scrubbed them on her dress.

"Wait. Stop. Use this." Justine reached into the pocket of a pair of slim-fitting capris and pulled out a bottle of hand sanitizer. Apparently familiar with the routine, Gracie cupped her hands while Justine poured a few drops into her palms. "Rub good. We'll wash with real soap as soon as I get you inside." She titled her head, her gaze shifting from her daughter to him. "Did she say you gave her juice?"

The way her voice rose on that last word sounded almost as though she was accusing him of feeding her daughter poison. "A couple of drops." He shrugged. "No big deal. She saw me testing the fruit and wanted to know what it tasted like."

"No big deal? How do you know? Maybe she's allergic. Maybe she swallowed some of the pesticides you use on the trees. Say ah." Justine alternated between staring into Gracie's mouth and hugging her close.

Nate backpedaled. Her missing daughter had put Justine through parent hell. So, yeah, she was upset. Any mother would be. But that didn't explain her shrill overreaction. Especially not about something as pure and simple as a little juice. Had she completely forgotten how they used to bet a week's allowance on who could eat the most unripened fruit? Or how she'd won those contests every damn time?

"Look, she's fine," he said, trying to put her fears to rest. "From the time she walked off the porch, she was never out of my sight, never in any danger. As for the juice"—he shuffled his feet—"maybe I should have asked first, but we raise organic citrus here on Castle Grove. No pesticides. No harsh chemicals."

Justine's shoulders rounded the tiniest bit. Her head came up. Her eyes slid over his face, probing, searching. "You're sure?"

"Who would know better than me?" It was another reason he had to keep her from selling out to Fresh Picked. There was no place for an organic grove in the big juicing conglomerate's five-year plan. But a second glance at Justine convinced him that, in her present state of mind, trying to get her to see his side of *that* argument was a waste of time and effort. It was time for him to leave.

"If you'll excuse me, now that you know Gracie's safe, I'll be heading back to work." Certain he needed to put some distance between them, he slapped his hands on his jeans and was only moderately surprised when getting his boots moving in the right direction took a bit more effort than he wanted to admit.

Should she yell at Gracie for leaving the house? Or smother her with kisses?

Read Nate the riot act for giving her child something to eat? Or hail him as her hero?

Torn between choices, Justine clutched her daughter closer to her chest. "Oh, sweet baby. Mommy was so scared," she whispered. "Don't ever do that to me again."

She ran her fingers over Gracie's arms and down her legs, searching for scrapes, bruises, any sign that she should rush the child to the ER. When she didn't find a single mark, the stranglehold of panic that had held her in a tight grip ever since she'd realized her pride and joy was missing finally began to loosen its hold. She gave Gracie another squeeze.

Remembering Nate, she stared at the spot where he'd been. But the man who'd returned her baby to her was rapidly moving toward the grove.

"Nate, hold up a sec." Behind him, the sun dropped toward the treetops, silhouetting his tall, muscular form against a blinding light. The sight stole the words right out of her mouth, and she cleared her throat. "I left a message on your voice mail, but I wanted to thank you in person, too. I can't believe you installed air conditioners in the house." She shifted Gracie around to one hip. Air conditioning meant the difference between sleeping through the night and spending hours tossing and turning in the stifling heat. It meant Gracie could play with her dolls without having their hair stick to her hands. Or color in her coloring books without sweat dripping onto the pages. The difference it would make in their lives was monumental, but why would Nate go out of his way...for her? "I don't understand why you did it."

As if he shouldn't have to explain, Nate tipped his head to the child in her arms. Now that they were standing in the full sun instead of the cool shade of the grove, sweat trickled down the long part between her daughter's braids and dampened the fabric around the little girl's neck.

He'd spent all that money, done all that work, for a child he'd never even met?

Trying to make sense of such a huge act of kindness, she traced his outline to a set of wide shoulders. "Much as I appreciate the gesture—and I do—I can't afford them." Two expensive air conditioners simply didn't fit into her budget. Shielding her eyes against the sun, she frowned. "Can you return them?"

"No returns on sale items. Besides, I didn't ask you to pay for 'em." In a move that was pure Nate, he hitched his jeans higher on his slim hips. A grasshopper buzzed out of the grass when he tapped his heel against the ground. "I'm afraid you're stuck with the screens, too. I was able to save a couple of the old ones. The doors, well, those were a different story. They all had to be replaced. Caulked a couple of holes while I was at it."

Justine felt her jaw unhinge. "It's too much. I can't let you do all that for us." Heat crawled up her neck and onto her cheeks. She'd been so busy unpacking and putting away Gracie's clothes that she hadn't actually noticed the repairs Nate had made. She probably would have, but when she stepped out onto the porch with an iced tea for herself and a juice box for her daughter, she'd discovered that Gracie had wandered off. After that, everything was kind of a blur.

"Too late. The job's already done." Nate rocked back on his heels, his eyes twinkling. "Besides, I didn't do it all myself. I had help. I recruited a couple of the boys from the football team who needed some community service hours." He held up a hand. "After the snake episode the other night, I look at anything I can do to keep the critters at bay as an act of self-preservation. Running to your rescue is tough on the ol' ticker, you know."

Mirth danced in Nate's eyes as his hand slid over his heart, and she had no choice but to laugh along with him.

"Why are you laughing, Mommy? Did Mr. Nate tell a joke?" Gracie's two small hands on either side of her cheeks demanded Justine's attention.

She started to explain, but the words got stuck in her throat. Telling a five-year-old that she'd found a snake in their kitchen probably wasn't a good idea. "It's grown-up stuff, baby," she hedged. "You wouldn't understand."

"I'm hot. I want to get down." Gracie pushed her way out of Justine's arms and slid to the ground.

"Hold my hand," she ordered, determined not to lose sight of her daughter again. Little fingers firmly in her grasp, she studied Nate. "Whatever your motive, I can't thank you enough." But she could think of one way to show her gratitude, and brushing the ends of her ponytail off her shoulder, she said, "Look, Penny and Sarah are coming over tonight. We're going to light a fire in the backyard, roast some marshmallows. If you're not doing anything else, why don't you join us?"

"Sounds like a hen party." He shook his head. "I'm not sure I'd fit in."

"Haven't heard that term in ages." The smile that rose to her lips spread across her face. Suddenly aware of how much she wanted to see Nate again, she rushed to explain. "But, no. That's not what it's all about tonight. You know Sarah's sister Mandy," she said, not bothering to ask since, as the mayor of Orange Blossom, Nate was probably on a first-name basis with practically everyone in the county. "She and her husband are coming and bringing their little girl. SueEllen will be in the same kindergarten class as Gracie. I ran into Jack while I was in town this afternoon. He said he might swing by, too."

"If you don't think I'd be intruding..." Nate hooked his fingers on his waistband. "Maybe I'll break out the churn and whip up a batch of my dad's ice cream. I've had a hankering for it ever since the weather turned hot."

"There's nothing better in the world," she murmured, recalling the blend of vanilla and cream on Nate's lips as they'd traded kisses over a bowl of freshly churned ice cream. For a split second, she wondered if they could ever be that close again. Then her sensible side weighed in, arguing that she and Nate were on opposite sides of a fight neither of them could afford to lose. It reminded her of other considerations as well, and she frowned at her memory of the prep work involved in making the sweet treat. "Doesn't your recipe call for raw eggs?"

When Nate confirmed her suspicions, she shuddered. "I'm sorry, but I can't risk anyone getting sick. If you want ice cream, we should pick up a couple of gallons from the store."

"It's not the same, and you know it. Just forget it." Nate widened the distance between them.

"We'll have plenty of other goodies," she offered, attempting to smooth his bruised ego. "I bought all the fixings for s'mores."

The hint of a smile tugged at Nate's lips. "I've never been one to turn those down."

Neither had she, though in the years since their breakup, she'd never enjoyed the chocolaty treat quite as much as she had with him. Her heart beating faster, she asked, "So you'll come, then?"

"I'll be there." His smile widened just a smidge as he bent low to talk to Gracie. "And you, missy. I'll see you later, too. In the meantime, you listen to your mom and don't go wandering off again. It upsets the adults."

At Gracie's solemn nod, Nate touched the bill of his cap and retraced his steps into the grove. Unable to tear her eyes away from his disappearing figure, Justine's mouth gaped. Nate was her enemy, the man who threatened the one thing she wanted most out of life—her daughter's health. And yet he'd gone out of his way, pulled money out of his pocket, to make sure she and Gracie were not just safe, but also comfortable, for as long as they stayed in her uncle's house.

"Can we go inside now? It's hot, and I want to play with my dolls." Gracie tugged on her hand. "I like Mr. Nate, Mommy. He's nice."

"Yes, he is." Justine hugged her daughter close. What would have happened if Nate hadn't been there for them today? Not wanting to know the answer, she turned toward the house. She owed Nate more than she could ever repay, but she couldn't afford to let her guard down around him.

One of the logs in the fire pit burned through. The ends tipped up. The center collapsed, sending a shower of sparks into the dark night air.

"Ooooh, fireworks!" Pointing, Gracie scrambled to the ground. She hadn't taken more than a step or two before Justine hauled the little girl back onto a lawn chair.

"This is close enough. You stay right here where it's safe." Justine stomped on a dying ember that had fallen beyond the rock liner. "How about another s'more? I'll make one for you."

Sending her curls tumbling, Gracie shook her head. "I want to do it myself. I can hold the stick, Mommy. Let me." She grabbed the skewer from Justine's hand.

"No, Gracie," Justine said firmly. "It's too dangerous for you to get that close to the fire. You could get burned."

"She's on quite a tear, isn't she?" Jack ambled over to the tree where Nate had propped one shoulder against the trunk and quietly sipped iced tea.

"I thought it was just me, but yeah, she's a little on edge."

Justine had been repeating the same litany of no-no-nos ever since he'd shown up carrying a pile of sharpened sticks that were perfect for the marshmallow roast. Perfect in his mind anyway. Muttering something about poisonous sap, she'd insisted on tossing his contribution into the fire. Instead, she'd put him to work straightening coat hangers and washing them in hot, soapy water. Wearing gloves, no less.

If that had been all, he might have chalked her behavior up to a mother hen fretting over her sole chick. But the nos just kept on coming. First, Justine refused to let Gracie get within a mile of the fire pit. Then, while everyone else opted for seats on one of the split logs that circled the bonfire, she made her daughter use a lawn chair. The awesome spinach dip Sarah brought for the party got a big ol' two thumbs down the minute Justine learned the dish contained mayonnaise.

"You hear what went down between her and Mandy?" Jack tipped his red cup to an empty spot in the parking area. When Nate admitted he hadn't, Jack leaned closer. "Evidently, SueEllen had a stomachache this afternoon. Justine heard about it and asked Mandy to take the child home. Said she didn't want to take a chance that Gracie might catch whatever was going around."

"Did the kid look sick?"

"Nah. SueEllen was running around with her brothers. It didn't matter. Justine wouldn't budge. Wouldn't even listen to Sarah, who said it was probably from all the lemonade SueEllen drank at lunch. Mandy and her family packed up their gear and left in a huff right after."

So that was where all the kids had gone. One minute, Sarah's three nephews and her niece had been playing tag in the front yard. The next, they'd disappeared. He'd wondered why the sudden departure. Now that he knew, Nate knit his brows.

The conversation lagged while Jack took a long pull from his cup. "Don't get me wrong," the new father said at last. "I'd kill to protect my kid. But a stomachache? Don't kids get those all the time?" He looked away. "You don't think Mary Beth will be that overprotective with Jack Junior, do you?"

"Beats me." As a general rule, Nate tended to steer clear of dating women with young children. Not that there were many single moms in Orange Blossom. "Mary Beth has a good head on her shoulders. Plus, she has you to keep her straight."

"You got that right."

Over the rim of his cup, Nate studied the woman who'd knelt down to speak with her daughter. What had happened to the free-spirited girl he'd once known? The one who dashed between the orange trees and ran barefoot through the grass. The girl who'd swung from the old tire swing and loved homemade ice cream. *That* girl had never quibbled over raw eggs. She had never loosed a blood-curdling scream at the mere sight of a snake. Never shied away from a bonfire. In fact, in her quest to build the best s'more, she'd often scooted closer to the fire than he'd even dared. He resettled his ball cap, unable to shake the feeling that something more than the responsibilities of single parenthood had transformed Justine into the ultra-careful, terribly cautious person she was now.

"Maybe I'll sit with Sarah and Penny for a while," he said. "See if they can shed any light on why Justine's got her panties in a wad." That was one of the side benefits of friendships in a small town. He and Jack and the two girls had been thick as thieves all through high school. Though graduation had marked a turning point and the group had splintered soon after, whenever the four of them got together again, it was almost as if the intervening years had never happened. "You coming?"

"I think I'll keep Grady company." Jack nodded to a tall white-haired gentleman who sat apart from the rest of the group. Penny's dad alternated between sips of iced tea and furtive drinks from a bottle he'd stashed in a brown bag. "I'll make sure he doesn't plan on getting behind the wheel tonight. Plus, I hear he got a shipment of Lee Child's latest thriller. Thought I'd ask him to set one aside for me."

"Doing a lot of reading, are you?"

"Little Jack doesn't sleep much at night. Which means neither do I. What else is there to do?"

Nate had a hard time wrapping his head around the image his wide receiver voluntarily reading anything more than the coach's playbook. Everyone changed, he guessed. Determined to find out why Justine had, he pushed away from the tree. It was time for a heart-to-heart with Sarah and Penny.

"Hey!" he called, heading for the spot where the two women sat with their heads together. "Can I get you anything?"

Penny looked up long enough for a quick smile. "More tea would be nice."

"Coke for me," Sarah added.

The snack table stood not far from where they sat.

Detouring to it, he raised the lid on the cooler.

"Cut her some slack. She's going through a lot right now." The humid night air carried Penny's throaty whisper like a feather.

Penny made a good point, he supposed. Justine had uprooted her entire life by moving to Orange Blossom, even if the move was only temporary. Friends, her career, her home—it had to be tough to trade all she had going for her in the big city for a run-down shack on the outskirts of a small town. Not that the folks around here had treated her like an outsider. Far from it. The summers she'd spent here as a kid had earned her a place in the hearts of the locals. Despite the threat she posed to their whole way of life, they'd banded together to transform Jimmy's house for her. She'd landed a great job, and for as long as she stayed in Orange Blossom, she'd have people looking out for her. It seemed like a pretty sweet deal to him, especially considering that, if things went her way, she'd wind up the owner of the largest privately-owned citrus grove in this part of the state. Still, change—even good change—was hard for some people to handle.

Is that what Penny meant? Hoping to hear better, Nate angled closer.

"I get it. If I were in her shoes, I'd be a basket case. But try telling that to Mandy," Sarah countered. "If I know my sister, she's still in a snit about having to take her brood home." A puff of steam rose from the fire when Sarah tossed the last of her iced tea into the flames. "Now I'm going to have to swing by her place tomorrow to calm her ruffled feathers."

Penny leaned down to retrieve a small stone, which she sent skipping into the darkness beyond the glow of firelight. "It's the uncertainty that gets to me. She might need that kidney tomorrow. Or ten years from now."

Nate froze, one hand wrapped around a can of tea, the other halfway to a bag of chips. A slow burn started somewhere in his midsection and rapidly spread into his throat. Straining to hear more of the conversation, he slowly lowered his hands to the table.

"At least they have some time to find a donor."

"And if they can't find a match?"

"I guess she'll go on dialysis."

"Jeez," Sarah swore. "Remember Mr. Reynard from grade school? He was on dialysis for a while last year. Four hours a day, three times a week, they'd hook him up to all those tubes and literally wash his blood. He had three broken ribs and his leg was in a cast for six months, but he said the dialysis was the worst."

"At least he was an adult. Can you imagine trying to explain that to a child?"

"Makes me glad I don't have children, you know?" Sarah's pointed glance landed on the little girl who waited while her mom roasted a marshmallow on a long skewer. "Poor kid."

Startled, Nate lost his grip on Penny's tea. Taking his stomach with it, the can dropped into the ice chest where it rattled over the cubes. Bile rose in his throat, and he swallowed. Hard. He risked a quick look over his shoulder at the child confined to a lawn chair and the woman who guarded her like a hawk.

That vibrant little girl was critically ill? He paused for a long minute, trying to catch his breath while the world spun around him. No wonder Justine was on edge. If her child really did have a life-threatening condition, he couldn't blame her for overreacting to anything she saw as a threat to her daughter's health. Whether the danger was real or imagined.

"Speaking of kids, did I mention that Mandy's pregnant?"

"What?" Swatting at her friend, Penny leaned away from Sarah. "No one said a thing."

"Yep. I'm going to be an aunt again. I guess my big sis took me at my word when I told her she was in charge of providing all our folks' grandchildren."

"Five." Penny shook her head. "I can't even imagine."

His movements as slow and deliberate as an old man's, Nate popped the top on Sarah's soda and poured iced tea for Penny. He trudged the short distance from the table to the girls' chairs, feeling as though he was moving through cement.

"Here you go," he said, delivering the drinks and a bag of chips. "I'll catch y'all later."

"You're not going to stay?" Penny raised a questioning glance.

The weight of Gracie's illness was a ten-pound rock in the center of his chest. Knowing what he knew, he couldn't sit and make small talk. "Thought I'd catch a couple of innings of the game before I call it a night." With the Braves making a run for the playoffs, ordinarily he'd be glued to the set, cheering on his favorite team. Tonight, though, the crack of a bat wouldn't hold his attention.

Penny unfolded her long legs and stood, dusting off the back of her shorts. "Well, you'd best give me a hug now, then. My flight leaves first thing tomorrow."

"You have a safe trip, hear?" They hugged like only two people who'd never known a wisp of attraction for each other could. Stepping back, he added, "Don't stay away so long next time."

"I have a feeling I'll be back sooner rather than later."

Nate followed Penny's gaze when it drifted to the spot where her father sat nursing his bottle. "Something I should know about?" he asked in a low voice.

"Not really. He's just not getting any younger, if you know what I mean."

"None of us are," he murmured, bending under the weight of all he'd overheard. The urge to retreat to his den and howl pressed hard on his shoulders. Taking the coward's way out, since he couldn't face Justine or Gracie just yet, he waved good-bye to the rest of the group.

Jack had drifted off next to Grady. He snapped awake. As careful as Nate was to mask his feelings, some glimmer of emotion must have broken through, because Jack took one look at him and stood.

"I'll walk out with you," he insisted over Nate's protests. "I need to get home to Mary Beth and Jack Junior anyway." When they'd stepped well out of the hearing range of the others, Jack added, "You look like someone killed your best hunting dog."

"I found out what's made Justine so edgy." They walked several paces closer to Jack's truck, the gravel shifting beneath Nate's boots much like the world seemed to shift on its axis.

"You gonna keep it a secret, or what?"

"Her little girl is sick. Some kind of kidney disease or something. I didn't get all the details. But it sounds serious."

Jack's stride hitched. "That's gotta be tough."

"I was thinking the same thing."

"It also explains a lot."

"I guess." Nate paused. It could certainly account

for why Justine insisted on selling Castle Grove. Even with insurance, treating a chronically ill child had to cost a pretty penny. He ran a hand over his face. Gracie's illness also explained why Justine fussed over the child with such intensity. It was a shame, really. Gracie reminded him a lot of a much younger Justine—fearless, adventurous. But from the little he'd seen, Justine was determined to weed those feelings out of her daughter. He got that she felt compelled to shield the kid from illness and the like, but was the constant hovering really necessary? At what point did someone cross the line between concerned parenting and obsession? He didn't know the answer, but he knew someone who might. His college roommate had gone on to med school at Florida and worked in the ER at a hospital in Ocala.

"I was thinking I'd call Victor Spears. You remember him. He went fishing with us a couple of years back. Thought I'd ask him a few questions."

"He's a doctor," Jacks said, nodding agreeably. "He's got to know more than we do."

Nate pressed a button on his watch, and the time glowed on a dark screen. He felt like he'd aged ten years in the past hour, but time hadn't moved forward all that much.

"I'll try to reach him tonight." He needed answers, and he needed them fast.

The throaty roar of Jack's diesel had barely faded in the distance when Nate picked up his phone and scrolled through the contacts list for a number he hadn't dialed in over a year. An hour later, he hung up, having shared a lengthy conversation with his former roommate. Leaning back in his recliner, he closed his eyes and almost wished he hadn't made the call.

Almost.

Victor had given him a crash course in kidney disease, including the fact that, without a transplant, a patient in renal failure needed to have every drop of their blood cleansed several times a week. Designed as a stop-gap measure, the arduous process was a two-faced coin, prolonging the patient's life, while at the same time exposing them to antibodies that made it increasingly difficult to find a matching donor. The best solution, according to his friend, was to avoid dialysis altogether.

No wonder Justine was so hot to claim Castle Grove as her own and sell the land to the highest bidder. If he were in her shoes, he'd probably do the same thing. Which didn't mean he'd throw in the towel or sign his rights to the citrus grove over to her. He tapped the bend on the inside of his elbow. Tomorrow, he'd swing by the clinic for a simple blood test to see if he was a potential match for Gracie. And if he was? He bowed his head. If he was, he'd give up a kidney to save the child's life. He'd do that much.

But he wouldn't sacrifice the entire town of Orange Blossom to protect one little girl, no matter how sweet she was. Or how quickly she'd wormed her way into his heart. As heartless as it made him feel, he had to think of Orange Blossom and the people who depended on Castle Grove for their livelihoods.

Groaning, Nate mopped his face with his hand and made his way to the liquor cabinet, where he fixed himself a stiff drink. When one wasn't enough, he fixed another.

Justine looked away from the computer screen that displayed one of the 903 sections of Florida's statutes on wills and probate. She aimed a warm smile toward her daughter. Gracie sat on the red sofa in the anteroom of Royce's office, her head bent over a picture book she had insisted on reading to herself, even though she hadn't quite mastered her ABC's. Gracie's lower lip quivered. Turning away, she buried her head lower in her book.

Justine rubbed her temples where a headache threatened. She downed two aspirin with a sip of water while the red light on her desk phone continued to blink. Royce's conference call had begun before she'd taken Gracie's lunch box from the refrigerator in the break room and left to drop it off at school. She scrolled to the next screen and lost herself in Florida's complicated probate law. When she checked the phone at the end of the next page, Royce's call had ended. Finally. She rose and, motioning Gracie to stay put, headed for her boss's office.

"Mr. Enid, do you have a minute?" She leaned around the doorjamb.

"Unhnnn." Like someone who'd been caught napping, the rotund lawyer blinked owlishly. Straightening his propped elbows, he cleared his throat. "How many times do I have to tell you, it's just *Royce* when we're alone in the office?"

"Royce," she repeated, despite the odd feel of the word. At Jacoby & Sons, paralegals never referred to the partners by their first names—in private or otherwise. Of course, Royce Enid's small practice in Orange Blossom was nothing like a busy firm in the nation's capital. The lawyer hadn't been kidding when he'd said things were slow. She could count the number of clients who'd come into the office on the fingers of one hand.

So much for getting to know everyone in town, she thought.

Not that she was complaining. With nothing but free time on her hands, she'd spent the long, empty days educating herself on Florida's complex inheritance laws, studying the thick tomes until her eyes crossed. She'd put her skills as a paralegal to use in unearthing a dozen cases similar to her own. The good news was that in all but one of those, the court had eventually ruled in favor of the heir named in the will. The bad news was that it had taken years—in some instances, decades—for the courts to hand down their final decisions. Gracie's health might hold out that long. Fresh Picked's offer wouldn't.

All of which left her with two choices. She could either find proof that Uncle Jimmy had disinherited Nate, or somehow persuade the grove manager to drop his claim. Neither option was as easy as a walk in the park. Not that she had time to devote to either at the moment. Because, right now, a more pressing matter demanded her attention.

Namely, her five-year-old daughter.

"I need the afternoon off. I had to pick Gracie up from school at lunchtime."

"Is she sick again?"

Is she? No, thank goodness. But when she'd stopped by the school to drop off Gracie's lunch, she'd noticed that two of the kindergartners had runny noses, and a third had a bad cough. Hand wipes notwithstanding, she didn't dare leave her daughter in a classroom filled with germs.

"I think she might come down with something." Justine crossed her fingers and prayed she was wrong.

His chair groaned as Royce shifted his enormous girth. "This is the third time you've had to take off in the past three weeks. Have you taken Gracie to see a doctor?"

"As a matter of fact, we have an appointment next week," she offered, though she was pretty sure the pediatric nephrologist at Florida Hospital wasn't at all what her boss had in mind. "I'm sorry I won't be able to be in the office for the rest of the day. But I have my laptop. If you need anything, I can write it up at the house and bring it in first thing in the morning."

Not that she expected Royce to hand her a big assignment. In the month she'd been working as paralegal-slash-receptionist for the town's only attorney, he'd asked her to draft precisely one official letter. Royce had scrawled his name across the bottom without bothering to read a word.

"What about the phones? Who's going to handle appointments?"

"All taken care of," she said, pleased with herself for thinking ahead. "Your calendar is clear for the rest of the day. I've forwarded the office phone to my cell. If any important calls come in, I'll text you." Though, if today was anything like every other day in Royce's office, she wouldn't need to disturb him. Lunch dates were the only appointments her boss had in his date book. More often than not, those stretched until closing time. Anyone who wanted a word with the attorney simply stopped by his corner booth at the Ham Hut.

"I know you're new to Orange Blossom and all, but we don't do things here the way they do in those big corporate offices in the city." Instead of being impressed by her efficiency, her boss gave his head a jowl-jiggling shake. "Our clients expect the personal touch. When they drop by, they're used to seeing Mary Beth sitting behind that desk. It gives them confidence that we're here to help them with their problems."

A sense of dread wobbled uneasily in Justine's stomach while Royce drummed his fingers on the desk.

"Where's Gracie now?" Royce asked.

"Sitting on the couch in the waiting area." Her voice dropped to a whisper. "She's not very happy with me at the moment."

Although that probably qualified for the understatement of the year. Her daughter had been in a royal snit ever since Justine told her to pack up her bag and made her say good-bye to her classmates. Although the move would probably earn her another black mark in Gracie's book, she made a tentative offer. "I could set her up with a coloring book and crayons in the conference room if you need me to be here."

"A sick kid in the office?" Royce picked at his fingernails. He let out a heavy breath. "Since you've already taken her out of school, you can forward the phones and cover the calls this one time. But I want you to think long and hard about your position here. I need someone dependable. If you're not it, then you need to let me know so I can get someone who is."

She gulped as the fear in her stomach solidified. Talk about impossible situations. She'd given up what little sense of security she'd built in DC in order to find the proof she needed to dispute Nate's claim. But to stay in Orange Blossom, she needed her job...and the insurance benefits that came with it. Now, though, it sounded like staying on as Royce's assistant would require her to expose Gracie to germs that might make her sick, thus setting in motion the very thing she feared the most—that her daughter's condition would worsen sooner rather than later.

Her thoughts ricocheting off one another like Ping-Pong balls, she grabbed her stuff and shepherded her daughter out to Uncle Jimmy's pickup truck. A quick stop at the Ham Hut for French fries bought Gracie's forgiveness and loosed a flood tide of little-girl chatter that lasted all the way to Castle Grove. By the time they reached their temporary home, Justine's headache had eased enough that she almost felt up to dealing with the next challenge of the day.

The minute Justine had parked the truck in the shade of the oak tree, Gracie sprang from her seat. With Justine hot on her heels, she thundered up the steps and raced through the house, making a beeline for the kitchen table.

"We played with sand in school," she announced, flinging her tote bag onto the table.

"Mrs. Porcher gave us jars and little bowls of sand. One was green. One was red. One was purple. Like when we dyed Easter eggs. I poured my sand into my jar, one color at a time. I was very careful. I didn't spill any. Mrs. Porcher said I did a good job."

"I'm sure you did, honey." Though Gracie had never been a particularly messy child, she'd grown more cautious in recent months.

"The other kids got to do more. Mrs. Porcher said I could finish mine tomorrow." Gracie rooted around in her bag. She pulled out crumpled papers bearing gold stars and tossed them on the table. "But I wanted to bring it home today, Mommy. Wait till you see. It's so pretty." Gracie pulled an empty jar out of her bag. "Oh, no!" Her little face fell.

"What's the matter, baby?" Justine turned from the counter where she'd been unpacking her daughter's lunch bag.

"All my sand fell out!" Gracie upended the bag. Pencils and a crayon box clattered onto the table, followed by a waterfall of brightly colored grains. "It's ruined!" she howled.

Before Justine had a chance to say a sympathetic word, much less figure out how to fix things for her daughter, the angry little girl swept everything off the wooden surface and onto the floor. The jar bounced on the rug before skidding into a corner. One of the pencils broke with a sharp crack. With a cry of absolute anguish that nearly broke her mother's heart, Gracie drummed her feet.

"I want to go home! I want to go home! I want to go home!"

A sneakered foot connected with Justine's calf.

Stifling the sob that rose in her chest, she forced herself to remain calm and firm.

"Margaret Grace Gale, you need a time-out. You will march yourself into the bedroom. You will stay there for fifteen minutes."

"No! I won't! I don't want a time-out." Her face turning red, Gracie screamed. She jabbed a finger at Justine. "You get a time-out. You're a bad mommy."

Okay, she was all for understanding and compassion, but enough was enough.

Scooping her willful child into her arms, she carried a kicking and screaming Gracie down the hall. The cooler, drier air in the room they shared stoppered her daughter's wails. Fighting her own tears, Justine wrapped her arms around Gracie and plopped down on the rocking chair where she rocked until they both calmed. It didn't take long. Within minutes, the little girl's sobs tapered off. Gracie's thumb found its way into her mouth. Her long lashes lowered as her eyes drifted shut.

"I'm sorry, Mommy," she murmured.

"I know, baby. I know," Justine whispered, letting the heartbreak of the last few minutes wash over her. She waited until Gracie had fallen sound asleep before, moving slowly and quietly, she tucked her daughter into bed. Her little girl's temper tantrums were rare summer storms that blew up out of nowhere, dumped an inch of rain onto the hot pavement and disappeared while steam still rose in thin tendrils. Afterward, worn out by the emotion, Gracie usually slept for hours. Justine tucked a thin blanket around her shoulders and sucked in a thready breath.

Inheriting Castle Grove was supposed to have been the answer to all her prayers, but no matter which way she turned, there was only more heartache, more problems. Gracie certainly didn't understand why they'd moved to Orange Blossom. She didn't even understand that the move was temporary. In her five-year-old mind, she knew only that everything safe and routine in her world had been swept away, much like the schoolwork she'd swept off the table.

If Gracie were all she had to worry about, Justine told herself she could handle it. Unfortunately, she was picking up decidedly mixed signals from the friends she'd expected to have in her corner. Oh, Sarah had organized an army of women who'd transformed Uncle Jimmy's house into a comfortable home, while Penny had looked after Gracie for a week before bringing her to Florida. But Sarah's unspoken plea to hang on to the grove came through loud and clear in every reference to her family's pie shop. Penny's dad had sunk every penny of his savings into the bookstore on the square and would lose his shirt if the local economy faltered. The husbands and brothers of the women who'd shown up to help her—they all looked to the grove for jobs and support in one way or another. Yet, how could she give them what they wanted if doing so put her daughter's future in jeopardy?

She had to sell. Had to trust that Fresh Picked would honor its commitment to support Orange Blossom once the deal went through. Which couldn't happen until she dealt with Nate's threat to sue for partial ownership of the grove. And that meant searching through years' worth of clutter in Jimmy's office in hopes of finding something that would negate Nate's claim. Something that, between work and Gracie, she'd hadn't had time to do. By the time she picked Gracie up from school, fixed dinner for the two of them and spent a couple of hours entertaining her five-year-old, it was too late to delve into the boxes and file cabinets in Jimmy's office. She'd hoped to spend some time in there this afternoon, but Gracie's temper tantrum had thrown those plans into disarray.

Determined to not give in to her fears for the future, she squared her shoulders. She might not have the answer to all her problems, but she knew one thing for sure—the mess in the kitchen wasn't going to clean itself. She'd best get to it.

It didn't take long to wipe down the table and chairs. Stepping into the yard, she turned Gracie's backpack inside out and shook the last grains of sand from the cloth. In the kitchen, she eyed the rug covered in brightly colored sand. No amount of vacuuming would ever get out all the grit. The only way to do that was the old-fashioned way, and with a sigh, she rolled the thick carpet into a tube and hauled it through the door. It took some muscle to heave the heavy rug over the clothesline, but she managed. Then, grabbing the broom, she swung.

The first blow sent a cloud of multicolored sand into the air and loosened her shoulders. She put a good bit of her frustrations into the next swing. Sand rained down on the grass. Another whack produced a small puff of color and eased some of her tension. From then on, she simply whaled away. Finding her rhythm, she let the respective motion soothe her.

Lunge. Strike. Pull back. Lunge.

The world narrowed until it was just her and the broom and the rug. Until she no longer cared that the carpet had long since given up its last tiny grain of sand.

"Hey now, Justine."

An arm around her waist pulled her tight against a broad muscular chest.

Nate.

"What'd that poor, defenseless rug ever do to you? You better stop before you beat it to tatters."

Warm and teasing, his breath at her ear drew her to him. The broom thudded to the ground at her feet. For an instant, she let herself savor the once-familiar feel of Nate's arms around her. But only for an instant. He was, after all, the enemy. The one who'd thrown a king-sized monkey wrench into all her carefully crafted plans.

Turning, she pushed out of his arms.

"What are you doing here?" she asked, fighting to keep her voice even, her breathing steady so he wouldn't notice the effect he had on her.

"Everett Grimes needs to move a load of hay from his pole barn to the big barn behind his house. I promised I'd lend a hand. I thought Gracie—and you—might enjoy riding along."

Before she could stop them, her lips curved into a smile as memories of summer hayrides in the back of her uncle's truck surfaced. "She'd like that if..." She peered closely at Nate. "Has the hay been treated in any way? Pesticides? Poisons?"

"It's feed for his cattle, so no. It's perfectly safe. Speaking of which, we'll probably see some of Everett's cows. Gracie might even have a chance to pet one of them."

Riding around in the back of a truck with a load of hay was one thing. Brushing up against a cow was something else entirely. Who knew what diseases they harbored? "I don't think so." She started to move off, but Nate surprised her for the second time in five minutes when he caught her arm.

"I get that you're extra cautious with Gracie. Lord knows, I'd be, too, if I was—" Nate stopped to clear his throat.

"If you were...what?" Justine held her breath. Nate couldn't know, could he? Only her closest friends knew about Gracie's situation, and she wanted to keep it that way. She didn't want people to look at her daughter differently. To feel sorry for the poor little girl who needed a kidney transplant. Or worse, to mention it to Gracie. So far, her five-year-old didn't even know what a kidney was, much less that hers were in trouble. Part of her job in protecting her child was to keep that knowledge from Gracie as long as possible.

"If I had a daughter as sick as Gracie."

So much for keeping Gracie's condition a secret. Justine let her eyes narrow. "Who told you?" It had to have been either Penny or Sarah.

"No one. Not on purpose anyway." Nate scuffed one foot through the dirt. "Sarah and Penny didn't know I was close enough to overhear them when they were talking about it at the bonfire. I guess, from what they were saying, her father isn't in the picture."

"I tried to find him." Her ex was a world-class jerk, but even a jerk deserved to know he had a daughter. "He's a ghost."

The summer before law school, she'd treated herself to a sight-seeing tour of Italy where she'd been swept off her feet by Marco Abelli. The suave, sophisticated Italian had pursued her from one end of the country to the other, and by the time the tour ended in Rome, she'd convinced herself she was in love. When he popped the question at the top of the Gianicolo, she hadn't hesitated. Nor did she question it when Marco insisted on having his uncle perform the ceremony in front of the Trevi Fountain. The marriage had lasted all of two weeks before her wedding ring turned as green and ugly as her new husband's mood when his petition for an immigration visa was declared fraudulent and denied. Marco, it turned out, already had at least one other wife. His marriage to Justine was a sham. His lies exposed, he disappeared without a trace. Not quite seven months later, she'd given birth to Gracie and dropped out of law school. They'd been on their own ever since.

"You didn't deserve that any more than Gracie deserves to get sick," Nate said when she'd finished explaining. "She's the sweetest little girl I've ever met, but don't you ever get tired of being on guard all the time? It's got to wear you out."

"I do get tired. And frustrated. Sometimes, I take those frustrations out on a rug."

"Looked like you were doing a damn fine job of it. Look, I know it's not my place to tell you how to raise your child." Nate studied the grass that grew around his feet.

"But you're going to do it anyway," she said dryly.

"Nah. I wouldn't. I'll only ask you to consider this— what good does it do her if she lives to be a hundred, but she never gets to, you know, live? To taste an orange she picked fresh off a tree. To run around and play tag with her friends. To go on a hayride." Nate crossed his arms across his chest as if he'd said all he'd come to say.

Justine's shoulders slumped. How had Nate zeroed in on one of her biggest fears? "You're right. I know you're right," she said, conceding the point. "In my head, I get it. But when it comes down to the wire, I'm too afraid. Too scared that she'll get sick when I could have prevented it."

Astonishment showing in his gray-blue eyes, Nate's head came up. "They say knowing you have a problem is the first step in eliminating it. What if we do this? This time, we'll just go on the hayride. If we see cows, we'll wave to them. I'll make sure none of them get within touching distance. Do you trust me to do that?"

Surprised that she'd even consider trusting the man who'd sworn to fight her in court, she paused. Sure, she and Nate stood on opposite sides of an issue neither of them was willing—or could afford—to lose. But from the very beginning, he'd been honest with her. He'd told her from the start that he'd do everything in his power to overturn Uncle Jimmy's will. He'd explained exactly why he opposed the sale of Castle Grove to Fresh Picked. And when she'd burst in on him at the town council meeting, he'd defended her.

So, yes, she did trust him. And having said that, how could she say no? She couldn't, and nodding, she took a breath. "What time do we need to leave? I'll be sure and have Gracie ready."

If she'd expected Nate to gloat over his win, she was wrong. He merely named the time and said he'd see her later. As he moved off, she stared after him, wondering if she'd done the right thing by placing her daughter's fate in the enemy's hands.

"Wow! Look at that. I think you have a bite!" As much as he wanted to take the pole and help Gracie land the fish, Nate shoved his hands into the pockets of his jeans. Catching your first fish was something everyone—especially five-year-olds—needed to do on their own.

"I do?" Wonder filled Gracie's voice. Her tiny hands tightened their grip on the spinning reel. Ten feet from the shore, the red-and-white bobber dunked under the surface. It stayed down. The tip of the child-sized fishing rod bent toward the water. A pair of rosebud lips gaped open. "I do!"

"Yep. Now, reel the line in just like I showed you. Slow and steady. You don't want to pull the hook out of his mouth and let him get away." Especially not when, thinking of a certain little one's tender skin, Nate had carefully removed the barbs from the entire box of his best hooks.

"Get the camera ready, Mom," he called, more for Gracie's sake than Justine's. The willowy blonde had been snapping pictures of her daughter ever since they'd climbed out of his pickup truck twenty minutes earlier.

"Good job, Gracie!" Justine peeked out from behind the lens long enough to offer a word of encouragement. *Thank you,* she mouthed.

The curve of Justine's lips delivered a sucker punch straight into his middle. He hadn't actually recovered before Gracie clutched the handle on the reel and cranked it for all she was worth. Line spun. The bobber rose to the surface. Realizing he was being pulled in the wrong direction, the fish thrashed, a golden tail breaking the surface. Gracie screamed in delight, but kept reeling in, just as Nate had shown her.

246

"That's it, Gracie. You're doing great," he coached.

Seconds later, a small peacock bass flapped its amber-colored fins on the sandy bank.

"I caught it, Mr. Nate. I caught it!" Still holding her rod, Gracie jumped up and down. "Oh, look at all the pretty colors!" She pointed to the yellow-and-black stripes and orange belly. "Somebody used a lot of crayons on him."

"You did great, Gracie. It's a beauty." It was also an expensive fish, considering how much he'd paid to stock the small pond with dozens of peacock bass and dull-colored bream. He shrugged. The little girl's excitement was priceless, no matter what the cost. "Let's get a picture of you holding your fish. Then I'll show you how to put him back in the water."

"Can I, Mommy? Can I hold him?"

In answer, Justine lowered her camera and pinned him with a questioning gaze.

Mustering all the encouragement he had to offer, Nate shoved it into a confident smile. She didn't have to worry. They'd discussed this. Every fish Gracie caught today had been farm-raised and chosen especially for their lack of sharp spines and teeth. Still, he held his breath while Justine gave the fish a look that was at least one part apprehension before she swung back to him again. Her expression softened. She licked her lips and gave a quick nod.

"Of course!" she said at last. "You have to hold him. That's all part of the fun."

Nate puffed out a breath of air. Knowing how hard she was trying, he gave Justine a lot of credit. Every day, she grew a little more open to the idea of letting her daughter try new things, experience new activities. Gracie had bounced up and down on the hay bales, her excitement bubbling over, as they'd ridden through Everett's back forty. When that adventure had gone off without a hitch, the overprotective mom had agreed to another trip to the nearby farm, this time so Gracie could pet a cow. Not wanting to take any chances, Nate had snuck over to the neighbor's an hour or so before the scheduled visit. There, he'd treated one of the calves to a warm, soapy bath so the little girl could feed it a handful of hay and run her fingers through the young heifer's coat without giving her mom heart palpitations. When Justine had said she might be willing to take Gracie swimming in a spot that had once been one of their favorite haunts, he'd paid a visit to the pool of crystal-clear blue water fed by an artesian spring that ran deep into Florida's aquifer. Purer water wasn't to be found in the state, a fact he'd verified by having the water thoroughly tested at the ag center. Then, last week, the three of them had played tag in the grove, racing between the trees he'd brushed free of spider webs.

Now, with Justine throwing her support behind the idea of Gracie handling the fish, he hustled to the water's edge.

"Here you go, sweetheart," he said, picking up the wriggling peacock and placing it in her outstretched hands. "Don't squeeze too hard. We don't want to hurt him."

"He's slippy!" Gracie squealed with delight.

"Yep. He's slippery." Moving quickly, he positioned the fish in her hands. "Hold him out, so your mom can take your picture."

Justine dropped down on her knees for a better angle. As the fish wriggled, he hovered within arm's reach, ready to assist if anything went wrong. Which, he was reasonably certain, wouldn't happen.

Hadn't he taken every precaution? In preparation for today's outing, he'd waded into the water last week armed with heavy-duty plastic sheets and sturdy wooden posts. It had taken an entire afternoon of sloshing around in the mud and the muck, but the underwater fence he'd erected had discouraged the gators from entering their little corner of the pond. This morning, he'd scoured the entire area for wildlife, finding—and relocating—two grass snakes and a large snapping turtle. As for bait, he'd driven straight passed the shop where he normally bought worms. Instead, he'd invested in brightly colored, plastic lures that had delighted Gracie almost as much as her very own fishing rod and reel.

Had it been worth the effort?

If Gracie got any happier, she'd probably burst. As for Justine, she was no longer a bundle of nerves. No longer hovering over her daughter as if a single germ could lead to disaster. Seeing the woman he'd once loved relaxed and enjoying herself made his hours of preparation well worth the effort.

"Now that we have lots of pictures, let's put the fish back in the pond where he can grow up to be big and strong." With the tiny fish cupped in Gracie's hands, they swished it back and forth through the water. "Okay, let him go."

Gracie did as she'd been told, and in a flash of color, the peacock aimed for the slightly deeper water near the fence and disappeared. In deference to Justine, Nate whipped a hand wipe out of his back pocket and scoured two pairs of hands.

"Mommy, my fish swimmed off." Gracie dashed to the rod that lay on the beach. "I'm going to catch another one. This one will be hu-u-ge," she announced.

When Nate bent to help her with the artificial bait, she shouldered him aside. "I want to do it all by myself."

Adjusting the visor she wore over her ponytail, Justine gave him a knowing look. "See what I have to put up with?"

"Like mother, like daughter." Relegated to the sidelines by her daughter, Nate moved closer to the only woman who'd ever bent his thoughts toward home and family. Between the hayrides and playing in the grove and fishing, Gracie was having the time of her life, while he'd gotten used to carrying antiseptic wipes and Band-Aids wherever he went.

And Justine? He hoped—prayed, even—that she, too, was rediscovering all the things she'd enjoyed about Castle Grove when she was a kid.

"What are you talking about? I was never as bossy as she is."

He felt rather than saw her staring up at him and coughed to cover a laugh. "Sure you were. Don't you remember the time you insisted on digging for your own worms and found that nest of baby moccasins? You were going to use them for bait till I stopped you."

Justine cupped one hand over her mouth, her lips twitching as memories of that day danced in her eyes. "Those weren't snakes. You were jealous because I found more worms than you did. If I remember right, I caught the biggest fish that day, too."

"Right before you fell into the pond."

"When you pushed me." Justine bumped her slim hip against his.

"I did not," he argued, though they both knew he had. A grin started in the center of his chest and worked its way up and out until it spread across his face. There'd always been a bunch of other kids around, but he and Justine had been in competition with each other from the first day they'd met. Now, standing so close his thigh brushed against hers, it felt only right to slip his hand around her waist. When Justine made no effort to move away, when she, in fact, leaned a smidge closer, he nodded to the little girl who intently watched her bobber float in the water. "Next time we bring her out here, we'll bring a couple of her friends so they all can build their own memories of this place."

"We did have some good times, didn't we?" she asked, her voice wistful. "I'll always be grateful to Aunt Margaret and Uncle Jimmy for those summers. Sarah and Penny have been the best friends I could ever ask for."

Nate angled his head down until his chin brushed her hair. Drinking in the floral scent of her shampoo, he whispered, "I'd like to think you consider me a friend, too." At Justine's nod, he let go of a breath he hadn't realized he'd been holding.

"You deserve a special thanks for all you've done for Gracie these past few weeks."

She tipped her head, giving him a look that warmed him all the way to his toes. At his side, she stirred. Later, when he had time to think about it, he supposed she'd meant to peck his cheek, the way good friends rewarded each other with a warm embrace. He would never be certain, though, because in the instant before her lips met his jaw, he lowered his chin. Whatever she'd intended became something more when their lips met...and refused to part. As if they had a mind of their own, his arms wrapped around her. From Justine's firm breasts, to the angular planes of her ribs, to the bony outcropping of her hips, her body melded against his.

He drew her closer. The tip of his tongue traced the seam of lips that were at once both familiar and strange, firm and yielding. Justine's lips parted with the sigh of a traveler who'd just returned home after a long journey.

Her soft moan was all the invitation he needed. He pressed closer, exploring the warm recesses of her mouth while he traced the outlines of her curves. He caught a hint of bitter coffee mingled with the salty sweetness of the peanut butter and jelly sandwiches they'd had for lunch. The jasmine and gardenia in her cologne tickled his nose.

He groaned. His heart pounded against his chest. The urge to possess her built within him.

"Mommy, Mr. Nate. I caught another fish. All on my own. Look!"

An instant later, the hand that had cupped Justine's breast hovered in empty air. The tongue that had dueled with his had withdrawn and was firmly locked behind lips that no longer pressed against his. The body that had leaned insistently against him had turned away, leaving him aching and alone.

Okay, he admitted, he might have had more than Gracie in mind when he'd invited Justine and her daughter on the hayride or proposed a long walk through the orange groves as the sun set and dust motes floated in the air. There was a part of him— maybe a large part—that hoped every outing, every adventure might rekindle the love Justine had once felt for Castle Grove. That somehow, by doing the things they'd enjoyed doing as children, she'd fall so deeply in love with the land that selling her uncle's grove to complete strangers would be unthinkable.

To a certain extent, he'd succeeded. Every day, Justine seemed more relaxed in her new home. Lately, she'd taken to wandering out onto the front porch to drink her coffee in the mornings. But therein lay the problem. Because, while Justine enjoyed the stillness of the day, the peace and quiet of the grove, while she watched birds flit among the treetops and listened to their early morning songs, he enjoyed watching...her.

The more Justine fell in love with Castle Grove, the harder it became for him to deny the fact that he was falling for her, too. Which, as problems went, was a biggie. Yes, Justine was his onetime forever love. But she was also the girl who'd walked out on him. The one who'd stayed away for ten years. The woman threatened everything he'd spent his life working for.

He should hate her. Should, at the very least, stay away from her. Because there was absolutely no future for him with a woman bent on stealing the land out from under his feet.

Justine gathered empty boxes from the back porch and lined them up in the dining room. Ever since she'd come to Castle Grove, she'd been finding one excuse after another to avoid cleaning out her uncle's office. At first, it had been easy to blame the bugs and spiders hidden behind the closed door. After all, critters with six to eight legs did give her a mild case of the heebie-jeebies. But two bug bombs and a heavy application of peppermint oil had eradicated the critters. Still not up to the task of sorting and organizing, she'd used her job as an excuse. Working for Royce—though far from stressful—did eat up a large chunk of her daylight hours. She devoted late afternoons and evenings to Gracie.

Today, though, was Columbus Day, and the attorney's office had closed for the legal holiday. Schools, however, had not. And with Gracie going home with SueEllen for a play date, she had one entire day to sort through the office and find the proof she needed to support her claim to Castle Grove.

When she got right down to it, wasn't that the main reason she'd been dragging her heels in opening the door on what was left of Uncle Jimmy's life? Because once she had what she'd come for, once she proved that hers was the only valid claim to Castle Grove, her job here would be done. Over. Finis. As soon as Mary Beth was able to return to work for Royce, she'd be able to pack up Gracie and head back to Virginia, leaving the estate to sail through the rest of the probate process without her.

Wasn't that still what she wanted?

Her certainty waivered. The time she'd spent in Orange Blossom had been far more than she'd bargained for. The slower pace of small-town life had been a pleasant break from the hustle and bustle of life in the nation's capital. Her work for Royce had given her the chance to get to know the few clients who stopped by his office. Then, there was her renewed friendship with Sarah. To be honest, her relationship with Nate tempted her to stay on far more than it should, as well.

Still, she had to do whatever it took to ensure Gracie's future. And cleaning out her uncle's office was the next step in that journey.

You can do this.

Steeling herself against anything that might move, jump or scurry across the floor, she steadied her hand and opened the door. Perhaps the dust had grown a tiny bit deeper on the piles of books and papers that littered the small space. The floor might be a little bit grittier. Otherwise, nothing, not even a breath of air, stirred. Relief sent a shiver down her spine despite the warm October weather.

Armed with a broom and a dustpan, she made her

first foray into the office. The spider that not so long ago had sent her and Sarah screaming into the hall lay, eight bent legs up, behind the flowerpot. She dispatched it to the burn pile, along with the desiccated carcasses of roaches and other insects.

With that chore handled, she stood at the door and took stock. Evidence of a life that had veered slightly off the rails at the end showed in every stack of books, every out-of-place tool. Papers spilled haphazardly from the filing cabinet. A jumble of mail, magazines and who knew what else covered every inch of the desk. Where should she begin? The proof that Uncle Jimmy had changed his mind about leaving Castle Grove to Nate could be hidden anywhere in the room.

Nate.

She clenched her teeth. As much as she resisted it, just thinking of the boy she'd once loved—and the man he'd become—made her go weak at the knees. She pressed the back of her fist against her lips. As a teen, Nate had been a good kisser. As a grown man, he had skills. The velvety press of his tongue against hers when they'd kissed at the fishing hole had stirred desires she hadn't felt in so long, she'd nearly forgotten they even existed. He must have felt the same way, because over the course of the next three weeks, they'd taken advantage of every chance to be alone whenever Gracie wasn't looking.

Every single time, she told herself she shouldn't give in, shouldn't want Nate, shouldn't need him the way she did. Yet she was powerless to resist him. Whenever she saw him, she told herself that this would be the time she wouldn't succumb to Nate's charms, she wouldn't let him take her in his arms, she wouldn't press her lips to his or savor his touch until they were both panting and on the verge of something more.

And each time, she failed.

Maybe she could have resisted if her reaction had merely been physical. But whenever Nate held her, the world and all its troubles faded away. For a brief moment, she forgot that she'd let herself be taken in by a married man and had been forced to drop out of law school. She escaped the grueling life of a single mom. She nearly forgot that she had a seriously ill child. Whenever Nate's lips met hers, when their mouths melded while his hands drew her closer, in those moments, nothing else mattered but sending her tongue running across the smooth edges of his teeth, inhaling the woodsy, citrus smell that belonged only to him.

She was both stronger and weaker when they were apart. When Nate wasn't around, she sternly reminded herself of all the reasons they were wrong for each other. That things between them could never go any further than a kiss or two.

She dumped the lifeless plant into a large, plastic garbage bag. The empty vase went into a box destined for the sharing center. Jimmy's boots landed in the box beside it. His tools went into a pile for the garage.

If only she could get Nate out of her head as easily as she cleaned out her uncle's office. Being with him could only lead to heartbreak, but the more time they spent together, the more her heart begged her to consider a future with Nate in it.

What would happen if she was able to prove that Uncle Jimmy had reneged on his promise?

Nate was a reasonable man, a fair man. Eventually, he'd accept that she'd had nothing to do with her uncle's actions. He wouldn't blame her, would he?

As she cleaned and sorted and put things to rights, the idea that she and Nate might work things out rippled through her. Her imagination stirred. By the time she checked her watch, she was shocked to see how much of the day had passed while she worked and dreamed of a future with Nate. Taking a break, she surveyed all she'd accomplished. Three sturdy cardboard boxes overflowed with outdated bills, flyers and expired credit card offers. Another box held assorted tools and equipment slated for the barn or garage. At one point, she'd uncovered the remains of a long-forgotten dinner on a moldy plate. She'd promptly upended it into a bulging garbage bag.

By the time she finished clearing out the clutter, papers and cardboard boxes threatened to overflow the burn pile in the back yard. She tossed a final load into the drum and dusted her hands. With Nate out of town for the night, she decided to wait for his return before she started the fire. The recycling, though, that she could handle on her own and loaded it into the back of Jimmy's truck. She'd drop it off in one of the industrial-sized recycling bins behind the town hall on her way to pick up Gracie.

Returning to the office, she grabbed a can of furniture polish and treated the desk to a heavy spray. A vigorous rubbing erased what was left of the dirt and brought out the patina of the old wood. She smiled at the small red vase she'd placed on one corner of the desk. Gracie would enjoy gathering wildflowers to fill it before supper this evening.

Pleased with the progress she'd made, Justine tightened her ponytail. Not that she was anywhere near finished. There was still a lot left to do. Wondering what her uncle had stored in his desk, she tugged on one drawer and discovered a handful of cheap ballpoint pens and stubby pencils in the space above the knee hole. Bulging file folders filled the drawer beside it. Curious, she thumbed through a few. Nestled among manila folders bearing labels like *Warranties* and *Seeds*, a bright orange sleeve stood out like a stock of corn in Aunt Margaret's bean patch. She tugged it free and stared at Nate's name written in Uncle Jimmy's handwriting.

Is this the proof I need?

Her heart thumped. It couldn't be that easy, could it? Her fingers crossed, she opened the sturdy cardboard. Inside lay nearly a dozen cocktail napkins from The Crush on top of what looked like a pile of sales receipts. Perplexed, she lifted one of the napkins from the small stack and studied it.

A black felt-tip pen had snagged the soft paper. Beverage rings blurred some of the ink. A smear of unknown origin covered one corner, but last February's date was clearly legible, as was James C. Castle's signature scrawled across the bottom.

"Another ten," she read between the stains, while her stomach dropped like a stone thrown into a deep well.

Gently, she sifted through the rest of the napkins. All came from The Crush. All bore dates that corresponded with the end of the citrus harvest. All held some version of the same cryptic message. Official-looking receipts lay at the bottom of the stack. Here, Jimmy had taken more time, spelling out that the sum of ten acres of Castle Grove property was to be transferred to Nate as payment for what Jimmy called *services rendered*.

Feeling as if she might throw up, Justine paired napkins with receipts and added up the acreage. The total came to nearly half of Castle Grove. Hoping she was dreaming, she rubbed her eyes. When she opened them again, the proof was still spread out in front of her.

Since the day she'd wandered through the orange grove to find Nate, he'd consistently sworn he'd paid for a large portion of Castle Grove with sweat equity. Now, the indisputable proof of his claim lay before her. Her stomach tightened into a hard ball. It stood to reason that if Nate had been telling the truth about earning his ten acres each year, he'd been telling the truth about the rest, too. She had to face the fact that her uncle had planned to change his will and leave his estate to Nate instead of her.

Her heart sank. She'd wanted proof, hadn't she? Well, she'd found it, all right. Proof beyond a shadow of a doubt written in her uncle's scribbled notes on a dozen cocktail napkins.

Feeling as if she'd aged a hundred years in the past hour, she cupped her head in her hands. She'd been wrong to think that she and Nate could ever have a future together. That had been a pipe dream. No matter how fond Nate was of Gracie, he'd never part with his land, his inheritance. Not for her. As he'd said time and time again, he had the entire town of Orange Blossom to consider. He had to do right by them. As Castle Grove's rightful heir, now he could.

But where did that leave her?

There was nothing else to do but move forward. Do what was best for Gracie. She supposed that meant going back to Virginia without the one thing she'd come to Florida to get.

Heartbreak loomed in every direction. Her mouth went so dry it hurt to breathe. Tears stung her eyes. She automatically reached for one of the napkins, then stopped. It'd be easy, so easy, to destroy the folder, to stick it on the burn pile and light a match. But, no. The truth about what she'd done would be like a cancer, eating its way through her, destroying her from the inside out.

What good would she be to Gracie then?

Before she could chicken out, she tugged her cell phone from her back pocket and snapped pictures of each of the napkins and their corresponding receipts. Then, tucking her phone in her back pocket, she trudged out the door. Uncertainty gnawed at her. She shoved it away, her feet automatically aiming for the one person in Orange Blossom she trusted to help her do the right thing.

A blender whirred from somewhere deep in the recesses of the house Sarah shared with her mother and grandmother. Standing on the stoop outside the front door, Justine tapped her foot. "Sarah," she called the instant the motor stopped humming.

"Justine?" Drifting from the back of the house, Sarah's voice carried a lilting curiosity.

"Yeah, it's me." Justine raised her voice. "You have a minute to talk?" She shifted her weight from one foot to the other. She should have called. Or gone to Royce's by herself. Or buried Jimmy's notes under the old magnolia tree in the backyard, alone, in the dead of night.

On the other side of the screen, the sounds of someone rushing across hardwood floors grew louder. Seconds later, Sarah's petite figure emerged from the darkened interior of the house.

Too late now. She couldn't run if she wanted to. Her courage wavered. "Hey," she managed.

"Is everything okay? Gracie's not sick, is she?" Flipping the hook on an old-fashioned latch that wouldn't stop a determined eight-year-old, much less a burglar, Sarah ushered her inside.

"Gracie's fine. She's going over to Mandy's for a playdate after school. It's me who's a mess." Justine drew in a thready breath.

"Whatever's wrong, we'll fix it." Sarah's slim arms wrapped her in a warm hug.

"We can try, but I don't think anyone can fix this." Blinking, she fought back tears. She'd looked at the situation from every angle. Every possible solution broke her heart in one way or another.

"Sounds serious." Sarah gave her a final squeeze and, turning, linked their arms together. "Come on into the kitchen where we can talk. You want tea? Coffee? Maybe something to eat? How 'bout a slice of pound cake?"

In spite of herself, Justine grinned. It was just like Sarah to think that every problem could be resolved over dessert. "Coffee, thanks. I'll skip the pound cake...for now."

While Sarah went to fill two cups from an ancient percolator, Justine paused at the threshold of the cramped kitchen where the heady blend of sweet and savory floated in the air. And no wonder. Beneath cabinets hung from the ceiling, fruits and vegetables in various states of preparation littered the surface of a narrow island. Newer than every other appliance by at least a decade, the sleek blender in the middle of the pile looked slightly alien and as out of place as a professional chef in a kitchen that needed a major update. She swung toward Sarah. "You're cooking...here?"

"Not cooking, exactly. Juicing. I was fixing Mom a batch of smoothies." Sarah sighed. "The treatments are taking a lot out of her. Here." Lowering a mug of coffee to the counter, she cleared a space with the back of one hand. "Sit down and tell me what's going on."

Justine eased onto one of the high-backed rattan stools. Proud that her hands trembled only a little bit, she withdrew a slim folder from her shoulder bag. "I found these in Uncle Jimmy's desk drawer."

Sarah lifted the cover and frowned at the page on top. Wonder gathered in her blue eyes. "Are you serious?" She shot a brief glance across the counter at Justine before Jimmy's notes claimed her attention again. Stirring a finger through the thin sheets, she asked, "Are these what I think they are?"

"If you think they prove Uncle Jimmy meant to give Castle Grove to Nate, then yeah."

"Whoa." Sarah sank onto a chair on the opposite side of the island. Idly, she swirled a spoon through her coffee. "This changes everything. No wonder you're upset." As if she needed to gather her thoughts, she lifted a banana from the pile. Peeling it slowly, she asked, "What are you going to do with them?"

Justine breathed deeply. "I should have destroyed them."

"You didn't, though."

"As tempted as I was, no." Every time she considered it, she recalled the day Nate asked her what good it would do to save Gracie's life if her daughter never had the chance to really live. Still unable to answer that question, she took a sip of coffee that had spent far too long in a heated metal container. "Jeez. How do you drink this stuff?"

Sarah took a swig and wiggled her eyebrows. "Gotta love Gram's coffee."

Justine pushed her cup aside. "Fresh Picked's offer is still on the table. They had a courier deliver a revised contract to me this morning." She closed the folder. "I have to decide what to do about it...and Nate."

Sarah stood, grabbed the blender and set it on the counter next to the fridge. "Penny's going to want to weigh in on this. Get my laptop from the end table in the living room, will you?"

By the time Justine returned with the computer, her friend was swiftly dipping chunks of apples and carrots into lemon juice and tossing them in a bowl.

"I didn't mean for you to stop working," she protested.

Sarah wiped her hands on a dishrag and pitched it into the sink. "I'm probably wasting my time anyway. Mom just turns her nose up at whatever I fix and goes right back to living on potatoes and cookies. Sometimes I wonder why I even bother." She rolled her shoulders and leaned over the computer. "Enough about me," she said, clicking keys.

Minutes later, Penny's complexion paled on the computer screen as they brought her up to speed on the latest developments. "Fresh Picked will bury Nate," she cautioned. "You know that, don't you, Jus?"

Her lips trembled as the truth sank its claws a little deeper into her heart. Castle Grove had never belonged to her. Selling the land to secure her daughter's future had been nothing but a pipe dream. "Yeah. I know. I have to turn the papers over to Royce and tell Fresh Picked to take a flying leap. I don't think I'm strong enough to do it on my own, though."

Penny, ever logical, nodded. "That's easy enough to fix. Sarah, you'll go with her to Royce's, won't you?"

"You bet." Sarah gave her hand a squeeze. "Any time you're ready."

"Right after we finish here." Justine gave a tremulous smile. "Before I lose my nerve." With the notes as proof, half of Castle Grove would pass to Nate. He'd said Uncle Jimmy promised him the rest, and she'd see that request honored, even though it would leave her with nothing.

"Then what?" Penny asked.

She shook her head. "Frankly, I wish Royce had never gotten in touch with me." A few months ago, she'd had a modest savings account, a steady job and a roof over her and Gracie's head. Yes, she'd also had a pile of bills and a daughter who faced an uncertain future, but at least they'd had a little stability. And her heart had been intact.

"Don't say that," Sarah scolded. "Gracie has blossomed since you came here. She has friends. She's excelling in her schoolwork. You've changed, too. You've lost that frantic edge you had."

"Nate deserves most of the credit," Justine admitted. He'd helped her see that she couldn't control every aspect of Gracie's life, that sometimes she just had to let go.

"Well, I love having you around," Sarah said. "It reminds me of when we were kids. Orange Blossom will always be our home."

"That's just it. I don't think it will be." Justine massaged her forehead. "The money I was going to make from the sale of Castle Grove was supposed to wipe out my debts and provide for Gracie's future. With that out of the picture, I need a job. Oh, and a place to live, since I can't stay where I am."

"You don't think Nate'll kick you out, do you?" Sarah's jaw practically unhinged. "I don't believe that. You can't tell me you don't have feelings for each other. You're good together, and he's wild about Gracie."

Her headache tightened the band that circled her head. She'd spent two months falling in love with Nate, but it was over now. She'd risked her heart on a second-chance romance that wasn't going anywhere. "Castle Grove will always stand between Nate and me building a future together."

"Nate's not like that."

"Not now, maybe, but in time he'll start to wonder if I love him, or if I simply stayed with him to get what I want." She refused to put Nate through the months of self-doubt she'd endured after Marco's betrayal. "Plus, I have to think about Gracie."

On the screen, Penny's lips moved. A split second later, her voice rose from the speakers. "Like, if something happens to Gracie later on, you'd blame Nate."

Would I?

If she'd been anywhere else, with anyone else, she might have offered bland reassurances that, of course, she would never blame the man she loved. But Penny and Sarah were more than friends, closer than sisters. For nearly two decades—since they were youngsters— they'd kept each other's secrets. If she couldn't be honest with them, she had no one.

"I'd try not to. I wouldn't want to. But I don't think I'd ever be able to get past the fact that, when he had to choose between Gracie and Orange Blossom, he chose the town."

Sarah's expression fell as she grasped the inevitable truth. "You're going to leave."

"I don't see any other way. I can't stay here. Mary Beth will be back to work in a couple of weeks. Royce can manage on his own till then." Justine wiped her eyes. Her voice thinned. "Nate deserves happiness. But I can't watch him move on, find someone new and settle down. That'd be torture."

"I hear you," Penny said softly.

Sarah darted from the room. She returned quickly with a box of tissues. Handing one to Justine, she asked, "So what will you do?"

"I don't have a lot of options. Jacoby & Sons won't take me back." She'd loved the life she was building in Orange Blossom so much that she hadn't given the matter much thought when her leave of absence ran out. "Still, I stand a better chance of landing a job in Virginia than I do here. I hate to uproot Gracie again, but I have to go where I can find work and have a place to live. That's"—she nodded at the screen—"unless Penny rented out my room already."

"About that..." Penny frowned.

"What?" What else could go wrong?

"You gotta understand. I thought you were staying in Orange Blossom permanently. Otherwise, I might not have considered it. But it's too late to change things now."

Justine leaned closer to the monitor. "What did you do, Penny?" She watched her friend's mouth move, dreading the moment when the sound caught up.

"Coming down there in August only made me realize how much I miss Orange Blossom, miss the people there. I've talked with Dad. He wants to retire in a few years and has asked me to come home, help him out with the bookstore, learn the ropes."

"And?" Sarah prompted.

"And I've already given my notice at the library. You're welcome to stay here till my lease runs out, but after that…"

Penny's voice faded while Justine's stomach dropped like a stone in a well. She'd risked everything in coming to Orange Blossom, and what did she have to show for it? Nothing—not Nate, not Castle Grove, not even a small apartment in a run-down complex in the DC suburbs. Yet, she couldn't let her own troubles ruin things for her friend. She pasted a smile over her fears. "That's great, Penny. I'm happy for you."

"Me, too!" Her head swinging away from the screen, Sarah narrowed in on Justine. "What will you do?"

She shrugged. "Move forward and hope for the best. If that doesn't work, Gracie and I can go live with my mom and her new husband in Phoenix, I guess."

As if they'd practiced it, Penny and Sarah spoke at the same time. "That's too far away!"

"It'd only be a last resort." But the way her life was going, it might well come to that. "For now, we'll take it one step at a time. First step, I need to deliver these papers to Royce. Then, we'll call Fresh Picked and tell them the deal is off the table." She slipped the folder into her purse. "And then, I'll go to Castle Grove and pack, I guess. There's no sense in sticking around here any longer." Turning to Sarah, she asked, "Will you come with me? Make sure I don't chicken out?"

Sarah glanced at the towering bowl filled with cut fruit and vegetables. "Give me ten minutes to finish here and another five to change clothes, and you're on." She tossed a handful of the prepped food into the blender. "I can't stand to throw all this away, even if I'm probably wasting my time and money."

Justine nodded. "There's been a lot of that going around." Facing the computer screen once more, she looked past her own heartbreak to congratulate her friend on what had to have been a tough decision. "I'm glad you're coming home, Penny."

She swallowed a sob. "You'll love it here."

"Sounds like you're telling me I've led a dull and boring life." Nate leafed through the results of two intense days of medical tests, exams and lab work. Meaningless numbers filled long columns that stretched from a long list of foreign-sounding words. He threaded his fingers through his hair. Having a friend to walk him through the medical jargon nearly made up for all the nights his former roommate had kept the lights blazing while he studied.

"No. What I'm saying is, you've somehow managed to avoid the nasty germs and viruses most of the rest of us catch somewhere along the way." Even, white teeth flashed in Victor Spears's wide smile. "You're in excellent health, according to these results. Your blood is squeaky clean. Big plus, you're O-neg. That makes you a universal donor."

"I can donate a kidney to Gracie?" A sense of awe filled him.

"I wouldn't go quite that far. Let's say nothing in your blood work rules you out." Behind a spotless desk, Victor leaned forward in his office chair. "When the time comes, her doctors will want to do further testing."

"But maybe."

"Yeah, a definite maybe."

That was a whole lot better than an outright no, wasn't it?

"You'll want to think long and hard about this before you rush into making a commitment." Victor's smile melted into a concerned flat line. "Donating a kidney is no walk in the park. Besides the usual risks that accompany any major surgery, you'd need to pay a little more attention to your health for the rest of your life."

"You mean, I'd have to give up my dream of playing professional football? That might be a deal breaker." He'd meant the question in jest, but Victor evidently didn't see the humor.

"As a matter of fact, I'd recommend avoiding contact sports."

"Not to worry." He'd scoured the National Kidney Foundation's website and knew the score. "The only hockey I play is air hockey. Besides, who knows what will happen between now and then?" By the time Gracie's health deteriorated to the point where a transplant was necessary, most of the citizens of Orange Blossom would probably line up around the block to help her. None of them would be the first, though. Thanks to Victor's help, that privilege would always be his.

"I appreciate you running the tests for me and all. What do I owe you?" Whatever the cost, he'd gladly pay it.

"I can't waive the lab fees. That's a different

department. They'll send you a bill. As for the office visit, no charge. Although, if you have a good harvest, I wouldn't turn down a few navels and some grapefruit."

"You got it." Nate made a mental note to select the cream of the crop for his friend. He folded the lab report into fourths and stuck it in his back pocket. Their business concluded, he rose. "What say we grab some lunch together before I head back to Orange Blossom? My treat."

"Much as I'd like to, I'm on call and can't leave the building. Next time."

"Yeah, next time." He shook his friend's hand.

Whistling, Nate headed out. Exiting the building, he wondered what it would be like to know that a piece of himself had saved Justine's little girl from months, even years, of dialysis. He rubbed his lower back. Despite the nonchalant air he'd adopted with Victor, he had his doubts. What thinking man wouldn't? But how could he deny Gracie a chance at a normal, or nearly normal, life?

He couldn't. That's all there was to it.

After two nights away from home, he made the forty-mile trip from Ocala to Orange Blossom in record time. At the end of Castle Grove's long driveway, he spotted Jimmy's old pickup parked in its usual spot in the shade. Anxious to share his news with Justine as soon as possible, he detoured away from his own house.

The banister at the top of the stairs wobbled a bit as he mounted the wooden steps to the porch two at a time. Nate paused to prod the railing with his pocketknife. Rotted wood crumpled at his touch, and he tut-tutted. What was left of the railing had weakened since the last time he'd checked it. It'd have to go. While he was at it, he might as well pull out the warped floorboards and replace them. He propped one hand on his hip and stepped back to give the whole house a good look. The place sure could use a paint job, he thought, and mentally added the projects to a growing list of chores he'd tackle once the busy harvest season was behind him.

"Justine? Gracie?" He banged on the front door of Uncle Jimmy's house. He waited a beat, tried the knob. Unlocked, it turned easily in his hand. He eased the door open a crack and called again. "Justine? Gracie?"

His voice only echoed through a house that felt too empty. Where was everyone? Had something happened to Gracie?

His mouth went dry. If the child had fallen or wandered off or gotten hurt in any way... Stepping farther into the room, he called again.

Silence.

He glanced into the parlor where, in deference to slightly cooler temperatures, the air conditioner had been turned off, the windows opened to catch the breeze. Other than that, not so much as a throw pillow appeared out of place. Where were the crayons and coloring books that usually littered the floor? The dolls Gracie normally lined up on the couch?

On the other side of the dining room, the door to Jimmy's office stood ajar. Nate pushed slightly on it, his eyes widening as he stared at a room that had undergone a serious transition since he'd last stepped across the threshold. The clutter and dirt had been banished. Neatly arranged books had replaced the tools and equipment Jimmy had stored on bookcase shelves. Instead of piles of circulars and catalogs, a vase filled with wildflowers stood guard over two neat piles of papers on the desk. His gaze landed on the folder that held Gracie's medical records. It was far too thick for a child, and he swallowed against the taste of bile that clogged his throat. Propping his hands on the desk, he leaned forward, letting his arms bear his weight.

On the other side of the desk, the pages on top of a stack of important-looking documents rustled in time to an old-fashioned rotating fan. He reached for the off switch just as the paper on top lifted and went skittering. He snagged the errant page. An uneasy feeling stirred in the pit of his stomach as he slid it on top of others that bore the Fresh Picked logo.

Was Justine still talking with the juicing conglomerate?

A sense of betrayal unfurled low in his stomach. He shook his head at it. Justine wouldn't go behind his back and cut a deal with Fresh Picked. Though they hadn't discussed the conglomerate's offer in a while, he knew as sure as he was standing in Jimmy's office that she'd fallen in love with Castle Grove, with Orange Blossom, with him.

And yet...

His brow puckered as he skimmed over a cover letter offering new assurances that Fresh Picked was willing to overlook his own claim on Castle Grove. He swallowed, hard. Once Fresh Picked had legal standing in any fight for the grove, the big company would outspend, outmaneuver him every day of the week and twice on Sunday. And the funny thing was, it didn't matter what the courts decided because, in the years it would take some judge to hand down a decision, Castle Grove would die. Without someone to weed or mow, thick kudzu vine would creep beyond the fences to strangle the trees. Without routine maintenance, the irrigation system would fail. Without water, the citrus would shrivel in the summer sun or freeze in the next cold snap. In the end, Fresh Picked would get exactly what it wanted all along—two hundred empty acres.

He ran a hand through his hair and thumbed to the end of the stack. Relief whispered through him as he stared down at the blank lines on the signature page. Justine hadn't signed the contract. He told himself she never would and smiled as the idea wrapped around his heart.

The woman he loved faced an impossible choice, but together, they'd figure things out. Especially now that he had information that could change everything. All he had to do was find Justine and reassure her that she had other options besides selling out to Fresh Picked—she had him.

By the time he reached the back of the house, though, emptiness pressed down around him. In the hallway outside the one air-conditioned bedroom, he paused hoping for the sound of girlish laughter, the soft murmur of a mother's voice. Nothing broke the silence. Not even the low buzz of the air conditioner. When no one answered his knock, he gave the doorknob a quick spin and pushed his way into the room Justine and Gracie shared.

Like soldiers standing at attention, suitcases stood beside the bed. The door to the small closet stood open, empty hangers still and silent on the rod. The drawers had been pulled halfway out of the dresser and left as empty as his heart.

He was too late.

Earlier, he'd fought off a sense of betrayal by reminding himself that Justine loved him, loved Castle Grove. Now, he had no choice but to accept the proof that stood before him. Justine had made up her mind. She had decided to take Fresh Picked up on their offer. She was leaving.

He told himself he shouldn't be surprised. That the sharp pruning knife shouldn't cut so deeply into his heart. Justine had left him before, hadn't she?

His cell phone issued a harsh bleat that reminded him of the town council meeting this afternoon. Fumbling for the device at his hip, he ignored the dozens of messages that scrolled across the screen. He thumbed the ringer off. Whoever wanted to reach him could wait. He had to get out of the house, get outside where he could breathe.

Mechanically placing one foot in front of the other, he made it to the front porch where he collapsed onto the swing. Everything was gone. The woman of his dreams. The daughter he'd come to think of as his own. The land he'd given his life's blood to preserve. He'd lost it all to a woman who'd gone behind his back and planned to sell out to the highest bidder.

Nate leaned his head against the back brace and howled.

"Do you have my special orange, Mommy?"

Walking through the grove, Justine hefted the sack Gracie had insisted on filling with fruit for Aunt Penny. Her daughter had polished one of the oranges with the hem of her shirt. The bright navel practically sparkled in the autumn sun. "Yep. It's right where you put it. Right on top."

Gracie ducked under a low-hanging tree branch. She squeezed her own orange and sucked at the hole Justine had cut in the thick skin. Juice dribbled off the little girl's chin. "Mr. Nate was right. The oranges did change colors. They taste better, too. Mine is soooo sweet. We need more of them." Nearing the edge of the grove, she stopped to study the citrus trees where plump orange balls hung like Christmas tree decorations.

Justine corralled the little girl before she could pick them. "We probably ought to leave a few for Mr. Nate." She reached for a hand wipe, thought better of it, and relaxed. There was plenty of time to get Gracie cleaned up before Sarah came to see them off.

"Mr. Nate says people are coming soon to pick all the oranges and load them into big trucks. Can I stay home from school that day, Mommy? I want to see the big trucks."

Determined to make her daughter's last day at Castle Grove a memorable one, Justine kept her smile firmly in place. She probably ought to tell Gracie the truth, she thought. But she dared not say a word. If she tried to explain that they were leaving Castle Grove for good, the tears she'd held at bay would overflow the dam she'd erected to restrain them. For now, it was better that Gracie think they were simply going to pay Aunt Penny a visit. Once they settled into their old apartment, their old lives, there'd be plenty of time for explanations. Though Justine had no idea how she'd ever tell her daughter that they'd never see Mr. Nate again.

"Look, Mommy!" Gracie cried as they stepped from the last row of trees into the sunlight. "It's Mr. Nate."

Speak of the devil.

Justine shook out of her reverie. Sure enough, a familiar long, lean figure slowly rocked back and forth on the porch swing. Her heart skipped a beat. *Nate.* For a half second she allowed herself to dream of the future she'd longed to share with him. Of taking their coffee out onto the porch where they'd sit and watch the sun rise. Of the brother or sister they might give Gracie, and the early morning rush that went along with getting children and adults out the door to school and work. Of the nights she and Nate would spend wrapped in each other's arms.

Her breath caught, and she gave her head a tiny shake. No matter how much she wanted to spend her life with Nate, no matter how much she loved him, they had no future. In order for them to find happiness together, one of them had to sacrifice the one thing that was most precious to them. The resentment that went hand-in-hand with that decision would eventually destroy their love. With their own personal Swords of Damocles hanging over their heads, staying around would only be asking for more heartache.

She had no choice. She had to leave. And leave now, while she still had the courage.

Hustling to keep pace with Gracie, Justine neared the steps that led to the porch as Nate stood. Above a stark white T-shirt, his features darkened.

"I see your bags are packed. Going somewhere?" he asked, his voice bland and unfeeling.

Justine's footsteps faltered. The question was not what she'd expected, and she hiked an eyebrow. She'd wanted to reach Nate, to explain her decision. Had tried to speak with him, but he'd been out of town for the past two days. Her messages had gone straight to his voice mail. He hadn't returned any of her calls.

"I guess we should talk about it," she offered, though she wasn't sure her heart was strong enough to handle breaking up with Nate in person.

"Why bother? You've gotten everything you came here to get."

"What on earth are you talking about?" The words she'd rehearsed melted from the tip of her tongue. As much as it absolutely killed her to know she'd come so close to providing for Gracie's future and failed, a part of her had cheered for Nate when she'd found Uncle Jimmy's folder. A thousand times, she'd imagined Nate's handsome face as she told him what she'd discovered. His dark eyes would widen the way they always did whenever something took him by surprise. His chest would seize. Weight would melt from his shoulders as the truth that Uncle Jimmy had never meant to do him wrong sank in.

To be honest, she'd expected Nate to show more than a little gratitude. After all, she could have thrown Jimmy's paperwork in the garbage. Or tossed the entire folder on the burn pile and lit a match. She might have hidden it away where no one would ever find it.

She hadn't done any of those things. Instead, she'd made the toughest decision of her life. And while she hadn't expected Nate to turn handsprings over her departure, the least he could do was say, *Thank you.*

But from the thunderclouds that gathered in his slate-colored eyes, *thanks* was not the word Nate was reaching for.

"Mommy?"

At her side, Gracie's thin arms wrapped around Justine's leg, trapping her in place.

"It's okay, baby. Mr. Nate and I are just talking." She patted Gracie's curls despite the way her breath shuddered in her chest.

Didn't he get the messages she'd left on his phone? Hadn't he heard the news?

She shook her head. This was Orange Blossom. Where everyone knew everything and no one had secrets. She'd bet good money that Royce had picked up the phone and dialed Nate the minute she and Sarah left his office yesterday afternoon. Almost twenty-four hours later, by now he'd surely heard about the folder Royce had stashed in his safe, the one that guaranteed Nate's ownership of Castle Grove.

Or maybe not, she thought, as he glared down at her from the porch.

"How could you?" he demanded.

Biting her tongue, she settled the sack of fruit on the ground. Aware that little ears were listening, she ruffled Gracie's hair. Keeping her voice low and even, she faced Nate. "How could I what?"

"You accepted Fresh Picked's offer. That's why you're leaving, isn't it? You got what you came here for?"

"You snooped through my stuff?" Never mind that the house was hers for only another few hours. He had no right. She'd done nothing wrong. Had, in fact, the best of intentions as far as Nate was concerned.

"I thought we had something going, you and me." He mopped his face with one hand. "Yet the moment my back was turned, you sold me out to Ken Thomas. You've been talking to him all along, haven't you?"

"You know me better than that," she protested. Her words ground to a halt. Clearly, neither of them knew each other as well as they'd thought they did. The man she'd fallen in love with would never jump to the conclusions Nate had reached.

"I thought I did. I convinced myself that you'd changed. But you're the same Justine you always were. Always looking out for number one. Why did I think things were different this time?" Nate's posture slumped. "I wish you'd come to me first. Trusted me. But you didn't. You betrayed me—betrayed *us*—by talking to Fresh Picked."

If he only knew how wrong he is.

His words stabbed her heart, each cut shearing off another piece of their love. He didn't trust her. That hurt as much, maybe more, than losing the land and all that that loss meant. Choosing her words carefully, she started to explain. "As a matter of fact..."

She swallowed the rest of what she'd been about to say. Sooner or later, Nate would learn the truth but, as for them, it was already too late. "You obviously don't trust me and never did," she said, biting off each syllable.

She pressed Gracie's head against her thigh. She'd been a fool to even consider a future with Nate. Gracie was her only priority and always would be. "I've had enough of this conversation. Enough of you."

"I could say the same thing. I have a meeting I need to get to. I'm sure the town council will have plenty to say about how their mayor let the town die on his watch." Nate jammed his hands in his pockets. "Thanks for that, too, by the way."

"Mr. Nate, don't go. I have to give you your orange first." Gracie broke her hold on Justine's legs. Snatching the brightest, shiniest fruit from the sack, she darted up the rickety stairs. While Justine watched, her daughter skidded to a halt in front of the man who stared down at her. An odd expression crossed his face.

"Don't you want it, Mr. Nate?" She held the shiny globe out to him.

Nate's features softened. "You have some juice on your chin, Gracie," he said, pulling a package of wipes from the pocket of his jeans.

Maybe Gracie didn't expect Nate to reach toward her. Maybe the move startled her. Whatever the reason, the little girl sidestepped...straight off the unprotected edge of the porch.

As Justine watched in horror, Nate lunged, but the fall happened so quickly, his hand closed on nothing but thin air. With a hard thump, Gracie landed on the unforgiving ground. For three long seconds, absolute silence reigned. Not a bird chirped. The cicadas quit their incessant chirping. The leaves in the trees stilled. So did Justine's heart.

Then everything happened at once.

"Oh, God!" Nate thundered down the steps.

"Aaaaaaaa!" Gracie's scream cut through the quiet like a hot knife through butter.

She's alive. She's alive.

Justine managed a sharp intake. "Don't touch her. Don't move her. Call an ambulance!" She brushed past the man who hunkered over her daughter. "Baby. Don't move, baby. Stay right where you are. Let Mama look at you. Show me where it hurts."

Her eyes squeezed shut, her mouth wide open, Gracie loosed another wordless scream.

"Oh, honey, tell Mama where it hurts."

"My arm! My arm. Owww! Mommy, my arm hurts!" Gracie cradled her left arm.

Slowly, carefully, Justine ran her hands from her daughter's shoulder to her fingertips, searching for a cut or any sign of broken bones. She didn't find any, but so what? She wasn't a doctor or a nurse.

"What about your legs? Can you move your legs?"

When Gracie flexed her toes, bent her legs at the knees, Justine allowed herself a tiny, relieved sigh.

"Hold me, Mommy."

Gracie's hiccuppy sobs broke her heart, and she swore she'd never let go of her daughter's hand again for the rest of her life. What had she been thinking, letting a five-year-old go up the stairs alone like that? Now her daughter was injured and she had no one to blame but herself.

Herself and Nate.

She glanced up at the man who stood with his arms folded across his chest, staring at the scene before him like a spectator at a movie. "Is that the best you can do? Stand there? Did you at least call an ambulance?"

"She got the wind knocked out of her. It happens." He shrugged. "You might want to see if she's hurt bad before you call the paramedics."

Nate's well-intentioned advice poured salt on Justine's wounded heart. "Can't you hear her? She's hurt! She's hurt, and it's all your fault."

Nate reeled away as if she'd struck him. "What the..."

But Justine wasn't about to back off. He'd had his say. It was her turn to strike out. "You were supposed to fix the railing. If you had done what you promised, my daughter wouldn't be lying on the ground."

"No one feels worse about that than I do."

"And that's supposed to make everything all right? It doesn't, you know."

"What can I say, Justine? I don't have anything left."

"There's nothing you can say, except *good-bye*." From the look on Nate's face, her response didn't come as any great surprise. She clutched Gracie to her chest. "We'll be out of your hair before you get back."

Nate reached out to ruffle Gracie's hair. "I'll never understand why you coddle her so. With all she's got ahead of her, I'd think you'd want to toughen her up a bit."

The man had a point. Not one she wanted to hear, but he had a point. She stilled her own reaction and searched Gracie's face. Not a single tear glistened in her daughter's eyes.

If she were truly hurt, wouldn't there be tears?

Scooping her daughter into her arms, she pressed Gracie's head to her shoulder. "You're okay, baby," she whispered. "You're okay. Lemme see your arm. Is it all right?"

Gracie bent her right arm. "It hurts, Mommy. It really hurts."

Justine cocked her head. She would have sworn Gracie had hurt her *left* arm in the fall. She turned, slowly, intent on telling Nate that Gracie appeared to be okay, but the man she'd once loved had turned his back on them both and headed across the yard. Without a single glance their way, he slipped behind the wheel of his truck. Gravel sprayed from his tires. Dust rose in clouds behind him as Nate drove out of her life.

This time, he was gone forever.

Nate managed to keep his feelings tightly wrapped until he reached the crowned arch that marked the exit from Castle Grove. A cool dread filled him as he thought of walking into the council meeting that was due to start any minute. He stopped shy of the two-lane highway. A glance in either direction revealed a road as vacant as the spot in his chest where his heart used to be. In the distance, black tar disappeared into distant heat mirages. The undeniable truth washed over him.

It was over between him and Justine. This time, there'd be no second chance, no rekindling of the love they'd once shared. His feelings for her, for the woman he wanted her to be, had blinded him. He'd thought they could work things out. That she'd see how the town had rallied behind her and know that, when the time came, the good citizens of Orange Blossom would support her and Gracie.

But had she been willing to give them a chance? *No.* Instead she'd sold him out and was about to leave him behind. Just as she'd done the first time around.

His plans for the future dissolving into a red mist, he took out his frustrations on the steering wheel. When he'd blown off enough steam that he could think straight, he shifted his foot to the gas...and stopped again.

Where to now?

Turning left would take him to Orlando, a city with roots so deep in the citrus industry that it hosted the Citrus Bowl and Citrus Parade. Yet, the average tourist had a hard time finding an orange or lemon tree in an area that had grown more famous for its theme parks. A big city like that had no place for a man who'd poured his life's blood into Castle Grove.

But had he worn out his welcome in Orange Blossom?

He ran a hand through his hair. From one end of Orange Blossom to the other, people had trusted him enough to put him in charge after Jimmy died. As their acting mayor, his only task had been to safeguard the land and trees that were Orange Blossom's main income source. And he'd failed them. He'd given his heart to the last person he should have ever fallen for. And what had she done? She'd betrayed them all by selling out to Fresh Picked.

No wonder his cell phone had been blowing up with messages this morning. Well, Justine might have won that battle, but the war was far from over.

Not that he'd fool himself into thinking he could win. He didn't have the resources for a prolonged fight. He'd never outlast the juicing conglomerate. Not with its bottomless pockets. But he wouldn't tuck his tail between his legs and slink off into the bushes either. He'd put every dime he owned into fighting the sale of Castle Grove. And who knew? Maybe a miracle would happen. Maybe the judge assigned to their case would award him, if not the entire estate, at least what was owed him. That alone wouldn't be enough to save Orange Blossom, but it might slow the town's decline long enough for the city fathers to come up with a different plan.

Of course, it was a given that he'd have to resign his post as mayor. When word got around about what he'd done—how he'd trusted Justine—the new mayor, whoever it was, would probably ask him to resign from the town council, too. It was just as well. Much as he'd enjoyed helping shape Orange Blossom's future, he could use the extra time to prepare for the day he faced Justine and Fresh Picked in court. The thought was small consolation, but it was all he had left. It would have to be enough.

First, though, he had to face the wrath of the town council. And feeling like a man on his way to face a firing squad, he put his truck in gear and turned right.

A short while later, he slowly drove down Main Street looking for a parking space in a town that seemed uncommonly crowded for a Wednesday afternoon. As he gazed at the cars and trucks that lined both sides of the street, Nate wondered if someone was throwing a party and had left his name off the guest list. He grimaced. The way his life was going, that was probably the best he could hope for.

Another ten minutes passed before he located a lone, empty space behind the hardware store. He strode across the street and into the town hall where he was a half hour late for a town council meeting. He hustled through the empty office area. Outside the meeting room, he paused. His personal life might be in the crapper, but until the council replaced him, Orange Blossom deserved its mayor to look and act the part. Squaring his shoulders, Nate stepped through the double doors and stopped dead in his tracks.

What the...?

His thoughts dried up as he scanned a room where every seat was taken and people stood in clumps along the walls. Conversation surged around him. Instead of dread and anger, an air of anticipation hummed through the crowded space. The meeting that should have been well underway hadn't even started. Why hadn't the vice mayor taken charge? He searched for answers, relief seeping through him when he spotted Jack standing nearby. Sidling closer to his friend, he whispered, "What's going on?"

"The harvest estimates came out this morning." Jack pitched his voice low. "Growers throughout the rest of the country are predicting small yields this year."

"No wonder everyone's beaming." Smaller crops meant skyrocketing prices for citrus in a year when Castle Grove should have its best harvest ever. For a town that relied on fruit for most of its income, the news couldn't get any better. But it could definitely get worse. Nate hung his head as he prepared to tell the crowd that the bumper crop might also be Castle Grove's last.

Feeling more and more like a fraud with every step, he suffered through a round of back-slapping congratulations on his way to the dais where George, the vice mayor, chatted amicably with council members. Halfway to his goal, he caught George's eye and nodded pointedly toward the microphone. He might as well have saved the effort. Instead of rapping the gavel on the table, George sprang to his feet.

"Here's our mayor now!" he exclaimed.

As if the man had thrown a switch, the buzz of conversation died. A pregnant pause lasted a full five seconds before the rest of the council pushed back their chairs and rose. Someone clapped their hands. A smattering of others joined in. The applause grew until it thundered through the room.

Wanting nothing more than to turn and run, Nate dredged up a frozen smile. His feet were lead weights, but somehow he found the strength to mount the steps to the dais. He passed a hand over his eyes, knowing he was about to break the hearts of the men and women who'd come to help the town celebrate its good fortune. But he had no choice. If Orange Blossom had any chance of survival, its citizens needed to start preparing for a future that didn't include Castle Grove...or him.

Gaining the podium, he tapped the microphone. "Well, that was good news, wasn't it?" he asked once the room quieted. "Between the harvest reports and the Orange Fest, this is turning out to be a pretty good year for Orange Blossom."

"All thanks to our mayor," interjected Bill Smalley. "You got my vote for re-election."

"Mine, too." Miss Bertie's soft voice sent another round of applause rippling through the room.

"Now, now. It's a little early to be talking about next November. A lot can happen between now and then." Motioning for quiet, Nate settled the crowd. "I, uh—" His throat closed, cutting off the bad news he'd intended to deliver. He couldn't go on. Couldn't destroy the bright future everyone in the room envisioned. Not yet anyway. Buying time to get his thoughts together, he cleared his throat. "I call this meeting of Orange Blossom's town council to order. We have a lot of ground to cover today, so let's get to it, shall we?"

Taking the coward's way out, he made it to his seat without planting his face on the floor. The agenda required little of him but to nod and look attentive. He managed that much, until the topic turned to the Orange Fest. He had to admit that threw him. One minute, he was nodding with pretend interest while one committee member after another reported on their progress. The next, his thoughts snarled on the plans he'd made to spend the day with Justine and Gracie.

His eyes stung. He pinched the bridge of his nose, warding off the threat of tears. So what if he wouldn't see Gracie get her face painted in the children's booth? Or watch her eyes light up when she spotted towering cones of cotton candy sold by the Sweet Shop? He wouldn't be beside her when she took her first ride on the Ferris wheel, but that wasn't the worst of it. Not when he considered all the other milestones he'd miss in her life. One day, someone else would lead Gracie onto the floor at her grade school's Daddy-Daughter Dance. Some other guy would put the fear of God into her prom date.

He shifted in his seat. He'd still play a role in the

life of the little girl he'd come to think of as his own, wouldn't he? If it turned out that he was a match, wouldn't he'd go through with the transplant? Folding his arms across his chest, he nodded.

Yes, yes, I will.

"I'm glad you agree, Mr. Mayor. We need that extra three thousand dollars in prize money to make the Orange 5K one of the premier races in the South." Clara Johnson's voice severed his line of thinking.

Nate gave himself a shake. *What did I just agree to?*

From her seat at the opposite end of the conference table, the treasurer glowered. "For this year, maybe, but what about in the future?"

"I don't see why you're so worried." Clara thumbed through the pages of her report. "With Castle Grove filling our coffers, we'll have plenty of money to expand the Orange Fest."

Suddenly aware that the meeting had taken an unexpected turn while he was lost in dreams of what might have been, Nate gave his head a rueful shake. He might not be the mayor of Orange Blossom for much longer, but for whatever time he had left, he'd give his best to the job. He leaned forward. Much as he hated to break it to them, the people deserved to know how short-lived the town's prosperity was going to be.

"Pardon me, Clara, but if I could have the floor..." A glance at Karen assured him he'd spoken in accordance with the rules.

Confidence radiated in Clara's smile. "Of course, Mr. Mayor."

Bending under the weight of responsibility, Nate stood. He scanned the crowded room, his gaze lighting on friends and associates. The muscles across his stomach tightened. His dad used to say it was best to swallow strong medicine in one big gulp. Figuring he might as well get it over with, he began.

"Before we go any further with plans for the Orange Fest—and especially before we commit extra funding to the event—I need to make you aware of a few new developments concerning Castle Grove's ownership." Taking a swig from the bottle of water Karen had thoughtfully placed in front of every council member, he swallowed past the lump in his throat. "See, the thing is…"

"Oh, for heaven's sake. Just get on with it." Erlene, Nate's former on-again/off-again girlfriend, leaned away from the wall at the back of the room. She propped one hand on a cocked hip.

Karen glanced up from her notepad and frowned. "Point of order, Erlene. The mayor has the floor."

With a saucy look that said it'd take more than a mere objection to stop her, Erlene struck a pose. "We all know Royce Enid was over to Oviedo this morning. Word around the courthouse was Justine Gale dropped her claim to Castle Grove."

A whispery rustle passed through the room, giving Nate a much-needed chance to get his bearings. One of the town's biggest gossips had gotten her facts wrong. He guessed there was a first time for everything. "Are you sure about that, Erlene? 'Cause that's not what I heard."

As if to prove her point, Erlene thrust out a hip. "I had lunch with Melody Ann in probate. She said new evidence supporting your claim had come to light. In-con-tro-vertible evidence."

Nate held on to the table as he tried to make sense of what he'd just heard. He swung toward a spot on the second row that Royce Enid had claimed as his own. "What's she talking about, Royce?" he demanded.

"Point of order, Mr. Mayor. This discussion is not on the agenda." Karen objected, but everyone knew her heart wasn't in it.

Nate ignored her, his eyes on Royce as the big man lifted both hands in a sign of surrender.

"Erlene left out a few details, but yeah, she got the gist of it right." In a few words, he described Justine and Sarah's visit to his office the day before. "I expect the judge to hand down his final ruling tomorrow, a ruling that will award you all of Castle Grove."

"All?" Nate's voice croaked.

"Woulda been eighty acres, but Justine wrote up a bill of sale for the rest of the place and signed it over to you for the princely sum of one dollar. If I were you, son, I'd pay the lady."

What the...

Air whooshed out of Nate's mouth as if someone had punched him in the stomach. His shoulders slumped. After all these months, Castle Grove was finally his. Why hadn't Justine told him? His gut tightened. He hadn't exactly given her the chance, had he? He'd been so certain, so sure she'd sold out to the highest bidder, when all along she'd had his back. And now—he gulped—now, she was leaving.

He stood. "I'm sorry. I have to go." He glanced down the row of council members. "George, you're in charge."

Over Karen's sputtered objections, he sped from the room. As he gained the sidewalk, Jack fell in beside him.

"Where're we headed?" Jack asked, matching Nate's hurried footsteps stride for stride.

"To Castle Grove. I only hope I'm not too late. She's leaving, going back to Virginia. I have to stop her." He swerved left around a trash can. "I need a chance to apologize. To make things right between us."

"Afternoon, Mrs. Basher." Jack tipped his hat to a passing matron. "Sounds like you could use a police escort. Where's your truck?"

Nate gestured toward the narrow alley that ran between two buildings. "I'm behind the hardware store."

"I'll meet you there in two shakes. Don't leave without me. Last thing you need is a speeding ticket." Jack spun to the side, heading for the cruiser parked in a reserved spot in front of the town hall.

The road to Castle Grove had never seemed longer as Nate followed the flashing lights and wailing sirens. At the entrance, he watched Jack pump the air with one fist before the deputy sheriff peeled off, leaving him to face the woman he'd loved and lost again. Aware of the hollow space where his heart used to be, Nate swung beneath the gates and drew in a breath that he didn't release until he spotted Sarah's car parked alongside a rental in front of Jimmy's house. He closed his eyes and thanked the powers above that he'd made it on time.

Now, if Justine would only give him a chance to make things right.

Justine wedged the bag of oranges between the tire well and an overstuffed suitcase. She dusted her hands. "That's the last of it. One more walk-through, and we're out of here."

"I wish you didn't have to go." Her arms folded across her chest, Sarah frowned. "Since you're leaving no matter what I say, take this. For the road." Reaching through her car window, Sarah retrieved a basket of homemade treats.

"What is it? Let me see." At Justine's side, Gracie bounced up and down, trying to peer over the basket's sides.

While Sarah knelt so her daughter could see the array of goodies, Justine squelched the sob that built in her chest. There'd be time enough for tears after they got where they were going. If she broke down now, they'd never get on the road before dark. And she needed to go. Needed to put Castle Grove and her failed hopes for the future behind her. Even more uncertainty lay ahead, but at least in Virginia, she wouldn't face the constant reminder of what might have been between her and Nate, the home they could have made in Orange Blossom.

"Thanks so much for—for everything. I wish—"

A throaty rumble on the gravel track that led from the main road drew her attention. Her breath stalled as a familiar truck rounded the corner of the barn and slewed to a stop. Whatever she'd been about to say forgotten, she watched Nate bound from the vehicle. In three long strides, he closed the gap between them.

"We need to talk," he announced, his slate eyes pinning Justine with a look that brooked no argument.

"The last time we tried that, things didn't go so well." In case he needed the reminder, she ran her hand through Gracie's curls.

"Still..." Nate nodded to Sarah. "Can you give us a minute?"

The urge to tell her friend to stay put danced on the tip of Justine's tongue. Sarah never gave her the chance to say a single word. Grabbing Gracie's hand, Sarah made it sound like they were embarking on a grand adventure when she suggested the two of them go inside. "We need to check every cupboard and closet and look under all the beds. Maybe we'll find something fun!"

"Can I, Mommy?" Eager to start on the unexpected scavenger hunt, Gracie pulled on Justine's hand. "I'm gonna find a treasure."

Justine bit back a smile. The granola bar she'd seen Sarah swipe from the gift basket practically guaranteed a dream come true for her daughter. "Sure," she said, ruffling Gracie's dark curls. "You two go ahead while I talk with Mr. Nate." She shot a pointed look at her friend. "This won't take long."

"Right." Sarah gave Nate a stern look. "If you ever want another slice of orange meringue pie, Nate Rhodes, you behave yourself."

At Nate's abashed nod, Sarah shifted into aunt mode. A loopy grin on her face, she skipped toward the house, Gracie racing alongside her. Their laughter died at the bottom of the steps, though, and Justine caught her bottom lip between her teeth while her daughter carefully negotiated the short flight of stairs, then raced across the porch. A new fear of heights showed in the way she clung to the door. The fall had clearly left its mark. Justine crossed her fingers and hoped her daughter's fears would fade along with her memories of Castle Grove. Counting to ten, she waited until Sarah and Gracie slipped inside before she turned to Nate.

"What brought you here?" she asked the man who gazed at the porch with pinched features.

"I can't tell you how sorry I am that she fell," he said, finally wrenching his gaze from the closed door. "I wouldn't for the world do anything to hurt her. You know that, don't you?"

When he looked at her with the pain of Gracie's accident so clearly etched across his face, she couldn't deny him, no matter what their differences. "I do. I know it wasn't your fault. And I'm sorry for what I said. I shouldn't have flown off the handle at you like I did."

"You had every right. I shoulda replaced that railing long ago." He scuffed his foot along the ground. "If anything, I'm the one that should be asking for forgiveness."

"Consider it given." Having said what she suspected he'd come here to say, she cocked one eyebrow when

Nate remained rooted to the ground where he stood. "Is there something more?" She waited for him to get on with it.

"Hell of a thing I found out in the middle of the town council meeting." Nate stared at a distant spot. "Royce said you didn't sell Castle Grove, after all. He said you and Sarah waltzed into his office pretty as you please with a folder crammed full of Jimmy's notes and receipts. Dropped them in his lap and told him to file 'em with the probate court." Humor tugged at the lips she'd once considered perfect. "I wish I'd been there to see that. I bet Royce 'bout had a heart attack."

Justine bit down on her lower lip to keep from smiling. She'd never actually seen anyone's face turn such a lovely shade of purple before. "You could say he was surprised."

Nate's gaze bounced off the house and landed squarely on her. "If I'd been in your shoes, I'm not sure I'd have been strong enough to do the same thing."

"It was the hardest thing I've ever done." She dropped her head, her breath sawing against her throat. "It was the right thing to do, though. The only thing. As someone once told me, going through life always being afraid is no way to live."

"I mighta heard the same thing." A knowing smile brightened a tiny corner of her heart as Nate thrust his hands into the pockets of his jeans. "Royce also said you'd sell me the rest of the grove. Did he hear that right?"

"Better you than Fresh Picked." She met his gaze head on. "They can't be trusted, Nate."

"Huh! That's for damn sure."

A grin that matched her own slid across Nate's

mouth. Justine held hers in place despite the pain that lanced her heart. She'd miss this. Miss having someone in her life who was so in tune with her thoughts. She told herself to savor the moment, that once her heart stopped hurting so much it pained her to breathe, she'd want to take out the memory of this moment and relive it.

Gracie's laughter echoed from somewhere in the house. The sound must have reminded Nate that they didn't have much time, because he sobered quickly.

"Let me get this straight, you want me to pay you a dollar for the rest?"

"It's a formality, but yeah." The amount wasn't the issue, as she'd learned during her first—and only— year of law school. "Since Jimmy didn't leave the land to you in his will, legal tender must be exchanged in order to make the deal legit."

"There's only one problem with that." Nate tugged his pockets inside out. "I'm fresh out of dollar bills."

The move, combined with his sheepish grin, startled a laugh that began deep in her chest and bubbled to the surface. She shook her head, the loose ends of her hair sifting over her shoulders. "You'd short me a dollar?"

"Well, no. Not exactly. I have a check around here somewheres." He patted himself down, apparently not finding what he wanted. At last, tugging his wallet from a back pocket, he carefully withdrew a wrinkled slip of paper and handed it across. "You could get far more for the land on the open market, but I hope you'll accept my offer."

Curious, she glanced down at the check he'd placed in her hand. Her heart stilled. She gaped up at him. "It's blank."

"Name your price. Whatever I have, it's yours." Nate's words came in a rush. "I started saving for my own place the day I went to work for Jimmy. With no rent to pay and no family to support, I was able to bank a big part of my salary. As of today, I have a little over a hundred grand in savings. It's yours. If you don't think that's a fair price—and it isn't, not around here—I'll pay you whatever you ask." He studied his feet for a long moment before he looked up. "Do we have a deal?"

Justine rubbed her eyes. Nate's offer would let her pay off every hospital and doctor bill dating back to Gracie's birth. But it wasn't right. She couldn't take his money. Sadly, she shook her head. "Jimmy left that land to you free and clear."

"Maybe. Or maybe he knew what he was doing all along. Either way, as someone once told *me*, an oral contract isn't worth the paper it's written on."

"You remembered," she said, her mind spinning.

"I remember everything about you, Justine." As if he knew he'd said too much, Nate hitched his jeans. "So do we have a deal?"

She swallowed, drinking in freedom like a rare wine as the oppressive weight of five years' worth of debt slid from her shoulders. Carefully, she folded the check and tucked it into the pocket of her jeans before she stuck out her hand. "Deal," she said simply as Nate's callused hand gripped hers and they shook.

Instead of giving her hand a single pump and releasing it, Nate's grip tightened. His gaze bore into hers. "Thank you. You didn't have to do what you've done, especially after I doubted you. I made a huge mistake by thinking you'd gone behind my back to

Fresh Picked. I want you to know, for as long as I live, I'll never misjudge you again."

Tears stung her eyes. "We've both made mistakes. Maybe now, we can put ours behind us and move on."

One day, maybe they could be friends again. In a decade or so, maybe they'd bump into each other on the street somewhere and laugh about the time she'd spent in Castle Grove. Her heart lurched.

A decade, huh? Who was she fooling? She'd need far longer than that to get over loving Nate.

He gave her a sideways smile. "I'll look forward to that day." He fell silent for an instant while the urge to linger flickered across his face. "There's something else."

Justine ran a hand over her ponytail. "You've already given me more than I deserve." What else was there?

"I think you'll want this."

While she watched in confused silence, Nate withdrew a folded sheet from his shirt pocket. Taking her hand, he pressed a page that had been handled so often it had gone soft around the edges into her palm.

"Open it," he whispered.

Puzzled, Justine slipped a fingernail beneath one crease, then another. When the paper lay flat, she stared down at an ordinary lab report. Mild disappointment rippled through her. She gave the sheet a careless shake that fluttered the corners. "Nate, I..."

"Look again." He shifted close enough to point to the paper.

As if following a lighthouse beacon, her eyes shifted to the section he'd indicated. Wondering what she'd missed, if anything, she gave the results a second, more intense scrutiny. The world slowed as she noted two names on the report—Gracie's and Nate's. Willing her hand not to shake, she ran a trembling finger down two long columns of results to the bottom of the page. There, in a box labeled Composite Predictions, she stared at a number that made her head throb.

Ninety-nine percent.

"You're a match for Gracie?" Disbelief shuddered through her.

"Not a perfect one, but the doctors say it's close enough. We have the same blood type. According to that"—Nate tapped the paper—"we're pretty compatible."

Trying to wrap her mind around a possibility that could change *everything*, she shook her head. "You'd be willing to donate? She's not even yours, and you'd be willing to give her a kidney?"

Nate's voice dropped into a register that erased all her doubts. "When the time comes, you can count on me, Justine. You always could. If I have my way, you always will."

A sob gathered in her throat. Slowly, she shook her head. Nate had already given her more than she deserved. Now he was offering to save her daughter's life. Yet, his generosity didn't change a thing between them. The fact remained that he didn't love her, not the way she loved him. Because of that, she had no choice. She had to leave. But no matter how hard she tried to tell him, the words wouldn't come. Time stretched out. She probably would have gone on standing there, gaping at Nate like a fish out of water for another impossibly long minute, if Gracie hadn't chosen that exact moment to put in an appearance.

"I found a candy bar!" Her daughter burst through

the screen door and onto the porch with the exuberance only a five-year-old possessed. "Aunt Sarah said I could eat it. It was good."

Gracie tromped down the stairs and sped across the grass. At the last minute, the little girl veered toward Nate, smacking into the tall man with enough momentum to nearly bring him to his knees. Despite the serious nature of the conversation she'd been having, Justine laughed out loud.

"We're going to see Aunt Penny, Mr. Nate. Why don't you come with us? There's plenty of room in the front seat with Mommy."

"Much as I'd like to keep you company, I have work to do here, Little Bit." Nate lifted Gracie into his arms and spun the delighted child in a circle. "Before you go, though, I was hoping to take you and your mom to see something in the grove."

Justine bit her lower lip. Spending more time with Nate was merely delaying the inevitable heartbreak she'd feel when she put Castle Grove in her rearview mirror. She shared a knowing glance with Sarah, trusting her friend to know the score and back her play. "I don't think so. I can't hold Sarah up. Not after she came all this way out here to say good-bye."

"It's a lovely afternoon." Deliberately, Sarah crossed to the front porch swing. "I think I'll just sit here for a while and enjoy it."

Justine stared daggers at the woman who was supposed to take her side. "Thanks for the support," she muttered.

Sarah's voice dripped honey. "Y'all just go along now. I'll be waiting for you when you get back."

Justine pressed her lips together. She supposed she owed Nate a few minutes, at least. After all, the man had not only erased all her debts, he was offering her daughter a kidney. But it was more than that, and she heaved a long sigh and slowly let it out.

Why bother fighting it? She might as well admit she wanted to spend more time with Nate. Wanted to pretend—even if it was only for a little while—that he and Gracie and she were the family she'd once hoped they could be. Her heartache would still be here waiting for her when she got back. It wasn't going anywhere.

"What do you say, Gracie?" She turned to her daughter. "Want to see what Mr. Nate wants to show us?"

For an answer, Gracie gave Nate's hand a tug. "Is it a surprise? I like surprises. Let's go, Mr. Nate."

With Gracie perched on Nate's wide shoulders, Justine ducked beneath waxy green leaves and sidestepped branches heavily laden with fruit. She drank in the scent of ripening citrus, listened to fat bees buzzing in the treetops. While Nate's long strides led them deeper and deeper into the grove, she struggled to get her bearings, to figure out where they were headed. It was no use. Too much time had passed since she'd wandered this far beyond the first row of trees. The landmarks had all changed.

Ten minutes passed. Then fifteen, before their little group left young trees behind and entered a section of the grove where gnarled trunks of older citrus bent like arthritic senior citizens. There, tall grass formed a hedge of sorts along a well-beaten path. Justine's heart skipped a beat when she recognized the tree where she and Nate had carved their initials one long-ago summer afternoon. Stepping onto the narrow trail behind him, she looked ahead to a spot where dark green leaves and branches blocked their way. Gracie, who'd been chattering nonstop since Nate lifted her onto his shoulders, hushed.

Slowly, Nate reached out to part the green curtain. Shafts of sunlight slanted through overhead branches, illuminating a small clearing beyond where they stood. A breeze stirred through the topmost branches. At its soft sigh, hundreds of delicate wings fluttered.

"Ohhhhhhh!" Gracie's whole face lit up. "Butterflies!" As nimble as a squirrel, she climbed down from Nate's shoulders and darted into the glen. A cloud of orange and yellow wings took flight around her.

Justine's heart trembled. Her lips parted. "How is any of this even possible?" she asked, breathless. Weeds and kudzu should have reclaimed their private garden ages ago. Even so, butterflies hatched in the spring and summer, not this time of year.

Nate's full lips curved. "Remember that hot spell we had last week?"

She nodded. They'd taken advantage of the return of summer-like temperatures by making an excursion to the spring.

"I reckon it got hot enough for this handful to emerge." He extended an arm and held it steady. Seconds later, a pair of bright yellow sulphur wings landed in his palm.

Shaking her head, Justine studied gossamer wings that coated low-lying plants like a blanket. "This is more than a few." A spark of hope ignited in her chest. She stared into Nate's hooded eyes. "That night, when we broke up. You destroyed all this. There wasn't anything left."

Of their love or the garden he'd so tenderly nurtured.

Purple petals dribbled onto the ground from the lacy flower Nate had plucked off a nearby bush. "With enough TLC, plants grow back." His breath hitched. "So does love, if you give it a chance."

She glanced around, noting small, wooden signs that identified the different patches of flowers. The weathered markers had been as fresh and new as her love for Nate a decade ago. Had his love for her remained so steadfast that he'd maintained their private spot all this time? Did he love her still? Her mind stuttered. After all they'd been through, could she and Nate really have a future? She blinked as hope seared across her chest.

Second only to Gracie, she wanted the forever kind of love she'd once shared with Nate.

She turned to face the man who'd once meant the world to her...and always would. Tipping her head, she stared into his slate-colored eyes. She had to hear the truth from his lips. "Why?" she asked, unable to form more than a single word.

"Because I've always loved you. I always will. Gracie, too. In fact..."

Nate stepped closer. His strong arms circled her waist and snugged her to his chest.

"If you'll have me," he whispered, "I never want us to be apart again."

A delicious shiver shuddered through her midsection. *This.* This was what she'd come back to Castle Grove for. Not for the land. Not for money or riches. Not even for her daughter's health. Being here, wrapped in Nate's arms, listening to the steady beat of his heart, it was enough. It was everything.

She stole a glance at Gracie. Grinning widely, her daughter spun in lazy circles through flowers while fragile wings beat the air above her head. Wonder stole Justine's breath.

"Wait till you see them in the spring. You've never seen anything like it," Nate murmured.

"I'll be here," she promised, lifting her lips to his.

The kiss that followed settled every question, erased every doubt. In Nate's arms, she was right where she was supposed to be, right where she belonged.

A tug on the hem of her shirt interrupted just as things were getting interesting. "I'm sorry," she whispered, breaking the kiss.

"Don't be." Nate's throaty voice purred in her ear as he traced one finger over her lips. "We'll pick this up where we left off...later. We have all the time in the world."

"I'll hold you to that," Justine sighed as another tug demanded her attention. "What is it, baby?" she asked, looking down.

"I want to hold a butterfly, but they keep flying away," Gracie pouted.

"I got this," Nate said, grinning like a man who'd just won the lottery.

Leaning down, he unfurled Gracie's fingers and held her hand out flat. Less than a minute later, wonder filled the little girl's face as a queen monarch lit on her palm. Aware that three months ago, she would have raced forward brandishing antiseptic cleaners, Justine leaned against a nearby trunk. A lot had changed since she'd returned to Castle Grove, and it was all thanks to the man who'd always held her heart.

"I love you, Nate," she whispered, while Gracie giggled at the tickle of wings on her bare skin.

"I love you, too. You and Gracie," he said with a tender look for the child at his side. "I just have one more question."

"Only one?" Justine raised an eyebrow.

"What are we going to tell Sarah?"

Justine nodded thoughtfully. "The truth. That we've loved each other from the beginning, and we always will." A delicious shiver shimmied through her. "I can't wait to show you how much."

"Then I guess we'd better get to it."

The corners of Nate's eyes crinkled as a smile bracketed his lips. Overcoming Gracie's protests with promises that they'd return to the butterfly garden the next day and stay all day if she wanted, he ripped open a hand-sanitizer packet and quickly wiped it over the girl's arms and face.

"How'd you like to play with Aunt Sarah for the rest of the day?" he asked, sweeping Gracie high onto his shoulders while Justine laced her fingers through those of the man she loved and retraced her steps through the orange trees, home at last.

If you loved *Butterfly Kisses*, tell a friend about this book and take a few minutes to leave a review!

Want to get the latest news and be among the first to learn when Leigh's next book goes on sale? Sign up for her newsletter: https://leighduncan.com/newsletter/

Behind every book is an amazing team.

Many thanks to those who made
Butterfly Kisses possible:

Cover design:
An amazing friend

Interior formatting:
Amy Atwell and the Author E.M.S. team

Copy and Content Edits:
Joyce Lamb

Proofs:
Marlene Engle at the Book Mama Blog

If you enjoyed *Butterfly Kisses*
look for the next book in the Orange Blossom Series

Sweet Dreams

"We've all been so worried about your mom, Sugar. It's good to see her getting back to her old self again. I'm sure you're relieved."

In a move she'd probably learned at her mother's knees, Dottie Carruthers managed to envelop Sarah in a fleshy hug without putting so much as a single dent in her own bouffant hair-do or smearing her pancake make-up. "Ya'll let me know if I can do anything more for her, you hear?"

Though Sarah's mouth ached from the smile she'd held for the last two hours, she widened her grin. "Thanks for all you've done for her, Ms. Carruthers. Mom, Gram and I—we all appreciate it."

"It was the least I could do, Sug. I—Well, would you look a'there. It's Mary Louise. I haven't seen her in a coon's age. I just *have* to say hello."

With a final, quick squeeze, Dottie hurried across the wooden floor of the Grange Hall toward a new glut of people who'd just entered the already crowded room. Sarah waved a hand through the air to dispel

315

the cloying sweet scent that drifted in the older woman's wake.

"Hmmph. Meddling old biddy." Penny hissed the pronouncement from Sarah's left. "All those years, she was in your face about your mom, and now she's relieved when Belle's on the mend? A little hypocritical, don't you think?"

"You live in a town as small as Orange Blossom, somebody's always up in your business." Sarah sighed. Much as she couldn't wait to experience life outside the confines of Seminole County, Florida, she had to hand it to her neighbors. As soon as the word got out about her mother's diagnosis—and in a town this size, word always got around—it was as though everyone had wiped Belle's slate clean. Rumors about the town's bad girl had evaporated like the morning dew did after the sun came up. People who once crossed the street rather than speak to her had lined up to drive Belle to chemo and radiation treatments. "Dottie brought us dinner once a week and organized a car pool to get Mom to all her appointments. With me working double-time at the bakery to cover both our shifts, I don't know what we'd have done without her help." Even with the extra help, the last two years had been tough. But with so many people counting on their jobs at Miss June's Pie Shop, Sarah and her grandmother had kept the family business going.

"That's not something that would ever happen in D.C., for sure." Beneath thick glasses, Penny's hazel eyes took on a dull sheen. "Except for Ms. Morrison and her dog, Brutus, I don't know any of my neighbors."

"Yeah, I'm going to miss that about this place," Sarah murmured agreeably.

"When you go away to culinary school?" Penny's voice dropped into a patronizing tone.

The remark stung, but knowing her friend had a point, Sarah consciously relaxed her shoulders. From the time Margaret Castle put a paring knife in her hand and showed her how to julienne carrots, she'd dreamed of becoming a chef. All through the long, hot summers she spent at the informal camp the Castle's ran for kids who had nothing else to do but get in trouble, she'd delighted in stirring simmering pots in the overheated kitchen while her two besties, Justine and Penny, tackled other chores. In high school, Sarah had concocted new recipes during long, cross-country runs and raced home afterwards to try out her latest experiments. While her friends applied to colleges and universities, she'd dutifully filled out her own application...to the Institute for Culinary Perfection. Along about then, she supposed she'd begun starting every conversation with, "Once I finish training at the ICP and become a chef..." But, as the years passed and one delay after another kept her from attending culinary school, even her best friends had gradually stopped asking when she was going to do more than just talk about her dreams.

Giving herself a little shake, pushed her regrets aside. Tonight was supposed to be all about celebrating her mom's recovery. It was time she joined the party.

"Where's Justine with our drinks?" she asked. Too much time had passed since the other member of their trio had waded into the crowd, promising to return bearing glasses of punch.

"Who knows?" Penny shrugged. "I saw Nate pull her aside a minute ago. They're probably smooching up a storm in some out-of-the-way spot."

A smile tugged at Sarah's lips. Maybe, now that she was going away, she'd find that special somebody of her own. "Can't blame 'em for that. It isn't often they leave Gracie with a babysitter." Though Justine had relaxed a bit since moving to Orange Blossom, she still watched over her five-year-old with more intensity than a cook gave a Béchamel sauce. "As soon as she gets back, let's find a quiet place to talk. I have news."

Standing on tip-toe, Sarah stiffened her spine to take advantage of every centimeter of her five-foot-two-inch frame. She searched the crowded room for their friend. Beneath colorful helium-filled balloons and crepe streamers, practically the entire town of Orange Blossom had turned out to help Belle Bowen celebrate the end of a two-year struggle against cancer. No more surgery. No more chemo. No more radiation. Finally free to pick up her life where she'd left off after the diagnosis, Belle had announced to one and all that she intended to resume her place behind the counter of the family business first thing Monday morning. A move that freed Sarah to put long-delayed plans in motion.

Minutes later, her hair slightly mussed, Justine emerged from the crowd carrying the promised drinks.

"It's about time," Penny called as the slender blonde approached. "Sarah wants to talk."

"Oh? Something exciting?" Justine's blue eyes glistened. "Are you in love? Heavy like?" The diamond ring on her finger sparkled as she lifted three goblets toward her friends.

"Better," Sarah promised. She retrieved two of the glasses and passed one to Penny. Then, eager to share her news, she ducked around a corner and led the way down a hall to an alcove outside an office. Shooting a glance over her shoulder, she made sure they hadn't been followed.

"Oooh, this is all very cloak and dagger-y," Penny announced over the hushed buzz of conversation that drifted from the other room. "It better be worth it."

Justine elbowed their friend. "I'm sure Sarah has a perfectly good explanation."

"You both know how much I've wanted to study in New York. Become a real chef." Sarah skipped the rest. Her besties knew the story as well as she did. Reality had crushed her like a clove of garlic when, with no work experience to speak of, she didn't qualify for a scholarship to the prestigious ICP. She hadn't given up, though. While her friends went off to the colleges of their choice, she'd tugged one of Miss June's aprons over her head and gone to work in the family bakery. Each week, she'd socked away a portion of her salary for her schooling. But she'd been doing that for ten years, and here she was, still stuck in Orange Blossom where she'd churned out so many of Miss June's signature pies they blurred together in a vast sea of orange meringue.

Oh, she'd almost made it. That was before the fire that nearly destroyed the family business three years ago. Grams had barely re-built the bakery when Belle was diagnosed with cancer. Now that she'd received a clean bill of health, though, it was finally time for Sarah to fulfill the dream she'd put on hold.

Her fingers trembled as she slid an envelope from her pocket. "I..." Her voice squeaked. She cleared her throat and tried again. "I've been accepted."

"Accepted?" Penny's eyebrows rose. "Where?"

"To the Culinary Institute?" A radiant smile broke across Justine's face. Beaming, she leaned in for a hug.

Penny-the-practical merely rocked back on her heels and fired questions. "In New York? When do you leave? How long will you be there? Do you have a place to stay?"

"Come on, you. Get in here and tell Sarah how proud you are of her." Justine broke her embrace long enough to pull Penny forward.

The other girl stiffened for a second before melting into the group hug with an effusive, "Of course. Of course. I'm so, so happy for you."

"A toast," Justine proclaimed, raising her glass. "To America's next top chef!"

Glasses clinked and the three friends downed generous gulps of their drinks.

"Start at the beginning and tell us everything," Justine prompted.

"Yeah, spill, girl. We want all the deets," Penny seconded. "When did you find out? What did your mom and Gram say? I bet they were thrilled for you."

Placing a finger to her lips, Sarah shot her friends a meaningful look. "Shhh. Not so loud. You're the first ones to hear. No one else knows."

"Ooooh, I have chill bumps." Justine held out her arm for them to see the tiny raised bumps. "Whatever made you finally take the plunge, I'm happy for you."

"Let's just say my mother's cancer was the wake-up call I needed," Sarah confessed.

"How so?" Penny's eyebrows rose.

"You know that seven minute frosting I make for coconut cakes?"

While Justine gave a tentative nod, Penny's blank stare told her the red-head didn't follow. Explaining the complicated recipe to someone who didn't cook was tricky, but she had to try. She took a breath. "I throw sugar and corn syrup and egg whites together and then I stand there, whipping and stirring this ugly goo over a double-boiler for, like, for-ever." She tugged on a loose curl. "They should have called it ten-minute frosting, or maybe twelve-minute frosting. Anyway, I'm stirring and whipping and nothing is happening and then, all of a sudden, the sugar melts and the mess becomes the most luscious, delicious frosting. But if it's left on the heat for just a second too long, it all falls apart. Then, there's nothing to do but throw it out and start all over."

Penny tucked a wisp of hair into a severe bun that added ten years to her face. "Icing. Cancer. Only you would draw the analogy."

"Yeah, well." Maybe she'd never been to college like her friends, but she knew food. "The thing is, Mom's diagnosis made me realize that I can't wait any more. If I don't make my move now, I'll be stuck here the rest of my life. Just like that seven-minute frosting, I'll go back to being a soupy mess." She might have spent her entire life in Orange Blossom, but she had big dreams. Dreams that were finally going to come true. And not a moment too soon. Though her thirties were still a couple of years away, they loomed on the horizon. She'd already have a hard time keeping up with the fresh-faced youths in her class. She couldn't afford to wait any longer.

"So—" She sucked in air until her lungs expanded— "So, once we knew for sure that Mom was going to make it, I submitted my application. This morning, I found out I got in. I start in March."

"So soon?" Justine's features drooped. "I was looking forward to the three of us hanging out again, now that Penny's thinking of moving back soon.

Orange Blossom won't be the same without you."

Penny removed her glasses and polished them on the edge of her sweater, a move Sarah recognized as the other girl's method of stalling. "I hate to mention it, but living in New York is expensive. Then, there's tuition, books and equipment. Are you sure you can swing it?"

"I'm sure," Sarah answered, wanting to put her friends' fears to rest. "With my savings, plus what Gram owes me, I'll have more than enough." Three years ago she'd emptied her bank account to help the family rebuild following the fire. Her grandmother had promised to pay her back—with interest. The time to collect on the debt had come. "I'll stick around long enough to help Mom get back in the swing of things at the pie shop. After that, though, I'm outta here."

In the second before silly grins broke across her friends' faces, Sarah thought she saw a flicker of doubt in their eyes. She looked again, just to be sure, but whatever she'd seen had given way to smiles and resounding congratulations. Relieved, she traded hugs with the two women who'd always had her back.

"When are you going to tell your Gram and your mom?" Peggy wanted to know. "If you want us there, you just say the word."

"No need." Sarah ran a hand through curls that refused to be tamed, no matter how much styling product she used. "While it's true that we haven't talked about anything but Mom's cancer for the past two years, they'll be happy for me. They've known all along this was my dream." Now that it was really happening, she closed her eyes and imagined the future. "In a few years, you'll all have to come and sit at the chef's table in my restaurant. I'll prepare my favorite dishes, just for you. We'll have a blast."

Tears stung her eyes as she let her gaze travel between the familiar faces of her two besties. She certainly hadn't expected to make life-long friends that first day when her mom dropped her off at Castle Grove for the summer. In fact, she'd never felt so alone. She'd sobbed as dust clouds rose from behind her mom's departing car. Then, Justine had slung an arm around her shoulders, picked up her battered suitcase and helped her settle in, and an instant friendship had been born. She hadn't shed another tear all summer, not until she had to say goodbye to Justine at the end of the summer. A few years later, Peggy had joined them when her dad took over the Book Nook, and the trio had formed their own version of the Three Musketeers. They'd been closer than sisters ever since.

Not that they were alike. In fact, they couldn't be more different if they'd tried. While she needed a footstool to reach the spice rack and had to run five miles every day or risk turning into a blimp, neither Penny or Justine ever hit the gym. Yet the slim figures that towered over her own petite frame didn't carry so much as an extra pound. From her coke-bottle glasses and the long red hair she always wore in a tight bun straight down over a figure-hiding cardigan to her sensible shoes, Penny had turned into the classic librarian after landing a prestigious job at the Library of Congress. And while everyone swore Justine—with her board straight blonde hair and classic features—could have made a fortune as a cover model, she'd set her sights on becoming a lawyer. Though she'd had to drop out of law school when her daughter was born, Justine had found a way to keep her dreams alive by becoming a paralegal.

Sarah took another sip of her drink. She'd made the right choice in sharing her news with Justine and Penny first. Her friends had given her just the shot of encouragement she needed. She slipped the acceptance letter into her pocket.

Nothing could stop her now.

Order your copy of *Sweet Dreams*, the second book in The Orange Blossom series:

https://leighduncan.com/books/

Want to get the latest news and be among the first to learn when the next book in The Orange Blossom Series goes on sale?

Sign up for my monthly newsletter:

https://leighduncan.com/newsletter/

About the Author

Leigh Duncan is the award-winning author of more than two dozen novels, novellas and short stories. First published in 2010, she wrote eight books for Harlequin American Romance. In addition to those heartwarming romances, Leigh writes more complex and emotional women's fiction. Some of her more popular titles include *The Orange Blossom Series* and *The Growing Season*.

The biggest thrill of her career to date came in 2017, when Hallmark Publishing chose Leigh as the lead author for their new line of romance novels and introduced her book *Journey Back To Christmas* on the Hallmark Channel's *Home and Family Show*. Leigh is currently working on more sweet romances for Hallmark, including the *Heart's Landing Series* which takes place in a small, New England town dedicated to providing "the perfect wedding for every bride."

An Amazon best-selling author and a National Readers' Choice Award winner, Leigh lives on Florida's East Coast where she loves to hear from readers.

Contact Leigh at: https://leighduncan.com

Or visit her at:
https://facebook.com/LeighDuncanBooks

Made in the USA
Coppell, TX
07 March 2023

13901843R00196